Praise for Lauren Dane's *Giving Chase*

Recommended Read! "I've long been a fan of Lauren Dane, grabbing whatever she writes as quickly as I can. In my opinion Giving Chase has to be the absolute best book she has ever written. Maggie is heroine who is spunky and independent while Kyle is just the kind of to-die-for hero that I love to read about. Lauren Dane has crafted not only the sensuous passion between them, but also the deepening emotional bonds, in such a way that I became enthralled. Add to this the knowledge that each of Kyle's three yummy brothers are slated to have books of their own and Giving Chase is a book that should be on the top every romance lovers list." – *Melissa, Joyfully Reviewed*

Five Blue Ribbons! "I absolutely love Lauren Dane's GIVING CHASE! While Kyle and Maggie's relationship is a joy to read about, it's really Maggie's developing self-esteem and the way she finally stands up for herself that had me eagerly devouring the pages... All the Chase boys are drool worthy and I can't wait to see what happens next in this promising series. Ms. Dane's GIVING CHASE is sure to be a hit with readers everywhere. It's definitely a book you'll want to add to your keeper shelf." ~ *Chrissy Dionne, The Romance Junkies*

Five Angels! "Lauren Dane's Giving Chase is an exhilarating ride from the first word. Maggie and Kyle are a wonderful couple that complement each other perfectly. While Maggie and Kyle are very passionate, friendship and respect are the cornerstone of their relationship. The mix of romance and mystery is perfect as Maggie and Kyle work together to insure their budding relationship...The entire Chase family are wonderful characters that I hope to see again." ~ *Fallen Angel Reviews*

Giving Chase

By Lauren Dane

A Samhain Publishing, Ltd. publication.

Samhain Publishing, Ltd.
2932 Ross Clark Circle, #384
Dothan, AL 36301
www.samhainpublishing.com

Giving Chase
Copyright © 2006 by Lauren Dane
Print ISBN: 1-59998-259-5
Digital ISBN: 1-59998-113-0
Cover by Scott Carpenter

First Samhain Publishing, Ltd. electronic publication: June 2006
First Samhain Publishing, Ltd. print publication: September 2006

Dedication

As always—for Ray, who is my heart. I love you. And to my incredibly wonderful beta readers—Tracy, Julia and Di, who help make all my books better. And speaking of making my books better—a big old thank you to my editor, Angie, who earns what I am sure can't be anywhere near what she's worth.

Chapter One

Friday night in Petal. Half the town—that is, those citizens sixty and under—were gathered inside The Pumphouse seeking refuge from the rain and enjoying three dollar pitchers of beer and burgers. The crowd noise was so loud, whatever song playing on the jukebox was indistinguishable. Still, Maggie, Dee and Liv sat at their usual table—the one by the window—so they could watch the goings on, They'd sat there, every Friday night, for the last four years. It should have seemed mundane, boring, but it was the time when each of the friends got to reconnect after a long week and it was a bright spot instead.

But the usually happy Maggie sighed into her beer before taking the last drink and setting her empty glass down on the table.

"So, I finally broke up with Sam. It's definitely over."

With an inelegant snort, Liv tried to catch the server's eye to order another pitcher. "Maggie, honey, it's been over for at least a month now. You just haven't been willing to admit it to yourself. And heaven knows our manners were too good to break it to you." It was Maggie's turn to snort at that.

Stifling a grin, Liv continued. "Anyway, he's an ass. He's been an ass since the fifth grade. You're too good for him."

"Way too good for him. He needs a momma, not a girlfriend." Dee's nose wrinkled in disgust.

"Well, the problem is this town is just too damned small! Who've I got to choose from? And let's keep it men between twenty-two and fifty who aren't married, living with his mother or gay." Maggie handed a five over to Patrick for the beer and began to pour out for everyone. "Keep the change, sugar."

She winked, getting a cheeky grin in return before he turned and headed back through the crowd to the bar.

"It really is a shame he's gay. He looks as good going as he does coming." Dee's voice trailed off as she watched him disappear into the crowd.

"Yeah, a shame for our team." Liv sighed. "But you know, you're failing to mention the hottest real estate in town. How about one of the Chase brothers?"

Maggie snorted. *Yeah right.* Those boys were mouthwateringly handsome. Tall, broad, boy–next-door gorgeous. The women of Petal had been lusting after them since preschool.

"Sure, why not! But no. I'd rather have Brad Pitt, he's about as available, although I suppose I'd have to fight Angelina for him." Maggie rolled her eyes. "Liv, *everyone* wants those boys. Even if a girl like me could catch their attention—I have no desire to be a notch on someone's bedpost. Maybe I just need to lower my standards. Roger Petrie has been asking me out for years. Maybe I should say yes. After all, he has a job, lives in his own home and has all of his teeth."

Liv and Dee burst out laughing. "Yeah but he's creepy! I mean, he's got like, what, fifty cats and a goat living *in* his house?"

"On the other hand," Liv said, breathless from laughing, "an animal lover can't be all that bad."

"Question is, how much of a *lover* is he? I mean, he sleeps with the goat!" Maggie's words dissolved into laughter.

"*Eww!* Time to change the subject. You don't need to lower your standards, Margaret Elizabeth Wright! There are plenty of decent men in Petal. You just have to be patient." Sweet as she was, Dee didn't know she said it in that way women do when *they* have a boyfriend.

"And what do you mean, *a girl like you?* Are you suggesting that those Chase boys are too good for you? Because you are dead wrong. My God, Maggie, you're beautiful! It pisses me off that you can't see it. I blame your mother." Liv shook her head as she looked at her oldest friend.

Petite and blessed with fine, almost delicate features, Maggie had a head of gorgeous strawberry blonde hair. She usually wore it in a tight knot at the back of her head but when she let it free, it hung past her waist. Tortoise shell glasses often hid the big amber-brown eyes fringed with long lashes. Hell, Maggie was pretty when she looked like a buttoned up school teacher. But Liv knew Maggie had a knock-out figure lurking under those clothes and itched to cut and style the hair, get rid of the glasses and show a bit of skin.

"Liv, those Chase boys are out of my league. Men that handsome and well—manly—don't notice high school history teachers." And she had to admit that they were all so powerfully vital and masculine that it intimidated her.

"Speak of the devils..." Liv nodded her head and the three turned to watch the Chase brothers stroll into the bar. In fact, every single woman—and even the not-so-single ones—noticed the four impossibly handsome brothers.

"My, my, my. Those boys sure are fine." Maggie's gut tightened at the sight.

"Yepper." Liv fanned her face with a napkin.

"Mmm hmmm." Dee nodded.

Once they'd disappeared into the back where the pool tables were, the women turned back to their conversation.

"Go on, Dee, tell us about Arthur. We know you want to." Every Friday night Dee did a weekly "Arthur is so wonderful" update.

Arthur Jones was Dee's boyfriend. One of the good guys. They were planning a wedding for Valentine's Day.

"He planted a magnolia tree in the backyard earlier this week and put in an arbor with yellow climbing roses. Three of them because you know, we've been together three years. He's so sweet."

Smiling through the sudden lump in her throat, Maggie stood and patted Dee's shoulder. "Yeah, he is." She stood up. "I'll be back. I have to make a pit stop."

It didn't use to bother her so much that she didn't have someone. Dating around was fine. Fun even. But lately, Maggie had begun to want the kind of love and connection that Dee had with Arthur. She wanted someone to make breakfast for. Someone to plant flowers with and take long walks hand-in-hand at the lake with. She now knew she was missing something and she wanted it.

On her way back from the ladies' room, she heard Patrick call out that their order of chili cheese fries was done. With a wave to thank him, she moved to grab them and save him a trip. Three steps from the kitchen window area someone slammed into her. Knocked sideways, the platter of gooey fries flipped over, dropping with a *splat* on the side of her blouse and down the leg of her pants.

"Hey! Watch where you're going!"

Maggie spun around, astounded at the tone. "Me? Did you just bark at me? You're the one who bumped into me! You made me drop this food all over my clothes and the floor. Last time I checked, it's the person walking backwards' job to watch out." Looking up, and then up some more, she came to the insanely gorgeous face of none other than Shane Chase.

"You were in the middle of the aisle," he growled at her, arms crossed over his chest.

"It's the walkway, dumbass! It's called that because it's where people *walk*." Unable to stop herself, she used a very slow voice and her heart sped a bit as his jaw clenched at her tone. And then her inner bitch wanted to snicker. Instead she couldn't resist. "Facing *forward*, I might add." This guy took the cake! A little bit of good looks turned him into a self-righteous jerk.

Narrowing his eyes, he leaned into her personal space to intimidate her. But she refused to step back. She did work with teenagers every day after all. And the man was acting like a big baby. "Did you just call the sheriff a dumbass?"

"No, I called *you* a dumbass. The dumbass who wasn't watching where he was going and slammed into me and then yelled at me, the dumbass who has NO manners—I'm calling *that* guy a dumbass. That you happen to be a cop is not relevant. Although one might expect a cop to actually act with civility and basic manners!" She huffed. But the impact was not as impressive as she'd hoped given that he was nearly a foot taller than she was. And all that distracting hard muscle and really nice smell. Why did a jerk like him have to smell so good she wanted to lean in and take a bite? It'd serve him right if she did. Shaking her head to dislodge the question about what he may taste like, the fog cleared a bit and she found her mad again.

"She's got you there, Shane." Kyle Chase approached, smiling at her apologetically. "Are you all right? That cheese stuff is pretty hot. Did you get burned?" He handed her some napkins but she just looked down at herself. If she tried to wipe it with the napkins the gooey mess would just get worse.

At least one of them had manners. He probably tasted good too. Stifling a smile she unclenched her fists and stepped back. "Thanks. It just stung a bit but my pants took the brunt. But I've got to go and get out of these clothes." Swinging her head to glare at Shane, she noted he was still glowering, only this time at his brother. "And you! I have sixteen year old boys in my class who have more manners. Take a civility training class or something." She harrumphed and spun around to stalk back to their table.

"Oh my god! What was that all about?" Liv handed Maggie her purse and raincoat.

"That moron Shane Chase slammed his gargantuan body into me and made me spill chili cheese fries all over myself! And *then* had the *nerve* to yell at me like it was my fault! Dumbass! I have to go. I'll talk to you two later." She tossed some money on the table.

"Now who's the dumbass? We're coming with you. I have plenty of take out menus at home. Let's go." Liv got up and Dee followed.

The three women headed out together into the evening, grousing about Shane Chase and his abominable manners.

ભ ભ ભ

"Well, that was really special, Shane. You were awful to that little woman. Happy now? Or do we need to go and search out some old ladies we can knock over or steal some candy from toddlers?" Kyle egged his brother on as they played pool in the back of the bar.

"She called me a dumbass!"

Kyle smirked when Shane missed the shot.

"That's because you are one. You rammed into her, made her spill food all over herself and then instead of apologizing, you yelled at her. You're lucky all she did was call you a dumbass. She had quite the vicious gleam in her eye." Kyle lined up his shot and missed.

"She's cute for someone so small. I don't think I ever noticed that spark behind those glasses and those stuffy shirts. I've seen her around town but who is she?"

"Maggie Wright. She was in my year in school." Matt looked up mildly before leaning back down to take his shot. "She's a teacher at the high school now. History I think. Clearly a real menace to society." He rolled his eyes as he straightened and grabbed his glass.

"Sarcasm doesn't suit you, Matt. You're too pretty. Anyway, she's a rude little woman." But Shane's voice didn't sound so sure anymore.

"*You're* rude, Shane. Mom's gonna kick your ass when she hears about this—and you know she will. Petal being Petal, I bet the story is weaving its way across town right this very moment," Marc taunted. "I don't envy you Momma's wrath, but I can't wait to see it."

೫ ೫ ೫

Maggie was up to her elbows in dirt, planting primroses when Polly Chase rolled up and got out of her car.

"Maggie? Honey, is that you?" Polly click-clacked up the front walk. The woman was a sight to see. She was not even five feet tall but that was the only thing small about her. A head of heavily lacquered hair stood several inches high, matched only by the spiked heels on her feet and a handbag bigger than a small country. All of this fit in the late 1970's Caddy she drove around town like a menace.

And her presence was big too. Polly Chase was the town matriarch. Her family was one of the oldest in Petal and her husband's just as old. Both the Chandlers and the Chases had a hand in the building and governance of Petal for five generations. When Polly married Edward Chase thirty-five years before, it had been the ultimate marriage.

Still, Maggie had always thought Polly—who sat with her on the historical society and Edward, an attorney in Petal—were very nice people. However, seeing how rude her oldest was, she began to wonder.

Standing up, Maggie took off her gardening gloves and tossed them on the walk. "Yes, Mrs. Chase, it is. What can I do for you?" As if she didn't know. "Why don't you come on in? I was just going to get myself some hot tea. Would you like a cup?"

"Oh that would be perfect, shug. Thank you." Polly followed Maggie into the large house that belonged to her parents at one time and now was hers.

"Please, sit down and I'll get the water on." Maggie swept into the large kitchen and lit the burner under the teakettle. While she waited, she prepared the teapot, measuring the loose tea, spooning it into the mesh ball. Hanging it into the pot she turned and put a few oatmeal cookies on a pretty plate.

Steeling herself, she took a deep breath before going back into the living room a few minutes later. She put the tray down on the coffee table and sat across from Polly.

"It'll need steeping for another three minutes or so. Would you like a cookie? They're fresh baked."

When Polly had taken a few bites of the cookie, Maggie poured her a steaming cup of green tea. "What can I do for you today, Mrs. Chase?"

"Honey, I heard what my boy did to you last night at The Pumphouse. I'm just mortified! So naturally I wanted to come by and apologize. Because it also came to my attention that he failed to do that on top of everything else."

Softening at the sight of Polly's distress, Maggie leaned across the space separating them. Reaching out, she squeezed the other woman's hand. "Mrs. Chase, please don't be upset. Whatever Shane did, he did on his own. You have nothing to do with it. I'd never think that."

"Honey, you're too nice. Now I'm just embarrassed. They weren't raised to talk to anyone that way, much less a woman! Don't think I haven't been on his tail all morning. He's managed to avoid me so far, but mark my words I'll find him before the day is through. And when I corner that rat, you can be assured I'm gonna tan his hide!"

Maggie stifled a laugh at the picture of Polly spanking her nearly thirty-year-old giant of a son, badge and all. "Well if it's any consolation to you, Kyle did come over with some napkins and asked me if I was all right."

"Oh he sang like a bird when I got out to his worksite this morning. He's a good boy, Kyle. Always treats people with kindness." Polly smiled with pride. "They might be big, giant boys but they're *my* boys and I'm still their momma. I heard you called Shane a dumbass."

Maggie blushed fiercely. "I'm sorry. I shouldn't have, it wasn't nice but he was just really obnoxious and I lost my temper."

Polly burst out laughing. "Honey, it sounds to me like he *was* being a dumbass. You don't have to apologize to me. They get it from their daddy you know." She gave Maggie a wink.

After tea and cookies and a discussion on the next historical society function, Polly excused herself. "I have to run now, Maggie honey. Rest assured I'll wrangle that boy into doing the right thing. Thank you for the tea and cookies." She gave Maggie a big hug and teetered on her spiky heels back down the front walk, giant handbag in tow and sped off.

ભ ભ ભ

"You and I have a double date." Liv stood on Maggie's doorstep several hours later.

Automatically, Maggie opened the door to let her in. "What?" Maggie took in the garment bag and the big train case in Liv's arms and tried not to panic. God only knew what her best friend was up to.

"Jeezus, Maggie, get the freaked out look off your face. I'm not going to kill you. Our dates are Shaun Stadey and Alex Parsons. I was shopping at the Piggly Wiggly earlier today and they asked if you and I had a date for the Homecoming Picnic tonight. Of course I told them they'd be filling the bill. And now you're getting a make-over. No argument. I brought some clothes by, too."

"A make-over?" Maggie's eyes moved to the train case and big garment bag. "No way! Liv, do you remember what Toots looked like when you got finished with her? I'd give you one of my kidneys but you don't have the best record with make-overs. Anyway, I have to get out to the car wash with the kids, I just came home on a break."

Unmoved, Liv stared for a long moment. "Okay, but Maggie, Toots was a dog and we were eight. So shaddup. And no, you don't need to get back to the car wash. It is pointless to try and think of ways out of this. Dee and

Arthur are over there now and doing just fine. You know how much that freaking precious Arthur loves kids. Honestly, sometimes don't you think he's got to be a pod person or something because he's so perfect?" Liv hustled Maggie up the stairs and into her bedroom.

Maggie couldn't deny herself a guilty snicker and then sobered up. Well, she tried anyway. "Aww, leave poor Arthur alone. He's a nice guy in a sea of asshats. And Dee, being a pod person herself, deserves someone equally as nice. Plus, he's kinda hot in a very nerdy way, dontcha think?"

One perfectly manicured eyebrow rose along with the corner of one side of Liv's mouth. "Whatever. In any case, there is no excuse for you not to let me do this." Liv laid the bags on Maggie's bed, unzipping them with military precision.

Stepping back, she glanced from the clothing to Maggie and back again several times. "Okay, clothes for tonight. Alice let me have a few things from her store to bring over here for you. They're all really cute and it would only be a couple hundred bucks and I think you should buy them all. But, I'm willing to leave you alone for a week if you buy at least one outfit. Come on, I know they'll all look great on you."

Despite her amusement at Liv's hard sell, Maggie broke out in a nervous sweat. "Didn't you just tell me how beautiful I was on Friday? Why do I need a make-over?"

"You *are* beautiful, Maggie. But these clothes will fit you. You've got a great body but you never let anyone see it because your clothes are all at least a size too big. This stuff isn't tight or slutty, it's just modern and it'll flatter your figure.

"A trim and style of your hair will frame your face. You don't need those glasses tonight because I'm driving anyway. Oh, and by the way, I made you an appointment at the eye doctor for Tuesday. I'll meet you there. You need new frames that better fit your face. Contacts would be nice too, don't you think?"

Cripes, the woman was a steamroller! Maggie eyed the door, considering her chances for escape. Liv caught it and shook her head as she stepped in front of it, blocking Maggie's way.

"Don't even think about it."

Maggie knew by the set of Liv's face that she wouldn't win this one. She sighed and Liv grinned, sensing imminent victory. Still she added a few things to sweeten the offer. "Sam will be there. Probably with some skanky date. You know you want him to see what he's missing. Better yet, Shane Chase will be there too. Let's show that dumbass what's what."

Unable to hold it back, Maggie let her grin spread over her face. "You play so dirty!" But she was already looking through the stack of clothes on her bed. She had to admit the stuff was really cute. Liv did have good taste for a girl who used grape kool-aide to dye a dog's fur back when they were kids.

Liv's eyes sparkled as she pulled out a dark blue scoop necked blouse and a denim skirt. "I like these the best. You have great legs. Not that anyone would know since you always wear those long teacher skirts. And ugh, worse, the mom-waisted pleated khaki pants. Pleats! Oh the agony of watching any woman under eighty wear pleats!"

Maggie burst out laughing at the look of disgust on Liv's face.

"To go with it, those cute boots we saw in the window of Radison's last week."

"But I didn't buy those boots, remember?"

"Yes you did. You can pay me back later." Not bothering to look up, Liv pulled them out of the bottom of one of the garment bags and put them on the floor. "It'll be perfect. The skirt is the perfect length and the boots will come to the top of your calf. Well, what are you waiting for? Try on the whole outfit."

"If I do this will you stop setting me up and trying to make me over?"

"Well, I hate to point out that if I do this, I *will* be making you over. But I promise to not try again for the next six months."

"I'll take whatever I can get. Fine, hand me the clothes. But I'm wearing my glasses. I'm not gonna be blind just to look cuter."

Liv grinned and handed the outfit over to Maggie. Once Maggie had undressed, Liv shook her head in amazement when she saw Maggie's underwear. "Girl, you're something else. Look at those undies! I always forget that you're wild beneath the clothes."

Fighting a blush, Maggie smiled. "What? A girl needs pretty undies." She looked down at the forest green, lacy, high cut panties and the matching demi-bra. Pretty panties and bras were somewhat of a weakness for her. She had drawers full of the stuff.

"Girl, you're a mess of contradictions. Now, get those clothes on."

Once changed, Maggie looked down at the outfit and back at her reflection in the mirror. Liv had been right. The clothes weren't tight but they showed her figure. She looked pretty. The skirt came to just below her knees and the boots weren't too high heeled that her feet would be dying in half an hour. She tugged the bodice of the blouse up a bit, it showed more boobs than she normally did. "Liv, jeez, you can see my boobs."

Rolling her eyes, Liv clucked her tongue. "Now, shug, don't exaggerate. You can see your *cleavage*, big difference. Even at that, it's just the very top of your cleavage. I promise you it doesn't look slutty or even daring. Wow, I'd forgotten that you had breasts with all those buttoned to the chin shirts you wear beneath the bulky sweaters."

"Janie is the sweater girl. She's the one with the great figure."

Startled, Liv gave Maggie an appraising look up and down. There were moments when Maggie revealed another small, but bone deep wound her mother and sister had laid on her and it broke Liv's heart.

"Mags, you've hidden your light under a bushel for far too long. You look so pretty dressed up like this. Jane Marie is not the only pretty sister. Stop letting her mess with your head." She motioned to the chair. "Come on now, let's get the rest of you done."

Putting a drape around Maggie's shoulders, Liv loosed Maggie's hair and wet it down. Quickly and efficiently, she trimmed about four inches, layered it to free the curls and cut the front to frame Maggie's face. The weight gone, the pretty strawberry-blonde hair was a riot of curls.

After the application of some goop to hold the curl and wall out the frizz inducing humidity, Liv opened up the train case.

With artful application of subtle colors, Liv emphasized Maggie's giant amber eyes and put a shine on her full lower lip. Maggie didn't need a lot of makeup and would have been uncomfortable in it anyway. Finished, Liv stood back and surveyed her work. Impressive. The mousy schoolteacher was gone. In her place, a pretty, fey looking woman with long legs and a nice bosom. Not bad for a few hours work.

Cocking her head, Liv met Maggie's eyes in the mirror. "Look at yourself, Maggie." Moving away, Liv changed her clothes and finished getting ready while Maggie just stared at herself in the mirror.

For so very long she'd only looked at herself in the mirror long enough to put her hair back. That wasn't her place in her family. The shock that she could be something else, *someone* other than the smart one in the Wright family hit her. Tears burned her eyes for a moment until she blinked them back. "Wow, Liv."

If Liv saw the tears she ignored them. Just one of the million reasons Maggie loved her. "Instead of saying, *I told you so*, I'll just say that you look fabulous. In fact, we need to go clothes shopping! Or you could just keep the outfits I brought over *and* we could go shopping. You can show me where you get all those fancy panties." Liv winked.

Maggie fingered the colorful clothing in the bags. "Well, maybe. I mean, looking at myself right now…I think that I much prefer this me."

"Hon, you're the same you. Clothes and a haircut don't make you into a different person. But these clothes do allow the world to see more of how gorgeous you are on the outside. Everyone already knows how beautiful you are on the inside." Liv paused a moment. "I don't want you to feel I didn't already think you were beautiful. Inside and out, even with those ugly assed schoolmarm clothes. You're the most beautiful woman I know."

Maggie stayed silent for long moments as she swallowed past the tears in her throat. Her emotions seemed to have chosen that moment to run riot. "It's just that you've always been the gorgeous, glamorous one. Dee's the sweet, pretty one and I was the smart one. It feels weird to see that I can be the pretty one, too. Heck, sexy even."

Arms encircled her from behind as Liv hugged her. "Aw, shug, your mom sure did a number on you. Yes, your sister is a beauty but she's not the only stunner in the family and on the inside, she's a troll."

"Janie's tall, blonde and married with two perfectly gorgeous children. She never looks unkempt. Her house is a freaking showplace and her husband adores her. She's perfect."

"Bleah! You want to be blonde like Janie? We'll get you some of the same blonde she has, it's out of a bottle. And beyond her looks what does she have? You're good and kind and smart and funny. You give back to this town and those kids. Honestly, sometimes I want to smack your momma for making you think that just because your sister was in pageants that you're not as good. Well, I'd like to smack her for a whole host of reasons but that's neither here nor there now. Now, we have a picnic to get to, let's go."

Chapter Two

Petal's Homecoming Week festivities were a major happening. Everyone from three months to a hundred and three came out to at least two of them—the picnic which set off the week and the football game against Crawford High.

The picnic was held down at the park, on the shore of the lake and the evening ended with fireworks. The entire town came out to eat themselves silly on barbecue, homemade ice cream and peach pie. As traditions went, it was one of Maggie's favorite.

Maggie had to admit, the attention Alex Parsons paid her was wildly flattering. When they'd approached he'd given an almost cartoonish double take as he'd realized who she was. He seemed nice enough and he certainly had no problems being on a date with her. It was really nice to have a man so clearly attracted to her. His arm casually circled her shoulders as he guided her through the park.

Stopping at the top of a rolling hill that led down to the water, Alex turned to her. "How about right here to spread the blanket?" The spot would provide a perfectly unobstructed view of the fireworks and was close but not in the path of the tables heaped with food.

"Perfect." Maggie helped spread out the large blanket. Straightening, she suggested that the guys stay to guard their spot while she and Liv went to grab the food.

"You sure you don't want us to do the food run?" Alex asked.

"No, that's okay. Maggie and I can get in and out quicker. Anyway, all of the old ladies love Maggie and will give her the royal treatment."

Blushing, Maggie couldn't deny it. After all the years she'd been volunteering and taking meals to the folks at the retirement home and senior center, they did love her. And she loved them too. They'd become her family in many ways.

As she walked away, Alex watched her with a dreamy smile on his face. A woman like Maggie would make a wonderful wife and mother. There'd been so many others, women he'd thought were the right one. Could Maggie be it? He didn't quite dare allow himself to believe he may have finally found her.

ଔ ଔ ଔ

"Who's that?" Intrigued, Kyle stared at the redhead in the skirt walking past them toward the food tables. He loved the way she moved, graceful but a little shy. That long curly hair was gorgeous. Hell, *she* was gorgeous. Was she visiting town? He recognized the dark haired woman as Olivia Davis, the mayor's secretary.

Chase men did not fail to notice beautiful women and the other two looked up as well.

"Oh my lord, that's her!" Marc burst out laughing.

"Her who?" Shane craned his neck to get a better look and blanched. "Oh no, it's the teacher."

"And it looks like she caught you drooling, too. Listen, why don't I go over and apologize to her for you, I know how much you don't like her." Kyle realized he was only halfway joking.

"I owe it to her. I was a jerk." Muttering to himself, Shane shoved himself past his brothers and stalked toward Maggie.

Catching sight of Dee and Arthur, Maggie waved them over. She pointed toward their blanket. "We're over there with Alex and Shaun. We just came to grab food."

"I'll come with you two. Arthur, can you take our stuff over there? I'll be back shortly, with extra potato salad." Dee smiled sweetly and Arthur kissed her nose before loping off toward the blanket.

Dee turned back to Maggie and gave her a once over. "My god! Girl, you look gorgeous!"

"It's all Liv, I had nothing to do with it."

"Shaddup. I cut your hair and helped you pick some clothes. I didn't give you a kidney or anything." Liv waved her comments off.

"Don't look now, Maggie, but I do believe the big bad sheriff is drooling," Dee murmured.

They didn't even bother to pretend not to look as Liv and Maggie turned in unison to look in his direction.

"Oh and look, he's coming over here." Liv smirked.

"Great, and the whole town is watching. Is the man incapable of doing anything without making a scene? God, this is going to get back to my mother, I know it." Maggie blushed scarlet as heads turned to take in Shane's progress toward the three women.

Coming to a halt before them, he stood, hands on his hips. Maggie had to crane her neck up to see his face. What a surprise, he was glowering. *Did the man have any other facial expression where she was concerned?*

Frustrated anger coursed through her. "Yes? Did you fall getting out of your car and have come to yell at me for it? Or wait, let me go and grab some food and you can crash into me and spill it. I know! Gas prices are my fault right?" Maggie narrowed her eyes at him.

Anger flashed in Shane's eyes. "No. I came to apologize but I can see that you aren't ready to hear it."

"That's right, turn it around on me. Make it my fault *again* that you didn't do the polite thing last night. Gee, you think that because you are so good looking that you get a free pass?"

Ohmigod, did I just tell him I think he's good looking? She groaned inwardly.

"What's your problem anyway? Are you just naturally cranky?"

"Me? *I'm* cranky? You take the cake, buster. If you'll excuse me, I have a picnic to attend with my *friend*." Maggie's teeth were clenched so tight her jaw ached. She, Liv and Dee snorted and turned and walked as one toward the food tables as if Shane didn't exist

"Smooth." Kyle approached, watching her as she walked away.

"What now? I came to apologize and she started in on me before I could say a single word."

"Shane, you're a giant. You stand at least a foot taller than the woman. You stalked over here with that look on your face and glared down at her. Of course she felt threatened! You are aware you're physically threatening right? It's one of the reasons you rarely get challenged as a cop. So if the bad guys won't take you on you think she's immune? And you do have a history of intimidating her."

Kyle's eyes wandered again to Maggie. Watching as she chatted animatedly with her friends and the women handing out heaping plates of food. "You know, she cleans up pretty nice. I had no idea."

"No."

"Huh?"

"I recognize that tone, Kyle. A woman like that is trouble. There are plenty of beautiful women in Petal. Stick with one of those." Shane's glower was back.

Kyle laughed heartily. "Hmm, you're sounding a mite jealous, Shane. You looking for a bit of trouble? If so, I'd happy to stand back and let you at her."

The two of them watched as the women walked back to their blanket. Alex got up and went to help with the plates of food she'd been carrying and then helped her down to the ground.

"Uh oh, looks like someone else got to her first. Who'd have thought that little schoolteacher with the conservative blouses and the bun would look like that underneath?"

"I stole Melissa Harken from Alex Parsons back in the eighth grade. I don't see why I can't snatch our pretty schoolteacher from him." Matt strolled up with Marc. The grin on his face made it obvious he was deliberately goading Shane.

"Yeah, right. And that would be before or after you admit to all of us you have a thing for Olivia?" Kyle winked at Matt who laughed.

"Yeah. Well. Anyway. I don't think it would be very hard to push Alex out of the picture."

"No one is snatching anyone!" Shane turned away, stalking back to their blanket, grumbling under his breath.

The other three broke into laughter. "Uh oh, this one has gotten under his skin big time," Kyle said. "She is a pretty little thing, isn't she?"

"Hot is more like it. Damn, look at those legs. It's always the quiet ones." Of all the brothers, Marc was the one who seemed to revel in female attention the most. He watched Maggie with a sly smile. "How come I never noticed her before?"

"You're three years younger than we are. Plus, she's not the tight jean wearing, belly button ring kind of girl you usually chase." Matt turned to find Shane back at their blanket, drinking a cider and staring in the direction of Maggie Wright. "We'd better get back over there before he pops a vein."

ରେ ରେ ରେ

In marked contrast, Maggie was having the time of her life. Alex Parsons was a nice guy and it was a treat to have a man pay that much attention to her. And when Alex leaned over and kissed her quickly on the lips—just a peck really—Sam walked by with his new girlfriend. He'd nearly fallen over himself as he'd done a double take. It wasn't like she wanted him back, but it was nice for him to see what he was missing.

"So, Alex, how do you like working at the library?"

"Oh, well I don't think I ever imagined being a librarian when I was a kid. But I do love it. The job here was a stroke of luck really, I'd been trying to decide whether or not to go to grad school and I got the offer." He shrugged. "But I found out that I love it. I may still go back at some point but for now, I'm really happy where I am." Alex took her hand in his. "It's really great to turn young people on to books, knowing I'm opening up new worlds for them. I bet it's like that for you as a teacher."

Maggie's eyes lit up. Teaching was her great passion. "It is. I'm so lucky to have two tracks. The advanced placement history class is filled with kids who are very disciplined, high achievers. They want to be there. God, the work they produce is amazing! They're a joy to teach. My other class is just your every day sophomore history class. There are so many kinds of kids in it.

Some are just biding time until they drop out, some just barely scraping by. But my favorites are the ones who start out bored and then I introduce something that totally excites them and they become history buffs." She felt shy suddenly as she'd revealed something so important to her. "I know it's goofy but I love it. Last year, I took my AP class on a trip to Washington, DC and I think that they were more excited than I was to see the Constitution and the Declaration of Independence."

"Are you cold?" he asked Maggie when she'd shivered a bit.

Maggie stood up. "A bit. It started out so warm. I just need to run back to the car to grab my jacket and an extra blanket to wrap us up in."

"I'll come with you," Alex said, standing with her.

"Okay. Thanks." She gave him a smile and caught the keys Liv threw her way. Maggie liked the way he held a gentle arm around her waist as they walked. Not too much, just enough to let her know he wanted to touch her.

After grabbing her jacket and the extra blankets, Maggie locked up. Turning back around, she ended up nose to nose with Alex.

"You smell really good." Alex's warm, cider scented breath caressed her face. He tucked a wayward curl back behind her ear.

"Thanks. That's why I wear it back."

Alex took her chin gently between his fingers and tipped it up. Slowly, he brought his lips to hers. He was warm and gentle and the kiss only lasted a few short seconds. Maggie blinked up into his face and smiled. He hugged her quickly before walking back to their blanket.

Back on the hill, Alex sat behind her, pulling her into the warm shelter of his body. Wrapping the fleece blanket around them both, he left his arms encircled about her as well. Warm and content, Maggie leaned back against him and they watched the sky for the fireworks.

Afterwards, it was with regret that Alex helped pack up the blanket and their possessions. He didn't want the date to be over. He didn't like the idea of having to say goodnight to Maggie. He'd liked seeing that she was cold and then taking care of her. She needed someone to take care of her. He could see that. He also knew she was a lady and he wanted to take it slow to show her that he appreciated that.

Back at the car, Liv and Shaun kissed quite deeply at the driver side door and Alex burned with embarrassment and anger on Maggie's behalf. Maggie shouldn't have to be exposed to that sort of thing. But clearly Olivia was her friend and had way too much influence on Maggie's life. After they'd dated a while, Alex would know how to best deal with Olivia's bad influence and help Maggie make better choices with her friends.

With an internal sigh, he smiled at her instead and held her door open. "Can I call you, Maggie? I'd like to take you out again."

"I'd like that." She dug out a pen and some paper from her bag and wrote out her phone number and handed it to him with a smile. "I had a really nice time tonight, Alex, thank you."

He leaned over and kissed her again, still gentle and brief. He wanted to show her what a total gentleman he was. She gave him a small wave and got into the car and finally that slut Olivia stopped kissing and joined her.

"That went well, didn't it!" Liv said as they drove away. "First of all, Shaun is a great kisser! Second of all, did you see the double take that Sam gave when he saw you with Alex? Man that was perfect. Lastly, did you notice Shane Chase staring at you all night like he was a hungry wolf and you were a T-bone steak?"

"Yes, I saw Sam and yes, it was quite satisfying. Alex is a nice kisser—no fireworks—but I did feel like he was taking things slow. He asked if he could call me again and I said yes. Lastly, no, I did not notice Sheriff Dumbass looking at me. Boy, is that man sour!" And incredibly handsome and he smelled as good as all those Chase boys seemed to. Including Kyle. A man with a goatee was so sexy. One with a uniform, the other with a goatee! Whooee.

ର ର ର

The next few days were hectic as the school year wore on towards midterm exams and the homecoming game approached. Still, not so busy that when Alex called Maggie couldn't find time to have dinner with him Wednesday night at El Cid.

The dinner with Alex was nice. He was attentive and smart and he loved many of the same things she did. Their conversation was lively as they discussed books and travel and history. Still, Maggie couldn't quite shake the odd feeling at the base of her spine at times during the evening. It wasn't that he ever did or said anything wrong though and Maggie was sure she was just trying to talk herself out of a nice guy as self sabotage.

At her front door she turned to him with a smile. "Um, would you like to come inside for some tea?"

Grabbing her hand, he brought it to his lips and kissed it. Moments later he pulled her close, holding her against his body. "If I come in, I'll want to never leave and I think that's moving a bit fast for you."

"It's not that I don't like you. I do. But yes, it would be a bit too fast for me." Still, she didn't make any move to stop him as he lowered his lips to hers for a kiss. This one more passionate than sweet and he held her tight for a few long moments afterward.

"Goodnight, Alex. I had a lovely time." Placing a hand in the middle of his chest, she moved him back from her gently.

"Would you like to go to the Homecoming Game with me on Friday night? Then maybe go out for a drink and a bite afterwards?" He admired how much of a lady she was. He liked that she was saving herself just for him. His sweet Maggie.

"Yes, I'd like that. Dee, Liv and I all meet on Fridays at the Pumphouse. It's an after Homecoming tradition for us, too. Arthur will be there and I'm guessing Liv will have a date but I don't know who. Shall we meet them there afterwards?"

"I like Arthur. He's a good guy and I think Shaun is planning to ask Olivia." He mentally ground his teeth at the thought of Olivia but smiled instead. "Shall I pick you up at six then? I'll bring the seat cushions and the blanket?"

She smiled and he was glad he'd let her know how much he liked taking care of her.

"Okay, I'll be here." With a last look, she went into her house and he walked to his car and went home.

୰ ୰ ୰

Alex led Maggie up the steps toward an empty spot on the bench seats, at the stadium. She looked so pretty in jeans and boots with a deep green turtleneck sweater. Instead of the bun, her hair was loose in back, held by a headband. Having it down in back left the pretty color around her face, making her eyes seem larger. He liked that she'd kept the glasses. Liked that she was lovely and modest, too.

Wanting to be sure she was comfortable and warm, placed the two seat cushions on the cold aluminum bench and sat down next to her. He grabbed her hand and held it in between his own.

After a while, Maggie stood up. "I'm going to go to the ladies' room. Shall I bring us back some stuff to snack on?"

Alex smiled at her thoughtfulness. "Sure. Some hot chocolate and some licorice."

"I'll be back in a few minutes then."

When Maggie exited the restrooms she saw Shane Chase waiting there and eyed him warily.

He held up his hands in the universal sign of surrender. "I mean no harm, I promise. I wanted to apologize to you for how I acted. At The Pumphouse last Friday and then Sunday at the picnic, as well."

Narrowing her eyes for a moment, Maggie let out the breath she hadn't realized she'd been holding. "Apology accepted. I'm sorry if I jumped to conclusions at the picnic. I'm usually not that big of a bitch."

"I do seem to bring out the best in you." He chuckled. "For such a little woman, you sure pack a mean punch." His smile melted her insides. The man was just flat out handsome. Perfect, white teeth. Chocolate brown hair that was just a bit too long in the back and looked really soft. But his eyes were startlingly blue. Like the blue of a cloudless summer day. Her stomach fluttered just looking at him.

"I did not punch you! But you would have deserved it if I had." She raised an eyebrow. "But according to Cecelia Wright, that's not what ladies do. We bake and butter wouldn't melt in our mouths. Oh, and know how to embroider. Too bad I can't embroider or know how to keep my mouth shut. I can bake though." She snorted. *I just snorted!* Horror roiled through her.

Instead of being disgusted, he threw back his head and laughed, a deep rich rumbling sound. "Embroidering is overrated anyway, Margaret. That is your name, right? I'm Shane Chase by the way. Otherwise known as dumbass." He held out his hand for her to shake and she pinked a bit. His grip was gentle but sure.

"I was getting rather fond of thinking of you as Sheriff Dumbass. You were being one you know," she mumbled and he laughed a bit more.

"So my mother, brothers, father and half of the town have said."

She laughed at that. "Yes, I'm Margaret but most other people call me Maggie." She looked around him toward the stands. "Thank you for the apology, Shane. I need to grab some snacks and drinks before heading back. The game'll be starting soon."

"Oh, of course. It was nice to meet you, Maggie. Glad we cleared the air. See ya around." With a wink and a grin, he put his hands in his pockets and strolled away whistling.

Was that disappointment she saw in his eyes or wishful thinking on her part? *Probably just gas,* she snorted to herself.

He certainly was something else. In truth, she'd never met someone with that kind of sheer masculinity and sex appeal before. It left her a bit breathless. Still, she couldn't help but watch his ass in those snug jeans as he retreated back toward the stands. And she didn't feel one bit guilty about it either.

When she got back she handed out the armful of goodies she'd purchased. "Were the lines long?" Alex put the blanket back over her lap once she'd sat back down.

"Oh, no, not really. I just saw someone I knew and started talking." She blew on her hot chocolate.

Alex frowned. "Oh. Well, I was worried, Maggie."

The sharpness of his tone brought her head around to look at him with surprise. Her mouth opened to issue an automatic apology but she clicked her teeth together to stop it. The more she was around him, the more proprietary and paternalistic he became. It troubled her and she doubted she'd be seeing him again after the night ended.

As they filed out after the game, Shane caught her eye and she waved, smiling as he waved back. Alex noticed and shot an angry glare at Shane.

In the car, on the way over to The Pumphouse, Alex started in on Maggie about it. "I saw you flirting with the sheriff."

She winced at his tone. Definitely wouldn't be seeing him again after the date ended. Red flags flew all over the place at his behavior.

"I wasn't flirting. I waved at him. I ran into him briefly tonight and he apologized for something he did last week. I saw him as we were leaving the stadium and I waved. If you notice, I waved at his mother and father, too."

"You're with me. You don't need to talk to other men." Angrily, he parked the car and got out, leaving Maggie to process her shock and discomfort over how he'd just acted.

They walked into the bar and went to their table. But before they sat down, Maggie swallowed her insulted fury and stopped him with a hand on his arm. "I want you to know it makes me uncomfortable that you talked to me that way, Alex. I haven't done anything wrong."

The rigidity in his posture loosened as he shot her a sheepish smile. "You're right. I'm sorry, Maggie. It's just that you're so beautiful and I really enjoy being with you. I got jealous. I apologize."

Relieved that he wasn't going to flip out, Maggie smiled back wanly, still uncomfortable with his behavior. "Apology accepted. Oh look, it's everyone else." Just wanting to get the rest of the evening finished, she waved at her friends.

The place was packed, more so than usual and Maggie didn't fail to notice when the Chase brothers and their dates came in about half an hour later. Still, she wasn't going to let Alex control her so when Shane nodded his head to her in greeting she smiled back and sent him a brief wave. She felt Alex tense up but he didn't say anything.

But later when Shane got up to go to the men's room, Alex excused himself and walked back there.

"Hey, Chase, you need to leave Maggie the hell alone." His voice was an angry hiss and it echoed from the bathroom walls. Maggie was *his* damn it. His and no one else's.

Shane turned around to stare at him, eyebrow raised. "Oh, is that so?"

"Yeah, that's so. She's mine, Shane. Back off."

"Huh, well here's the thing, Alex, I waved hello at her, twice. I didn't kiss her or anything. Now, just between you and me, I like her. I think she's a nice woman with a lot of spark. I'm thinking of asking her to dinner sometime but I certainly wouldn't do it when she was on a date with another man."

"She's too good for you. Maggie Wright is a lady and she needs a man to take care of her. You're a dog. You're slime and you don't deserve a special woman like her. I'm telling you, she's mine, Chase and you're upsetting her with your unwanted attentions."

"Um, I don't think so. From what I understand, you've gone out with her a few times. Sorry but that does not a girlfriend make. I had a girlfriend who cheated, I certainly know the difference. In any case, if that's how Maggie feels, I'll certainly respect that. If I hear it from her. Now if you'll excuse me, I have a nice cold beer to get back to. Have a nice night." Shane walked past Alex and out the door.

Alex stormed back to the table and put his arm around Maggie. "Alex, I need my arm to eat." She shrugged him off. He glowered at her for a moment and he saw the fear in her eyes—just a flash—before she went back to eating her cheeseburger.

He knew he'd moved too fast as he took her home. She sat against the door and wouldn't look at him, avoiding small talk. He had to win her back. Had to show her how well he'd take care of her.

"You don't need to walk me to the door," she said as she got out the moment he stopped the car. "The porch light is on, I'll be fine."

He got out quickly and went to her side. "Don't be silly. It's late and dark. And I like being with you, Maggie."

At her door she unlocked it but stood directly in front of it, blocking his way. "Well, good night, Alex."

Moving in for a kiss, he felt her stiffen and tried to show her how much he liked her but she pulled back and put a hand between them to push him back.

She was right of course. He shouldn't maul her on her front porch. What if her neighbors saw? He needed to protect her reputation. She was important in the community and people looked up to her. As her husband, he'd need to always keep such things in mind. "I'm sorry, let's take this inside, shall we?"

"I'm really tired, Alex. I think I'll pass on any company. Thanks for the game and dinner." She took a step back, fumbling with the door knob directly behind her.

He exhaled sharply. She held herself away from him and that was not all right. But he had to let her know he was there for good. She was just worried he'd love her and leave her. "Fine. I'll call you later. You know what, Maggie? You're my girlfriend, right?"

Her eyes darted around until finally coming back to look at his face. "Um, well, no. We've dated, yes, but to my mind, that takes a lot longer than a few dates."

"Goodnight, Maggie." He turned and walked away from her without another word before she could say anything else.

Moving into the house quickly, Maggie locked the door behind herself. She also threw the deadbolt. Her hands shook. He sat in her driveway for several minutes more and finally pulled away. With a sigh of relief, she sat in a heap on her couch.

After the nausea passed, she went through the house and checked to make sure her doors and windows were locked as she replayed the evening in her mind. The way he spoke to her, held onto her all the time—it was really frightening and totally inappropriate. It'd started out sort of nice but went right to patronizing, clingy and then outright scary in really short order.

No more dates with him, that was for sure. No, when she got up the next day she'd talk to Liv and work out a way to break things off that made it clear she wasn't interested but also didn't make things worse.

Chapter Three

The day started out pretty darned good when she was downtown picking up ingredients for the banana bread.

Distracted as she shopped for baking supplies, Maggie was walking down Main Street when she literally bumped into Shane.

"Sheriff Chase, you seem to make a habit of knocking into me." Her flirtatious laugh died in her throat as she looked up his body and into his face. Try as she might, she couldn't ignore the tightening in her stomach at the sight of his khaki colored uniform stretched tight across his muscles.

"You're a menace, Miz Wright." He laughed back. "Tell you what? To make up for crashing into me, yet again, why don't you buy me a cup of coffee and cinnamon roll?"

Unreality slid into her. Did the man just ask her for coffee? Still, she managed to hang on to her flirty tone. "All right, if it's that or go to jail, I suppose I'd better bribe you."

They walked the two blocks to the Honey Bear Bakery. "Why don't you grab a table and I'll get the drinks and cinnamon rolls?" Maggie waved at an open corner table.

Shane blushed. "Oh no! I was just kidding. I'll buy."

"Nope, not this time. It's my treat. Now go on, get a table, I'll be over in a sec." Maggie made shoo motions with her hands.

He hesitated for a moment and she could see him wrestling with how he could wrangle his way into paying but he soon gave up and sighed. "Fine. I'll get us a table."

At least being alone at the counter and getting the giant rolls and steaming cups of coffee to the table without spilling gave her the chance to concentrate on something other than the fit of his uniform and why in the world he'd be interested in her to begin with. But eventually, she arrived at their table and had to unload the tray and sit down.

"You know, when I went away to school, my dad would mail me these cinnamon rolls at my birthday and holidays." The pleasant memory of her father cut into the happiness she'd been feeling.

"That was nice. Sounds like something my mom would do."

"Your mother would bring them herself." She laughed, thinking about Polly Chase and that mile long car of hers.

He chuckled. "You know her pretty well then."

"I happen to think your mother is an amazing woman. So old world in many ways but she always surprises me with how modern she is. I have to laugh every time I hear the click clack of those heels coming down the hall when the Historical Society meets. Everyone stops messing around and waits patiently and quietly until she comes in. Every time she does the same thing— slams that massive purse of hers down on the table, gives her hair a primp and flops into the chair."

"According to my father, she started out with a tiny purse back before she had me and it's gotten bigger over the years. We all thought that when all of us moved out and it was just her and Dad again, it would get smaller." He shook his head. "But I swear she needs the car just to cart the purse around."

Maggie burst out laughing. "She came to my house you know—to apologize for you."

"She's the ultimate meddler but her heart is in the right place."

"Hey, don't complain, you could have Cecelia Wright as your mother." She winced as it came out, more bitter than she expected. "Oh god, never mind, that just sounded awful."

"How about this? Why don't you let me take you to dinner tonight and you can tell me the whole story?"

Her eyebrow went up and a smile played at the corner of her mouth. If she'd been watching herself from a distance she wouldn't even had suspected her stomach had just run riot with butterflies and she had a mental picture of herself doing the somersault of joy.

"Hmm, well, I'd love to do dinner but I'll skip the whole my-mother-doesn't-understand-me story."

"How about a movie afterwards?"

"Okay." *Okay? Yeah, soooo casual.* She snickered mentally.

"I'll pick you up at say, seven? Do you like Italian? We could go to Vincent's and then, um, I've seen the action flick at the Orpheum but there's a double feature at the drive-in, would that be all right?"

"Are you trying to get me to make out with you at the drive in, Shane Chase?" Apparently, aliens had taken over her body. Flirty aliens with nerves of steel. She hoped they'd stay until he left or she'd die on the spot.

He turned pink and laughed. "You've caught me!" He gave her a grin, white teeth making him look a bit wolfish. "But of course you know I'm a total gentleman now that I took that civility class you recommended."

She threw back her head and laughed at that. "Okay. I live on the corner of Fourth and Magnolia." She stood up. "I need to finish my errands. It was nice sharing a cup of coffee and this nine thousand calorie cinnamon roll with you. I'll see you tonight." He walked with her to the sidewalk and they each headed opposite ways. She hoped the smile he had on was half as big as hers.

Still, she continued to grin like a fool back at home and mixing the bread. She was pretty impressed with the way she'd held it together and stopped herself from jumping up and down squealing with delight.

Her good mood held on until she noticed that she had some messages. Playing them back, a sick feeling replaced her happiness. There were six from Alex. And he'd already called twice before she left the house to start with. Each message she listened to got more intense. The way his voice had started off calm and friendly but turned into something like a sharp snarl on the last message sent a cold chill down her spine. Especially the part where he ordered her to call him immediately and chided her for being gone without letting him know her whereabouts.

It had to end. She'd decided that the night before but she wanted to do it face to face. Freaked as she was, she didn't want to stop seeing him via voicemail, that seemed cruel. Picking up the phone with trembling hands,

Maggie called him back but ended up leaving a message that she wanted to talk to him.

She ran the loaves of bread over to the retirement home. She sucked it up and stopped by her parents' house and Janie's as well. Best to just get that out of the way. As it happened, she had enough of an emotional high from her afternoon and upcoming date that the visits weren't too bad and she escaped as quickly as she could.

Back at home, she called Liv and begged for her help to get ready for her big date.

Liv showed up breathless and eager less than five minutes later. "I can't believe you didn't call me immediately! Let's go and get you an outfit while you tell me every last detail."

Liv pushed Maggie upstairs and made all the right noises as Maggie told her about the afternoon coffee with Shane as she got dressed.

With her usually curly hair blown out straight and captured in a headband, the pleated skirt and sweater made Maggie feel vibrant and sexy too.

"Very collegiate and sassy. Damn I'm good." Liv looked her work over with a critical eye.

"I know, without this I wouldn't be going out with a man like Shane Chase at all."

"Maggie, you need to stop this. You're still you. I told you before, it's not like I turned you into something you weren't. So I added a bit of sparkle. Shane Chase has been mooning after you since that night at The Pumphouse. A night you were covered in chili cheese fries and had your hair in a bun."

Ducking her head, Maggie hid her blush. She knew it was true but it was hard to overcome what she'd been told all her life. But she was too old to let her mother still make her feel inadequate. Taking a deep breath she stood up straight and held her head up. "You're right. Thank you. He's going to be here any minute. I'd better go downstairs. You going out with Shaun tonight?"

"No, I'm going out with Tom Maddox, he's picking me up in an hour. I should get home now. Speaking of Shaun, what's up with Alex? What crawled up his ass last night?"

"Oh my god! I forgot that I hadn't told you about this yet." Maggie related the whole story of how Alex had acted the evening before as they went downstairs.

"Major red flags are waving with this guy, Liv. He's seriously creeping me out. He called me eight times today! This guy is seriously not right."

"No shit. Why didn't you tell me? You shouldn't have even let him bring you home last night. You could have slept at my place."

"I know. It just kept getting worse and worse and it wasn't until I was sitting here in the dark, wondering if all my locks were working that I realized how truly freaked out I was. Anyway, the little voice said get away and so I am."

"Well, that's a good idea, Maggie." Liv frowned. "Never ignore the little voice. Be extra careful around him, okay? You call 911 and then me if he comes around. You know you can come over any time if you're feeling scared, too. You have a key for a reason." Liv kissed Maggie's cheek. "But for now, have a good time and I'll see you at brunch tomorrow. I expect a full report!"

Grinning as she watched Liv jog down the block that separated their two houses, Maggie saw Shane's truck pull onto her street. She ducked back into the house to check her hair and lipstick and grab her coat.

She opened the door as he walked up onto the porch and she wasn't quite sure where her breath went. He seemed to steal all the oxygen from the area where he stood.

While she tried not to gawk, he looked her up and down and smiled. "Wow. You look beautiful." He reached out to touch her hair. "I like the curls but this is nice, too. You can see all of the different colors of red better this way."

She blushed. "You're really good at that. Thank you. You don't look so bad yourself, Sheriff." Dark denim jeans hugged his long muscled legs. A black and gray sweater brought out the blue in his eyes and contrasted the color of his hair. Man, he looked so good she wanted to grab him and jump on him.

One corner of his mouth rose. "Thank you, Maggie. Shall we then?" He indicated his truck with a tip of his head and she nodded. He helped her into his ridiculously large truck and they drove to Vincent's. They shared small talk on the way over. Maggie was surprised by how easy he was to talk to.

Heads turned as Shane led Maggie to a dark table in the back. But she soon forgot the scrutiny as they ordered. Dinner was good, conversation came easy and they finished and took off to get to the drive-in before the show started.

Shane parked toward the back as his truck was so high and big it would have blocked the view. He pushed the bench seat all the way back and moved away from the steering wheel and into the center. Bringing him very close to her.

"I brought a blanket. It's been getting so cold in the last few days. I would have brought beer but you know, being the sheriff means I can't do illegal things, even when they'd be fun. I did bring snacks, though." Reaching behind the seat into the rear cab, he pulled out a sack of chocolate, red vines and some bottled water.

"You think of everything, Shane Chase." Maggie moved in a bit closer. It was very nice to be there beside him.

The double feature, two action movies with Bruce Willis, was entertaining. It didn't matter that the audio wasn't that good if you could see things blowing up. It was easy enough to follow the plot. By the middle of the second movie Maggie had snuggled up against Shane's body. Her feet curled under her, his arm around her shoulders, she felt utterly lazy and warm—and very turned on by the way he felt against her. It had been a year since she'd slept with anyone. She'd dated but none of them were people she'd wanted to sleep with. Shane Chase brought a level of physical desire into her life that she wasn't sure she'd ever felt before.

"Shane?"

"Hmm?"

"I do believe you promised something regarding making out?"

He looked down at her, surprise on his face. She blushed as the surprise heated into something more. "Never mind. I can't believe I said that out loud. It's the sugar. I need to stop eating sugar, that's all there is to it."

"No way. You said it," he murmured, moving his head down to her, "and I aim to hold you to it." A gentle hand at her chin tipped her face to his just as his lips reached hers. Electricity sparked between them, firing her nerve endings to life.

He tasted so good she had to have more. Coming up to her knees, she moved to get better access to his lips. His growl of approval vibrated down her spine and he pulled her to him tightly.

The kiss deepened as his tongue swept out, tracing the curve of her bottom lip before taking it between his teeth and nipping it. She sighed into his mouth as desire roared through her. She didn't recognize the sound of need that came from deep inside her but he matched it when she sucked on his tongue.

Those big hands caressed her back, leaving tingling, heated flesh in their wake. She wanted them on her thighs, sliding higher, wanted them palming the nipples that throbbed to be touched.

When one of his hands slid up into her hair and fisted, violent shivers wracked her. So much need, she felt like she was drowning in it.

He'd been moving his hands down her back to her ass when his phone rang. Stiffening, he pulled back from her lips ever so reluctantly. "I'm sorry, that's my work phone. I have to get it."

Too desire stunned to speak, she nodded her understanding.

"Chase," he grunted as he answered.

She watched as he went into work mode and the gentle, sexy face turned serious. Straightening her clothes, she sat back down on the seat and reached to turn off the audio so he could hear better.

"Hang on, let me get something to write on." He grabbed a pad and pen from his overhead visor. "Go," he ordered and began to scribble information down on the pad. "Yeah, I'll do it." Sighing, he snapped the phone shut.

"I'm sorry, Maggie, but I have to go on a call. I'll drop you home on the way." Apology was clear on his face as he moved the seat back into place and slid back behind the wheel.

"Don't be sorry. It's your job." She admired her ability to not sound disappointed. She certainly didn't want the man to feel guilty about being a cop. "I had a really good time tonight. Thanks for dinner and the movies."

"How about the making out?" He gave her that wolfishly wicked grin—the one that sent a ball of heat straight to her gut—and she laughed.

Before too long they'd navigated out of the parking lot and were on their way back toward her house.

"That too." She tried not to grin so wide her face would split open. He made her feel giddy.

"So, did I pass?"

"Pass what?"

"Muster. As in, am I second date material?"

"Ask me and find out."

"Maggie, can I take you out again? Like say, for ice cream on Tuesday night?"

"Ice cream, huh? It seems you've found out my secret. Throw something sweet at me and I'm putty."

He pulled up in her drive way and started to get out but she patted his arm. "No, go on your call, I can walk to the door."

He rolled his eyes at her before getting out and walking around the car to help her down. "It's not so urgent that I'd just throw you at your door." At her door he kissed her quickly. "I'll see you Tuesday then? I'll pick you up at seven."

"Okay, be safe," she called out and waved at him as he drove away.

ങ ങ ങ

Maggie walked into the restaurant where she met Dee and Liv for brunch every Sunday and her smile was apparent from across the room.

"So?" Liv asked before Maggie had even finished sitting down.

Maggie looked at both her friends. "So, it was great. We had a lovely dinner and then we went to the drive-in. We watched most of both movies, had a major, *major* kiss but then he got a work call and had to go. He did ask me out again. We're having ice cream on Tuesday."

"Oh my god! Of course you said yes." Dee grinned back at Maggie.

"Of course she did!" Liv waved her hand as if it were a done deal. "So, is he a good kisser or what? Details, Maggie, we want details."

"Duh! I tell you I've been dreaming about kissing Shane Chase since I was in the fifth grade and he was in the seventh. It was better than any of the times I kissed my pillow, I can tell you that."

"Dreamy. It's so romantic, Maggie. You've got the man you've always wanted." Dee sighed.

"I don't *have* him. I'm dating him. Big difference, especially to a man like Shane Chase. I need to remember that superhot lust is not the same as love." Maggie shrugged. She had a tendency to wear her heart on her sleeve and she knew Shane Chase had warning signs all over his very delicious body.

Liv nodded. "I'm glad you said it. It's good to remember that, Maggie. Sam was a dolt but Shane is big league because he's a player. Not in a bad way, he's not a mimbo, but he's not a one woman man either. And he's one of those men who's sort of overwhelming with all that testosterone rolling off him. It's really hot, but heck, it would fry my circuits, too!"

"I know. And I feel like a total hoochie for saying this, but I want to have sex with him. I don't think I've been this horny. Ever."

"You're the farthest thing from a hoochie that I can think of. Jeez, woman, you haven't had sex in a year! And this big old hard-bodied studmuffin strolls into your life. What woman wouldn't want to have sex with Shane Chase?"

"Hey, if I didn't have Arthur, I'd totally agree. But I do agree with the assessment that Shane is a nice boy to play with but he's not the kind to set up housekeeping. You're old enough to eat dessert first every once in a while, Maggie." Dee laughed and turned to Liv. "And how was your date with Tom?"

"It was all right. I'd give the date a six and a half out of ten. Speaking of Chase brothers, I bumped into Matt this morning. He's gotten even better looking since high school."

"Yes indeed. He's grown into his looks." Dee waggled her eyebrows.

"Certainly doesn't hurt that he works with his body a lot as a firefighter."

"I've contemplated setting my back deck on fire to get him over to my place," Liv said around a mouthful of waffle.

They all laughed at the idea of Liv in her backyard with lighter fluid and a negligee on, waiting for Matt Chase to arrive.

"Why don't you just ask him out?"

"Nah, he's the kind of guy that needs to be in the lead."

"Hmm, well, I'll have to think of something to bring the two of you together," Maggie said thoughtfully.

"Don't you dare mention this to Shane!" Liv actually colored at the idea.

"Why not? Oh my god, did you just blush?"

"Because! Jeez, I'm not desperate, Maggie! I can trap a man without having you tell Matt's brother that I like him. That's so eighth grade."

"I guess a Halloween party at my house and a game of spin the bottle is out then?"

They all laughed at the memory of the Halloween party that Dee had at her house when they were in the ninth grade. "That was my first official French kiss. Andrew Johnson, in Dee's mom's broom closet. Good times," Liv said dreamily.

"Yeah well look what you did to him, Liv, he's gay." Maggie laughed. "Clearly you were too much woman for him and it spoiled him forever for the rest of us.

"Seriously, Liv, I'm on it. I'm going to think of something because let me attest that a taste of Chase is worth the work." Maggie waggled her brows suggestively and the laughter started anew.

Across the room, Matt and Kyle Chase ate their brunch while they watched the women laughing at their table. "What do you suppose all of that is about?" Kyle couldn't stop himself from looking at Maggie Wright. *Damn,* he liked the way she looked when she laughed. But his brother liked her first and so he backed off. There were rules about this sort of thing.

"Looks like trouble but the kind of trouble a man enjoys in the end." Matt sipped his coffee.

"So what did Shane say about their date last night?"

"I haven't seen him yet. Maggie looks pretty glowing though."

Maggie looked over and saw them. Smiling, she waved. The other two looked around and waved hello as well before huddling together, the laughter starting again.

"Hmm." Kyle grinned. "I do believe we're the object of some female giggling, Matt. I think I like it."

"Hell, Kyle, I *know* I like it."

When the women left they waved again. Kyle enjoyed the view through the big front windows as the three women walked together down the street.

ભ ભ ભ

Alex melted back into the doorway of the hardware store so he wouldn't be seen. Someone had to watch over her. He'd wanted to get Maggie alone but she was always with her damned friends. Or with that jerk Shane Chase. Oh he'd seen the man pick up *his* fiancée the night before. Saw the kiss when Maggie returned. But she did not let Shane in. His Maggie was still saving herself just for him. And Shane Chase was just a momentary distraction. Alex would make sure of that.

ભ ભ ભ

Olivia and Maggie decided to grab a bite at The Pumphouse before Maggie's ice cream date with Shane.

Arriving a bit early, Maggie saw Matt Chase across the street with Johnny Prentice. She gave a friendly wave hello and they returned the greeting with a few shouted hellos.

Still smiling as she turned back toward the door, she bumped into Alex. Fear slithered through her as she realized she hadn't even seen his approach.

Shit. She really hadn't wanted to deal with him that night. She'd tried to call him to arrange to see him face to face to break things off. But he hadn't returned any of her calls. It wasn't like she was avoiding the issue but she certainly didn't want to have the discussion in public in the middle of the sidewalk.

"Hi, Alex." She gave him a wary smile, not at all liking the look on his face.

He grabbed her arm in a grip so tight she winced. "Hi, Alex? Is that all you've got to say?"

"What the heck are you talking about?" Her voice rose as she struggled to get free.

"The way you can't help but talk to every man you see. I told you, *you're with me.* You don't need to talk to any other man. Are you trying to make me jealous, Maggie? You don't need to play games. All it's doing is really pissing me off. I don't like my woman to act that way."

Still keeping a tight grip on her arm, he steered her into The Pumphouse. That grip was the only thing that prevented him from getting slapped as she tried to get free and keep her balance.

"What the hell are you talking about? I don't need to talk to other men?" she demanded through clenched teeth. "Let me go this instant!"

"You heard me, Maggie. You're my girl, I don't want you all over other men like a slut." He hissed and his grip on her arm tightened and caused her to gasp in pain.

Hearing the words, she stilled for a moment. Fury replaced the fear. "You did *not* just call me a slut!" Her eyes narrowed at him. "And I said—Let. Me. Go. Now or I'm going to kick you in the junk!"

By that point, the conversations around them had gotten quiet and for the second time in a few weeks, she was the subject of attention at The Pumphouse.

Noting that they were being watched, he let go and she took the opportunity to move away from him. But he stepped closer, filling the space between them. "You don't need to be hanging all over other men."

"I *waved* at them. I didn't flash my boobs at them or blow a kiss. I waved hello. But even if I had, *you* don't get to decide what I need to be doing, Alex."

He grabbed her arm again and moved her toward her usual table. "You're making a scene. Sit down." He shoved her into the booth.

Her eyes widened at that. "In the first place, you will not touch me ever again or you'll draw back a stump. In the second place, you need to get a hold of yourself right now, Alex. No one talks to me this way. You don't own me. Hell, we've only gone on three dates."

"You don't tell me to get a hold of myself when you're the one acting like a whore!" he said in a stage whisper.

"*What?*" Grasping the water glass on the table, she dashed it in his face, taking his moment of surprise to push him back and scoot out of the booth. "I know you didn't just call me a whore! How dare you!" She pushed up into his face, seemingly undaunted by the fact that he was several inches taller than she was.

Liv and Dee came rushing in with the Chase boys right behind them. For a moment, they all stood and looked in the direction of the fracas. Kyle's face turned so red it was purple. He and his brothers, together with Arthur stalked over.

"How dare I? You're a tease, Maggie Wright. You come on to every man you meet and now you don't like it when you get called what you really are." The viciousness in his voice made her skin crawl. He was like a completely different person. Reaching out, he grabbed her arm and yanked her to sit back down.

Shane stalked forward and grabbed Alex's wrist, squeezing tightly until he blanched and let go of Maggie. "You need to let the lady go now, Alex," he said in a voice that was low and threatening

"Are you all right, Maggie?" Kyle had moved around Shane so he could kneel in front of her. Slowly, he reached out and took her hand.

"That asshole called me a whore!" Maggie fumed but she knew her trembling was so bad that anyone looking could see it.

"I think you need to leave the premises, Alex, before I have to arrest you for assault." Shane moved so that he stood between Alex and Maggie.

"Oh, so you can fuck her then? This is all about you getting into her bed isn't it?" Alex's voice broke, he screamed it so loud. Incensed, Maggie jumped up to get in his face but Kyle grabbed her, his arms around her waist, murmuring into her ear.

"You bastard! Don't you ever call me or contact me again."

Shane dragged Alex to the door and tossed him bodily outside. "You're lucky I'm here as the sheriff today, Alex. If I was just here as Shane Chase you'd be spitting out teeth right now. Now you leave her alone just as she's asked or you'll be asking for a world of hurt." Shane glowered at Alex and turned back into The Pumphouse.

Olivia and Dee spoke softly to Maggie, trying to calm her down. Shane approached and put a hand on her shoulder. "Maggie, are you all right?" he asked, concern evident in his voice.

Kyle looked at the staring crowd. "Okay, folks, I'm sure we don't want to upset Maggie any more so let's just get back to our beers and burgers."

"Thank god you came in when you did. What made you come in?" Maggie asked them gratefully.

"Matt saw you bump into Alex. He thought it looked like Alex had grabbed you. I was walking up the street with Kyle, Matt called out to us and we all came over. I'm sorry I didn't stop him sooner. What happened, Maggie?"

"I don't even know really. I was walking in here and saw Matt and John across the way and I waved. I turned around and bumped into Alex. I said hello and for whatever reason, it set him off. He started freaking out about me waving at Matt and John. He said I was acting like a slut, that I was his girl." She rubbed her arm where he'd grabbed it. "Then he grabbed me, twice, and shoved me into the booth and called me a whore. That creep called me, Margaret Elizabeth Wright, a whore! I should kick his sorry ass for that." On the outside she was livid but she burned with humiliation.

Kyle's face darkened. "Are you hurt?"

She shook her head. "I might have a bruise on my arm but other that I'm just pissed off."

"Would you like to press charges, Maggie? It's assault you know." Shane knelt on his haunches in front of her.

"No, I don't ever want to deal with him again." Her bottom lip was trembling.

"Come on, let's get you home. I have some time left on my shift." He looked to Kyle. "Can you run her home? Just go through her place?"

"It's not a problem. Really, don't go out of your way." Maggie chewed on her lip.

Kyle smiled gently at her. "Don't worry about it. It's not out of my way at all. And it's certainly not a chore to ferry a beautiful woman around town." He reached out to her to give her a hand that she took gratefully.

Liv and Dee hugged her and told her they'd call her the next day. "Do you want to stay with me?" Liv asked.

"No, Liv, I'll see you tomorrow, I just want to go home and take a bath and go to sleep."

With a gentle guiding hand, Kyle nodded to everyone and took her out to his car.

On the way to her house he stayed quiet, letting her pull herself together. She appreciated that space. She wasn't ready to talk about it any further at that point.

When he pulled into her driveway he got out and came around to help her get out. "I'm going to come in, Maggie. Just to do a quick check. I don't think there's a problem but let's just be safe. All right?" He took the key from her and unlocked the door.

"You think he might be here?" Nausea rolled over her at the idea. She'd always felt safe living alone, now she didn't.

"No, darlin' I just want to be safe." His voice was soothing as he reached in to turn on the light before walking into the foyer. "I'm just going to look around. I want you to stay here while I do. I'll be right back."

Leaving her there, trying to set aside how scared she looked, he walked through each room of the house. He checked window seals and locks, closets, doors and under beds. No one else was there or had tried to get in and he was pleased to note that her locks and other security were in good shape.

"It's all right," he called out, coming down the stairs. The scent of her bedroom was burned into his memory. Rain and vanilla. And the sight of her panties, folded in silky piles on her dresser had made him clutch his chest. The knowledge that the woman wore silky, lacy thong underwear in every color of the rainbow haunted him.

The woman was involved with his brother. His brother who hadn't bothered to call yet to check in.

"I know it sounds weird but I'm suddenly hungry. Care to see what I've got in my fridge? I know I need some food to go with that scotch I'm going to drink."

He didn't want to leave. "Sure. Sounds good." Following her into the large kitchen, he sat at her comfortable, worn table.

On her tip toes, she reached up into a cabinet and pulled out a bottle of scotch. "Why don't you do the honors?" She put the bottle on the counter. "I'm going to see what we've got to choose from." Turning quickly, she opened the fridge and began to examine the contents.

In companionable silence, Kyle poured them both two fingers of scotch, breathing in the smoky scent. He handed her a glass which she quickly drained and held the glass out to be refilled. With one eyebrow raised, he poured more but she merely took a sip and put the glass down and continued to work.

He went back to his place at the table and watched her as she moved through her kitchen. She pulled out vegetables, rice, some chicken and started preparing things. "How does chicken and rice sound?" She poked her head around the refrigerator door to ask.

"It sounds really good. Are you sure you wouldn't rather get take out? Or be alone? I don't want to impose."

She grinned at him. "Hey, it's no problem now that the scotch has kicked in. I'd love to cook for you as a thank you for coming home with me."

He laughed. "Okay then, lay it on me. Can I help?"

"Nah, I've got it down to a science."

And so he watched her as she moved with efficiency around her kitchen, chopping and sautéing. They made small talk but he let her lead, not pushing her to fill in every moment of the silence. He could tell she was still processing the events from earlier.

With a start, he realized he wanted to know her more. Wanted to spend time with her. And god, did he ever want to kiss her. He'd known he had an attraction to her but this was more.

Kyle knew in his gut that Shane would fuck up. He was of two minds about it. The mercenary side of him wanted Shane out of the way so he could take her out. Freely express to her just how much he enjoyed her company. But he also knew a woman as sweet as Maggie would be hurt when the inevitable happened and he hated the thought.

So he put his feelings away and decided that fate would out in the end. He had to step back. He didn't like it, but brothers had rules and he would not betray that.

After dinner he walked to her front door. "Are you going to be all right? He's wrong, you know." Kyle said quietly, touching her chin.

A lump formed in Maggie's throat, words couldn't get past it.

"You didn't do anything wrong. You're a good person, Maggie. A kind, beautiful woman. Alex is twisted, broken. This is about him, not you."

Swallowing her tears she nodded. "Thank you. Thank you so much for saying it. I'll be fine. My doors will be locked up tight and I have no problem calling 911 if I have to."

He smiled and leaned in, kissing her forehead. "If you need anything, you can call me. I'll talk you through or come over, whatever."

"That's very sweet. I appreciate it."

"Goodnight, Maggie Wright."

"Goodnight, Kyle Chase."

☙ ☙ ☙

Maggie cleaned up the kitchen, grateful to have something to do. Leaving a few lights on downstairs, she trudged toward her bathroom and took a long hot shower. With a butcher knife, her cell phone and a baseball bat all within reach.

It might have been an overreaction but she was alone and you got to overreact when some creep attacked you.

Clean and warm, she crawled between her sheets and left her bedside lamp burning. But as she lay there, it wasn't Alex she thought of, or Shane, it was Kyle.

He'd been so gentle with her, so kind and funny and considerate. On top of being marvelously handsome, he was such a beautiful person on the inside. She really liked his company.

For long moments, there with her eyes closed, she imagined that his attentions that evening had been more than a man helping out a woman in distress. He'd seemed attracted to her but that couldn't be right. It was absurd enough that Shane was attracted to her, there was simply no way that *two* Chases were interested in her. And anyway, she was dating Shane, she should be thinking about that.

Yeah.

☙ ☙ ☙

Maggie had to admit that she was slightly bothered by the fact that Shane hadn't really checked in with her after the incident at The Pumphouse.

Not that night when he was supposed to have taken her out and only one brief phone call in the week after. It was an effort but she reminded herself that they were just casual and that she'd be a broken hearted fool to get attached. That way lay pain and anguish.

So she'd told herself until Friday night. She and her friends sat at their normal Friday night table, drinking beers and talking when she saw Shane walk in the front door. Her heart skipped a beat and she smiled at him. A smile that quickly faded when she saw he was with Kendra Fosse. Tall, blonde regal Kendra. Maggie turned back to the table quickly.

"What?" Liv looked toward the door. A frown marred her face when she sighted Shane and Kendra. "Maggie, I'm sorry, hon. Don't worry about it. I was thinking that we should go and kick up our heels at the Honky Tonk tonight. What do you say?"

Dee nodded, standing up and throwing some money on the table. "Sounds good, I haven't danced in forever. Let's go!" She tugged on Maggie's arm and got a smile and an eye roll. Still, she thought it best to leave and allowed them to pull her out the front door.

In the back room, Kyle saw Shane's entrance with Kendra and Maggie's reaction and subsequent retreat. "You are some piece of work, Shane," he murmured as Kendra walked past them to hit the ladies' room, probably to apply more hairspray.

"What?"

"What? Jeez, you said you were going out with Maggie, right?"

"Yeah? So? It's not like we're serious. I like her and all but I'm not planning to marry the girl." Shane's voice was gruff. Kyle knew it was just to hide how freaked his brother was about being hurt again like he'd been with Sandra. But at the same time, it was bullshit that his brother protected his heart by being an asshole.

"I never made promises, Kyle. Stop making me out to be the bad guy here. I honestly didn't remember about her being in here on Fridays until I was already through the door. I'm not trying to hurt her."

"Oh, okay. I was under the impression you had a thing for Maggie. My bad. I didn't know she was just the next in a long line of women you toy with and move past because, god forbid, you actually allow yourself feelings about any of them." Scowling, Kyle took his shot.

Matt snorted in disgust at his oldest brother. "I think I'm going to go. I'm meeting the guys over at the Honky Tonk." He finished his soda and stalked out.

"Wait, I'll come too. Friday night's a good night at the Tonk. Lots of lovely ladies to dance with." Marc followed with a laugh, pointedly ignoring his oldest brother.

Kendra came back and draped herself over Shane's arm, looking bored. "Are you going to play pool?" she asked, a tiny bit of a whine in her voice.

"Yeah, you want to play?"

She looked horrified at the very idea. "No, why would I want to do that. The sticks are used by everyone. Eww."

"They're called cues," Kyle said under his breath and shot yet another ball into the pocket. He couldn't help but think that Maggie would have jumped at the chance to play with them. He imagined those big whiskey eyes glittering with delight after she'd sunk a ball.

Kyle cleared the table of the solids and put the cue back into the slot on the rack. "I think I'm for the Tonk, too. Nice seeing you, Kendra. Shane."

"You want to hit the Honky Tonk, too?" Shane asked her.

"Sure," she said, looking bored still. "At least they have a better quality of mixed drinks there."

રા રા રા

Maggie was glad she'd let them drag her to the Tonk. Instead of moping about Shane and gorgeous Kendra, she was kicking her heels up and dancing the night away. The Dixie Chicks were coming over the sound system and she had Ryan Jackson's fine body guiding her along the floor effortlessly. Okay, so he was as married as the day is long and his wife put him up to dancing with Maggie so she could rest her feet but he made her laugh and she was having fun.

"Maggie, do you want a drink, sugar?" Ryan asked, having to yell in her ear.

"That sounds good, my legs are tired!" She laughed as he spun her off the floor and back toward their table and his wife who had her shoes off and her feet up.

It took a few seconds to register that Matt and Marc were there with Darla as well. "Oh hi."

"Hey, Maggie. You sure were tearing it up out there." Matt said it with an easy smile and she relaxed a bit.

"Nah, it was all Ryan. Darla let me borrow him a bit."

Drinks had arrived and they'd all fallen into an easy back and forth, talking and laughing, when Kyle, Shane and Kendra came in. Marc waved at them and they started toward the table.

"Uh, I should go and find Liv and Dee." She moved to stand but Matt put his hand on her elbow to stay her.

"They're both out there dancing." He nodded with his head and waved at the other women who saw and waved back.

"Oh."

"Stay a while and visit, Maggie. Chuck's not showing any sign of letting Liv get away anyway." Darla laughed, not knowing why Maggie wanted to run and hide.

Kyle came and sat down next to her, giving her a warm hello. "Hey there, shug. You owe me a dance tonight." He stood up again. "In fact, why don't we hit it now?" He bowed slightly and extended a hand and after a brief hesitation she took it, never once looking at Shane.

"All right then. But remember excessively tall men have much longer legs than small women. Which means you'll be dragging me all over the place if you go too fast."

"Do I look like I don't know how to take it slow with the right woman?" he said with cheeky innuendo in his voice and she rolled her eyes.

"One of these days I need to meet your father to see if he's as full of it as you four are."

Kyle laughed as he led her down the steps and onto the floor. He twirled her once and into a slow two step as the tempo of the Martina McBride song came on and slowed the dancers down.

"You all right?" he asked her when they were away from the table.

"What do you mean?" He was so close to her it was hard to concentrate.

"Shane isn't a bad guy you know. He just got screwed over pretty severely a year and a half ago by his fiancée. Turns out she was sleeping with his best friend. Ran off with him a week before the wedding. Ever since, he's guarded his feelings with women—never goes out with them for longer than a few weeks."

"I really don't care. I have no say in what Shane does. I just went out with him officially once and chatted with him a few times. I'm just dating him casually, I know that. It's not like I have a vested interest in him or anything." Even she didn't believe it as she said it.

She liked Shane Chase, thought she might have been the one to settle him down. But okay, she knew it now. Knew it truly was just a casual dating relationship and she could do that. She was an adult woman after all. Liv did it all the time. There was no reason why she couldn't enjoy herself with people and date around casually.

Kyle smiled. *God, she was so genuine and in way over her head.* "Ah, Maggie, you're too sweet for this game. You're a wonderful woman but don't count on him coming around to that. He's not ready to let himself really care about anyone just yet. I'd hate to see you get hurt. I just want you to know this up front, to protect yourself."

"I appreciate the advice, Kyle." She ruthlessly tamped down the sinking feeling that he was right. At the same time, Kyle's arms around her made her feel warm and relaxed. The flesh just under his hand at her back tingled a bit. Maybe Alex was right, maybe she was a slut.

"If he wasn't my brother, I'd ask you out myself." He tried to sound lighthearted but it was the truth.

"Please don't."

"Don't what?"

She stopped and pulled away, turning to escape him and the dance floor. He followed, catching up quickly. Reaching out, he grabbed her hand to stay her but she jerked it away and ran for the back deck. Sighing, he followed, catching up with her in the much quieter, much cooler, night air.

"You want to tell me what the heck you're talking about? Don't what?" He hoisted himself up to sit on the wooden railing of the deck so that he could face her.

Throwing one hand up in frustration she sighed. "Don't pity me and throw a few false compliments my way because you feel sorry for me."

He was still confused. "I don't pity you and they aren't false compliments."

"Please! My god, you don't think I have mirrors at my house? I know what I am and I know what I'm not. I'm not Jane Marie, I'm not Kendra. I can't compete with that. But I sure as hell don't want some kind of pity thrown at me because Shane has gone back to his regular diet of tall, gorgeous women. It's okay that I was an aberration. I shouldn't have expected more, it's my own damned fault."

Kyle sat in stunned silence for a few moments. He didn't know whether to laugh or cry. This woman was so beautiful and so special and yet, she thought a vapid, shallow woman like Kendra, or worse, her own sister, was better than she was.

Grabbing her hand, he brought it to his lips. "Sugar, I can't believe you think you have to compete with any other woman. I don't believe you do have mirrors in your house. If you did, you'd see a beautiful woman looking back at you and it's clear you don't. Honey, take it from me—a lover of women—you are absolutely, positively gorgeous. I am not throwing pity at you. Honestly, the only thing that's keeping me from grabbing you and kissing those beautiful lips is the fact that Shane is my brother."

Sighing, she ran her hands through her hair and over her face. "I can see you need an example. I was a virgin until I was twenty-two. My first year of graduate school. I went out on dates sure, but no one ever showed any passion towards me. Like a lot of grad students I had an advisor. He was so nice, so attentive. He loved to read what I wrote. Praised my work, paid attention to me as a person." She hesitated and then continued. "No, as a woman. He made me feel sexy and desirable. The first time he made love to me was in a hotel room in Atlanta. We were there at a symposium. He was gentle and sweet and he took his time. We continued to see each other throughout that entire year.

"My family came out to see me, my mom and dad and Jane Marie. It was a pretty big deal. The first and only time they ever visited me, actually. Anyway, I'd invited Charles over to dinner at my apartment to meet them all. He came and was his charming self. My mother and dad went out for a walk and I thought I would too. Janie and Charles said they would stay back and have coffee. It was a lovely early spring day but at the last minute, I decided that I'd skip the walk and go back home. When I let myself back into the apartment, I saw that Jane Marie and Charles were on the couch."

Her eyes blurred, lost in the memory. "They were having sex. Her perfect pleated skirt up around her waist and his slacks on the floor. I just stood there for a moment, not understanding at all, you know? My mind just wasn't registering what the hell was happening. Anyway, I stood there until I felt sick and then I quietly and slowly backed out of the room like I was never there.

"I confronted him later about it and he told me that he'd never imagined that a girl like me would have a stunning sister like that and what did I expect? I never said anything to anyone else about it. It was a good lesson for me about things. And you know? I was a fool to ever pretend that any Chase brother would think I was worth more than a few amusing dates and maybe a quick fuck." She hugged her arms around herself.

"My god, Maggie. What a bitch your sister is! What a calculating bastard your professor was." He moved toward her but she backed up.

"I have to go. Please don't say anything, I've never told that story to another soul." She spun on her heel and stalked back inside to the table. Still refusing to look in Shane's direction, she grabbed her coat and purse, plead sick and pretty much dashed out the door.

Kyle started to follow her out but Shane came up behind him, grabbing his arm. "What is going on?"

Shaking Shane off Kyle glared at him. "It's none of your business, Shane." But it was too late, as Maggie sped out of the parking lot.

ও ও ও

Shane showed up after school on the next Wednesday. "Hey, Maggie, you have time for dinner?" he asked smiling.

Maggie looked at him, dumbstruck. Fine, if he wanted a casual thing she'd give it a try but there was no way she'd be some last minute drop in date. "Hi, Shane. No, I'm sorry, I have plans. Perhaps another time," she said casually.

"Oh. How about tomorrow night then?"

"Fine. Pick me up at seven." Keeping a smile on her face, she walked past him to her car.

She didn't have plans of course so she stopped by the bank and asked Dee to have dinner with her.

"Honey, what do you think you're doing?" Dee asked as they munched on pizza at Maggie's house.

"What do you mean?"

Dee made a disapproving sound and frowned. "Margaret Wright, being dishonest is not who you are. Don't lie to me and don't lie to yourself. I know you and Liv think I'm some silly virgin but I know enough to see you're in over your head with Shane Chase."

"What do you mean!" Maggie challenged. The truth stung.

"Oh, don't be stupid! Honey, you are more than good enough for him. He's the one who isn't good enough for you. You know what I mean. You are not the kind of woman who can do a casual affair. It's not part of your make up. I'm not talking down about women who can do it. But I've known you your whole life—you're not one of them. Your heart and head are too connected. You're only going to end up hurt because Shane Chase cannot give you what you want and deserve. Listen, it's still early, I can tell you like him but it's not that deep yet. But this is a dead end street. Shane Chase is a dead end man. You cannot save him."

The eyes she turned to Dee made Dee's heart ache. "I'm fine, Dee. I can handle it, I promise."

Dee sighed and squeezed her hand. "You know where to find me when you need me."

ଔ ଔ ଔ

Shane knocked on her door precisely at seven and looked delicious as usual. He looked up and back down her body, with a slow sexy smile. "You look gorgeous, Maggie." He bent down and stole a quick kiss. "Ready?"

"Sure."

They went to The Sands, just a normal small town diner. She felt so comfortable with him. He was attentive and charming but neither mentioned the incident with Kendra.

"Hey!" She slapped at his hand as he attempted to steal a fry off her plate. "Get your own fries, buster."

"You won't share them? Not even with the sheriff?"

"Hell no!" she said, eating the last fry with relish.

He leaned over and placed his mouth over her ear. "Can we go back to your house, Maggie? I'd really like to be alone with you."

His warm breath on her ear and his confession sent shivers down her spine. "I'd like that." No sooner had the soft words left her lips than he'd yanked her up, thrown money on the table and they hurried out to his car.

Once they were inside her house and on the couch he looked down at her with a grin. "I've wanted this since you spun around and started getting in my face at The Pumphouse that night. And definitely since I had to leave you on your doorstep after the movies."

Leaning up, she nuzzled his neck. He smelled good, his skin was warm. His head fell back against the couch. She really liked the moan he made when she nibbled his ear lobe and then down to the hollow of his throat.

"But you never noticed me before. Back in high school you dated girls with flashy bodies and perfect clothes." She looked up at him with a grin.

"I think we established that I was a dumbass. I'm an idiot for not noticing you but your attitude is what turned me on first." With a low growl, he brought his hands down her back and around to cup her breasts. Her breath caught as his thumbs moved up to flick over her nipples.

Her head tipped back for a moment as she enjoyed his touch. After a bit she moved so that she was looking into his eyes again. Slowly, he leaned her back onto the couch, settling himself into the cradle of her thighs.

His lips found the hollow of her throat and she arched, grinding into him.

"God, I love this," she sighed.

And he froze.

He sat up quickly and reached for his coat. "I have to go. Thanks." He rushed toward the front door.

"Wait! You're leaving?" she asked incredulous.

"I have to get to work first thing." She barely understood his words he said them so fast, not meeting her eyes.

She wished she could crawl into a hole and disappear.

"I'll call you," he mumbled as he let himself out.

"Don't bother, asshole!" she yelled out but heard the door slam has he scurried out like the rat he was.

Chapter Four

The next night, the three of them sat in their usual booth. "And he left scorch marks in my front hallway he ran out of there so fast!"

Dee and Liv had looked at her, incredulous, as Maggie told them the whole story.

"I didn't say I loved *him*, I said I loved *it*. I mean goodness, we were making out on my couch. It felt good!" She tossed back yet another beer and motioned to Patrick to bring them a fresh pitcher.

"I don't understand. What an ass." Liv's face showed her anger and concern for her friend.

"Me neither but I'm done. What does he think? That he can throw a burger at me and get a cheap silent screw? God, he made me feel so stupid!"

Dee winced as she squeezed Maggie's hand in sympathy. Both Liv and Dee froze, looking toward the door and Maggie knew that it was Shane. She slowly turned around and saw that he was there with Kendra. *Again.* This time his arm was around her and she was nuzzling into his neck. He saw her and didn't even flicker recognition in her direction.

For a moment her mouth hung open and tears stung the back of her eyes. "Don't!" Liv whispered urgently. "Don't you let him make you cry, Maggie! He's not worth your tears."

She turned to face them. "I can't believe how stupid I've been," she whispered back and wiped at her eyes. "Okay, I could accept that we weren't serious. But the way he just ran out like that and just now? My god, he makes me feel like nothing."

Kyle saw Maggie wipe at her eyes, after she'd stared, hurt and dismayed at Shane. Shane who'd unbelievably looked through her like she didn't even exist.

Matt and Marc saw it too. "Shane, what the hell is wrong with you? You're really going to blow something that could be so good because of Sandra?"

Expressionless, Shane stared back at him.

"Whatever, man, I never thought I'd see you act like such an asshole. You don't deserve her," Matt spat out as he swept past and toward the front of the bar.

"What is he talking about?" Kendra asked.

"Who knows?" Shane knew, but he couldn't afford to deal with that. He had to make a clean break and it was better for both of them if he did it harshly but quickly, like ripping a bandage off all at once. He could not let himself care for Maggie. If she hated him, that would never be a problem.

Matt walked over to Maggie's table and sat down, talking quietly with the three women. Kendra snorted with derision. "Why would a man like Matt waste his time with that woman? She thinks she can put on some new clothes and let her hair down and compete with the real women of Petal?" Her mouth twisted viciously "Janie might be worth it but not that bookworm."

Kyle stared at them both, mouth open. "You are one stone cold bitch, Kendra." Disgusted, he threw his cue down on the table. "And you are not the man I've always thought you were." He shook his head at Shane and walked past them to join Matt at the table with Maggie and her friends.

"What did he just call me?" Kendra's pretty face was pinched.

"Maggie is a friend to *some* of us. We don't appreciate people saying nasty things about her." Marc looked at Shane narrowed his eyes, looking away sadly before heading off as well.

"Hey, Maggie," Matt said as he approached the table and sat down. "Listen, I just…"

Shaking her head to stay him, Maggie held up a hand. "Please. Don't. It's not your fault. It wasn't like he and I were serious or anything. I was just mistaken about him being a nice person."

Kyle strolled over then and sat next to Maggie. "Hey, Red. My brother is an asshole. Please don't judge the rest of the Chase men by his actions."

Maggie stood up. The tears were right there but she'd be damned if she'd give Shane Chase the satisfaction of seeing them. "I have to go." She shoved at Kyle until he moved. Liv and Dee stood as well.

Liv handed Maggie her coat. "Let's go to my place. I stopped at the package store yesterday and I have a big old bottle of Jose Cuervo Gold just waiting for us. Heck, let's get some pizza delivered. I've got a few DVDs I've been meaning to watch, too. I'm pretty sure one of them is Thelma and Louise." She and Dee each grabbed one of Maggie's arms.

"Thanks, guys," she tried to say lightly to Kyle and Matt but her voice broke and she shook her head hard to keep them from saying anything. "I'll see you later." The tears sprang to her eyes, bottom lip trembling as she hurried out.

Kyle looked at Matt, scowling. "I can't believe Shane made her cry."

ଔ ଔ ଔ

The next weeks went by in a blur. Shane hadn't even bothered to call to apologize or even to say he didn't want to see her again. She supposed that was the message he sent by going out with Kendra.

But she'd be damned if she'd allow that asshat to chase her away from her own life or make her feel bad for thinking that she deserved to be respected by her dates. So she held her head up high and continued her Friday night Pumphouse-with-the-girls dates. Of course, he'd shown up with women. Different ones each Friday but at least Kendra was gone. For the most part, Maggie just made it her mission to pretend he didn't exist.

She bumped into Matt at the bank and they'd chatted for a few minutes. She also ended up sitting on the same bench as Kyle and eating lunch once at the park. He talked her ear off and was friendly and jovial. Admittedly, she found him wildly attractive. But he was way off the menu. It still didn't stop her from thinking of him or sneaking looks at him on Fridays when they were in the back playing pool.

Her life moved into a new stage. One where she was proud of herself for not letting Shane's actions get her down. For a long time, she'd let people run her over. But no more. From that point on, Maggie realized she had every right to be treated well. She put the Shane incident behind her and she'd moved on.

One thing that did bother her was seeing Alex lurking around her neighborhood several times a month. She did her best to ignore him but she had to admit it did scare her slightly. He usually was doing something that she'd been able to explain away to herself—jogging, riding a bike, that sort of thing—but he still gave her the creeps.

Halloween came and went and Maggie worked in her garden all day the first Sunday of November. She tore out the old beds in the side yard and finished installing the raised beds she'd begun to build during the early fall. After getting her spring bulbs in the ground, she trimmed her climbing roses and fertilized her grass and trees. By the end of the day she'd cleaned out her yard and felt like she'd cleaned out her life. It felt damned good.

Sore but pleased with a very hard day's work she showered before retiring to her back porch with a novel and a cup of hot tea.

"Wow, you've done some major work here."

She turned and saw Kyle Chase standing there, hands in his pockets. He looked so handsome it took her breath away.

"Idle hands and all of that." Her words were wary, even as her pulse sped at his presence.

He grinned and raised one hand in a casual wave. "Now that I've said, hey, you gonna invite me up there for a cup of tea? You're a southern woman after all—it's hardwired in your genetic code."

"Tea?" She began to lose her battle against a smile.

"No. Unfailing courtesy, even when you don't want to be courteous."

Laughing, she put her book down. "Come on up and sit, then. I'll go and get another cup." Motioning to the couch she disappeared into her house.

With a secretive smile of his own, Kyle made himself at home on the small couch gracing her back sun porch. As a landscaper, he knew just exactly how much work she must have done to make her yard look so great.

Somehow, knowing she was such a hard worker only made him want her more.

Within moments she appeared again, carrying a tray with two steaming mugs of tea and a plate of muffins. She bent to put it down on the low table in front of him.

He smiled, grabbed the tea and breathed deeply, letting the heat from the cup warm his hands.

She motioned to the plate of muffins. "Blueberry muffins. I've been baking for the retirement home. Have one, they're still warm."

The porch was enclosed and had a fireplace at one end that sported a warm blaze. The popping of the wood accompanied the soft clinking of his spoon against the mug as he stirred in sugar. She looked comfortable and beautiful as she sat, curled into her chair.

"These muffins are criminally good," he said around a mouthful. Hot damn, was there nothing this woman wasn't good at?

"Thanks." Her smile faded as she got down to business. "Okay, niceties out of the way. What brings you here, Kyle?"

"I don't know." He hesitated. "Yes I do. I wanted to see you."

She narrowed her eyes at him. "You wanted to see me?" she repeated blankly.

"Yes. Maggie Wright, I wanted to see you. I can't stop thinking about you. I should you know, but I can't."

She sat utterly still, staring at him for a few moments. Pleasure warred with panic inside her. She couldn't deny she'd been attracted to him from the start. But she kept telling herself he was out of her league and also related to someone she'd dated, however briefly.

"You should what? What do you mean?" Her voice was careful.

Leaning forward, he sat his mug down, wiping his hands on his jeans nervously. "I mean that I can't get you out of my mind. Your lips, your beautiful amber eyes. God, the way you smell—rain and vanilla. Is it a perfume or do you just naturally smell that way? Your skin, it's like milk. That dusting of freckles across the bridge of your nose, it makes my hands itch to want to run a finger over them. Your smile, you're so genuine, Maggie. It's a very appealing total package. And I can't stop thinking about you."

She closed her eyes slowly and put her head down. "Please don't do this. I can't take it."

He came to kneel in front of her and slowly raised her face to his with a hand on her chin. "Don't do what?"

"This! Damn it! You heard my story that night and now you feel even sorrier for me. You had to get on your white horse to come over here to try and make me feel better."

He brushed his lips along hers and she stilled again as his taste warmed her. "First of all that was way over a month ago. I don't feel sorry for you, Margaret Wright. I feel something else for you. I want you. I want to get to know you better. I've tried not to think about it because of Shane. But since that night when he made you spill those fries, I've been crazy about you. I've gone out with a dozen women since then to try and push you out of my mind and it hasn't worked.

"The story you told me about your sister and the professor, it did change things but not in the way you think. It made me realize just how stupid I was being for letting you go because of Shane. Especially when Shane was such an ass. Life can be about taking chances and finding really great things and yes, failing sometimes. Or it can be about wondering what if because you never dared to try. Now see, I look at you and I kick myself because I was willing to say *what if* because of Shane. And damn it, he doesn't deserve you." His eyes looked deeply into hers. Her heart quickened but not out of fear. Instead she let go and fell into his gaze.

"No more, Maggie. I want you. I don't care what Shane thinks at this point. I would have come earlier but I wanted to give you some time to deal with how he treated you. It was about the hardest thing I've done in my life so far, watching you and wanting you but waiting. But as far as I'm concerned, Shane's loss is my gain. Give me a chance to show you that not all Chase brothers are bad. Let me get to know you, show you who *I* am."

Maggie looked at him and she felt her heart open back up, just a tiny bit. "I don't know. What about Shane? He's your brother."

"What about him? Are you in love with him? If you are, I'll back off, but only for a while because I'll be waiting for it to wear off. If not? Well, I've talked with Matt and Marc about it, to get their opinion on the matter and they're under the same impression I am. If Shane wants to continually close himself off because of an ex-fiancée, the rest of us should be able to follow our own hearts."

Maggie eyed him warily. "Love? I went out with him a few times. No, I'm not in love with him. I liked him and he made me feel like less than nothing. It was cruel and I have no clue why he acted the way he did. Ex-fiancée or not, he was a total jerk. Contrary to what he may have thought, I knew what our situation was, I wasn't looking for a ring, for goodness' sake!" She rolled her eyes at Shane Chase's giant ego.

"But I don't want to cause any problems between you two, either. Plus, Kyle Chase, why are you interested in me anyway? How do I know you aren't just doing this out of some kind of sibling rivalry thing and will lose interest in a few days?"

"First of all, I'm going to be totally honest with you. I've never actually pursued a woman before. They always come to me. That should show you a bit about how interested I am. I like you. You intrigue me. You're beautiful and sweet and funny and a hell of a baker. Why shouldn't I be interested?

"Second of all, I have no need to compete with Shane over women. Pool? Sure. Baseball? Oh yeah. I would never use you like that." He drew a fingertip down her cheek. "Let me in, just a little bit. Get to know me. Let me know you. Come on, let me court you, woo you. I've never wooed before, it should be fun."

"I've never been wooed."

"See? We'll both learn something. Let the woo begin." He grinned and she smiled hesitantly. "We'll take it slow, Maggie," he whispered and kissed her softly, his lips feather light over hers.

Her body tightened, moisture pooled between her legs, her breasts grew heavy and her nipples hardened. All from a kiss. Wow, he was good.

Breaking the kiss, he leaned back to look into her eyes. "Your lips are softer than I'd imagined. And I've been imagining, a lot."

She had to clear her throat twice before she found words. "So um, this wooage? Does it mean casual dating, as in we'll be seeing and sleeping with other people? I've come to understand and accept that I'm just not the kind of woman who can do the casual each of us seeing other people thing. I'm not cut out for it. I know it's against all of the hot guy dating rules to discuss such things but I just want to get things crystal clear up front."

"Hot guy dating rules?" His grin was cocky and she narrowed her eyes.

"Yes, as in guys who look like you and have their pick of every beautiful woman who comes their way."

"And those rules are different from the non-hot guy rules?"

"Are you making fun of me?" One eyebrow slid up slowly.

"Yes," he said, starting to laugh.

She put her hands on her hips and glared at him, but she was sure she lost the effect she was going for when her lips slid into a smile.

He stopped, leaning in to give her a quick kiss to attempt to appease her. "Sugar, wooage—at least in my own hot guy dating rulebook—does state that there will be exactly two people in the relationship. You and me. No one else. You're different from the other women I've dated. And that's a good thing," he added quickly. "I have no desire to share you."

"Let's just say that I agree to this. How are we going to deal with Shane?"

"I'll tell him myself. No need for both of us to do it. Shug, I don't want to be mean and I'm not trying to hurt you for my own gain but has he even called you since your last date?"

"No. The ass ran out the door and never called me again. Whatever, I'm past it now." The hurt had passed but the humiliation and the anger still burned deep and pushed old buttons.

"I don't think he meant to disrespect you. Hell, I love my brother and he's a good person but ever since Sandra, he's been like this with women. I think anyone that he truly likes is someone he'll push away right quick. I don't know why I'm saying all of this, it only makes him look better but he is a nice guy, he's just wounded."

She touched his cheek with a finger and smiled at him. Wounded? She'd love to wound him herself, *the asshole*. Instead she took a deep breath and let the anger go. "No, I'm glad you said it. I have a major concern and it's not how I feel about Shane. It's about making problems between two such very close brothers."

"Let me worry about that. I'll tell him when I see him in an hour and a half. We have family dinners each Sunday, you know."

"God, your family is going to think I'm a major slut." She cringed and he began to laugh anew.

He laughed and laughed and then laughed some more. *If she only knew the women I'd dated in the past!* He saw her narrowed eyes and changed his mind, glad she didn't know. He kissed her hand. "They won't. They know you. My mother thinks you are the best thing since hush puppies. Secondly, Maggie, I've dated slutty women, they know the difference, as do I."

"Oh god, again! So not only have you dated gorgeous women but slutty ones, too? How can I compete?"

He stifled another laugh. "Sweetie, how many times do I need to tell you? *You* are a gorgeous woman. Plus, why on earth would you have to compete against slutty? I mean, it's fun and all when you're young and carefree but slutty is in my past."

"It is? Because although it seems like I'm a slut for seeing two brothers from the same family, I'm not, I've not been intimate with very many men, less than you can count on one hand."

He caressed her face and ran his thumb along her bottom lip. "Hell yes, it's in my past. And I know you're not a slut, Maggie. I never thought that. Now, if every once in a while you wanted to *play* at being slutty." An eyebrow rose and he grinned. "Yes indeed, that would be mighty nice. But I've recently developed a terrible yen for gorgeous redheads who bake cookies for seniors."

Sweet heavens, the man was irresistible. "Awfully sure you'll get me into bed aren't you?"

"Oh yeah," he purred. Putting his hands at her waist, he pulled her forward on her chair and into his body. Sliding up to her back, the heat of his palms spread languid desire through her body as he brought his lips to hers. He tasted like tea and blueberry muffins. His tongue swept into her mouth like it belonged there and she actually mewled with pleasure at the sensation when it slid along hers in a sensuous caress. Gone were the teasing, hesitant kisses he'd given her earlier. This was the real thing. Soft and hot and he clearly knew his way around a kiss. She wondered what that mouth would feel like against her pussy and her clit throbbed in approval.

His skin was hot to the touch and so very hard. Letting herself go, she moved her hands, stroking her palms across the muscles of his wide shoulders and back. She couldn't touch enough of him and moved to touch the bare flesh of his neck and slid her hands down his back a little. He groaned softly into her mouth.

"Oh," she said softly, her head lolling back when he moved his lips to kiss the hollow just below her ear. The edge of his teeth nipped her earlobe before he pulled back.

Slowly opening her eyes, his smile made her pulse speed up. The man was sex on legs. Shane who?

"Well, my, that was definitely worth waiting for. Damn, Maggie, you taste good."

She blushed and he cocked up the corner of his mouth into a sexy grin. "Can I take you dancing on Wednesday night?"

"I love to dance."

"Good, it's a date. I'll pick you up at seven so we can grab a bite first and then head over to the Tonk afterwards."

"All right."

He stood, drawing her up with him. "I have to go to dinner at my parents' house. I wish I could stay and smooch on you for another five hours or so." He sighed and then leaned down to kiss her again, thorough and quick. Enough to leave the weight of his lips tingling on hers.

"Have a nice time. I'll see you Wednesday." She watched as he quickly headed down her porch steps and into the yard. Yep, the man looked good going too.

ભ ભ ભ

"Shane, I need to talk to you." Kyle came into the living room where his dad and brothers watched the game.

"Yeah?" Shane said, distracted by the television.

No one made a move to leave. Kyle sighed and caught a thumbs up from Matt.

"I just wanted to let you know that I'm going to be dating Maggie."

Shane looked at him blankly for a moment, eyes blinking slowly. Then, a red flush crept up his neck. "*What?*" he bellowed, jumping to his feet.

Kyle looked at his brother but didn't react. He'd seen it before and he stayed calm because he was in the right. "I'm now dating Margaret Wright. I've just been with her at her house. She and I are going dancing on Wednesday. I've thought about this long and hard. I've liked her from the start but I backed off when you showed interest. However, since you have decided to treat her so badly, I figure all deals are now off."

"I'm dating Maggie, Kyle."

"No you aren't. You *dated* her and then you hurt her. You humiliated her and made her feel used. I waited six weeks for you to fix it and you haven't," Kyle shrugged, "so too bad for you. Hell, Shane, you didn't even have the decency to call her and apologize for the way you treated her the last time you saw her."

"Or the way you acted when you brought Kendra into The Pumphouse," Matt added.

"You too?" Shane turned to him.

"I happen to really like Maggie. She's a nice woman, Shane. You made her cry. You didn't have to see her anymore, but instead of treating her with respect, you toyed with her and then you tossed her away. You didn't show her any kindness at all." Matt shrugged.

Edward looked at his sons and shook his head. "Is this true, son? Did you treat her as poorly as it sounds?"

"She knew it was just casual. I like her but she had to push it."

"How?"

"When we were kissing on her couch, things got a little...heavy. And then she told me she loved it. I don't need any love damn it. I just wanted to go out on some dates and have a casual thing. She pushed it and I had to back off, for her sake and my own."

Kyle's face hardened with anger. "You dated her, made out with her and ran for the door and never called her again because she said she loved being touched by you? No! How dare she say that! My god, what a maneater she is! How dare she compliment you! Jeez, now that I know all of the facts, I'll be sure to run the other way." The sarcasm in Kyle's voice hung heavy in the air between them.

"Tell Dad the rest of it. How you've paraded other women in front of her and looked right through her like she didn't even exist. You could have just said you didn't want to see her anymore. But you set out to make her feel like nothing. I hate that you let Sandra turn you into such a prick."

"Son, I can't believe you'd behave in such a way," Edward said, interrupting before anything physical could erupt between his sons. He frowned at Shane. "In any case, it sounds to me like you'd broken up with Maggie before Kyle expressed an interest in her. I don't see what the problem is with him dating her."

"I don't want him dating her!"

"Why? You say you don't want to be with her, that you had to back off. You haven't called her in six weeks and I know you've been dating other women in the mean time."

"Because. Why are you taking his side anyway?"

"Because is not an acceptable reason, Shane. I'm taking Kyle's side because you have treated the girl shabbily and you yourself said you wanted to back off. I don't see why you should be bothered if your brother is going to take her out."

"What if I still want her?"

"What if, what if," Edward said with an agitated wave of his hands. He leaned forward, "Maggie is not a thing! She's not a toy you can hold back until you want to play with her again. She's a person. A person who deserves respect. I surely have raised men who love women but I have not raised men who treat women the way you've treated Margaret Wright. Shane, you know better and you should be ashamed. Let her go, son. Why hurt her any worse? As long as Kyle treats her well and respectfully—which he'd better or his mother will have both your heads—why not let it go? You get your freedom and he gets to date a woman he likes."

Shane leaned back in his chair, defeated. "Fine, Kyle, but if you hurt her I'm going to stomp on your neck," he growled grouchily.

Kyle's anger drained away. He wished like hell that Shane could get past what Sandra had done. "I like Maggie an awful lot. She's relationship material and that's what I've offered her. I intend to honor that promise."

"Kyle Maurice Chase a monogamous man?" Marc held his hand to his chest in mock disbelief. "Well, this ought to be good. Don't mess it up because I find Miss Margaret Wright to be enchanting. If you mess it up, she'll never give me a chance."

"Not a chance, monkey boy," Kyle growled. He looked toward Shane. "Are we okay? She was very worried that this would set us against each other. I promised her that we weren't competitive over women, just pool and baseball."

Shane sighed. "Yeah, but don't mess up like I did."

"Not a chance, I'm way smarter." Kyle stretched as he winked. Rolling his eyes, Shane continued to glower.

Chapter Five

Maggie hadn't told Liv or Dee about her date with Kyle. She didn't want to have to face their skepticism over the whole thing. Liv would no doubt make some loaded comment about brothers sharing women and Dee would just give her one of those patented sweet Dee looks.

She stood in front of her closet door for at least forty-five minutes trying to decide what to wear. Four outfits later, she finally chose a pair of low slung jeans, her cowboy boots and the bronze shirt that had a bit of a shimmer to it. It had three quarter sleeves and buttons such that a small sliver of her belly would show along with a bit of cleavage. Still, not too much of either.

Searching through her jewelry box she decided on the leather choker with the piece of turquoise that Dee had given her for her birthday a few years back and her silver hoop earrings. It was simple and not more glitz than she'd feel comfortable with.

Pulling a few strands of hair from her face, she twisted them and pinned them back from her face with pretty clips. The barest bit of makeup, a touch of Chanel No. 5 behind each ear and between her breasts—not that he'd be going there, no matter how tempted she was—and she was good to go. Except for the nervousness that threatened to make her stomach riot and turn itself out on her bedroom floor.

She jumped when the doorbell rang. He'd shown up five minutes early. Taking a deep breath she opened the door and her breath was gone.

Where Shane's looks were rough and almost savage, Kyle's were beautiful. He still had brown hair but it was more blond than chocolate. It was longer than Shane's, too. Kyle's eyes were a beautiful green, like the ocean on the day after a storm. His skin was golden from working in the sun all day. He was tall but rather than his older brother's six-and-a-half feet, Kyle towered at just under six feet. Tall—especially in comparison to Maggie who was an inch shy of five and a half feet—but not so tall she got a neck pain to look into his face.

And what a face! His nose was perfect, almost Roman. Full, sexy lips were framed by a mustache and goatee. Crisp blue jeans clung nicely to long legs and a body hugging red shirt showed off his upper body nicely. He was long, lean and mouthwateringly good looking. She stared at him, speechless for a few moments.

When she opened the door he almost fell to his knees. She was there, hair cascading around her face, just a hint of makeup, lips shiny. Her shirt was snug, breasts clearly outlined by the soft material the color of autumn leaves. Something about the shimmer of it brought out the highlights in her hair and made her eyes smokier. The thick leather choker around her neck was very, very sexy. A creamy expanse of skin peeked from between the waist of her low slung jeans and the hem of the shirt. For a short woman, her legs were quite long and capped off with some seriously sexy cowboy boots.

"Wow," they both said simultaneously.

"Jinx." She grinned. "You look really handsome."

"Ma'am, I'm just here to fight off the men who'll mob you for looking as sexy as you do."

Before they left for dinner, she gave him a brief tour of the house. Kyle was impressed with the work she'd done herself.

"You've done a heck of a lot of work, Maggie."

"Thanks. This house wasn't the most pleasant place to grow up at times. I feel like each time I do something to make it more my own, I chase some of that away."

"I'm gonna want to hear that story."

"Oh, it's not good for digestion. On the other hand, your momma is something special." She grinned at the image of his flamboyant mother. "She's one of a kind. You're lucky to have her."

"Don't I know it." He laughed and motioned toward the car. "Shall we go then?"

"Absolutely."

He opened her car door and she got in. "You know, you don't have to open my door for me. I'm a big girl."

He looked at her and laughed. "Believe me, I've noticed. But you do know my mother, right? If she even caught wind of me not opening your door she'd hunt me down. She's been known to come out to my job sites or my office to lecture me or interrogate me about my brothers. Secondly, I just want to take care of you a bit, part of the whole wooing thing, you know. I know you're capable of doing it, I just want to spoil you a little." He gave her a smile so sexy that she swore she could smell her insides boiling from the heat.

Taking a deep breath, her hands gripped the edge of the seat to keep herself from jumping on him.

Stifling a smug smile, he raised a brow, satisfied he caused such a response in her. "How does steak sound? I'm really in the mood for it today. The Oak Room's got a pretty varied menu if you don't want steak, though."

"The Oak Room sounds just fine, Kyle." Truth was, she'd always wanted to go there on a date and had never had the chance. It wasn't fancy really, it was *the* meeting spot for folks her age in Petal.

At the side of his car, in the faint light of the restaurant, he leaned down to kiss her. She stood on her tip toes and he bent his knees—they fit well. "You taste like strawberries," he murmured against her lips.

Warmth bloomed through her at the contact. "Flavored lip gloss." Her eyes were still closed as she replied. Still savoring the moment. With a small smile, she wrapped her arms around his back and brought his mouth back down to hers again for another kiss. She didn't know why she felt so wanton with him, she just did. There was something explosive about their chemistry.

Chuckling, he obliged her, his mouth covering hers, sucking her bottom lip in between his teeth and laving the sting with his tongue. A breathy moan of delight escaped her.

His hands slid to the small of her back and brought her body against his tighter. Damn it she tasted good. She felt right against him, in his arms. Her soft sounds of pleasure tightened his need for her. His cock was rock hard. He had to tamp down his impulse to roll his hips, grinding into her as he reached down to grab that stellar ass to pull her up and over him. He broke off before he lost that thin shred of control, not wanting to paw her in a parking lot.

Putting his forehead to hers he got his breath back until he was able to speak again. "Let's go inside, Maggie." He took her hand in his own and led her into the restaurant.

She felt out of place immediately once they got inside. Practically everyone there knew Kyle—servers, managers and patrons alike. The women eyed him appreciatively and looked at her speculatively. She recognized many of the people but many were from the crowd she'd never been included in. Suddenly, it was like high school and she hated the way it felt.

Kyle felt her tense up and, once they were seated at a small table, he scooted his chair nearer to her own. "Is everything all right, darlin'?"

"Fine. I'm just hungry." She smiled at him, relaxing at his nearness. He looked skeptical but she didn't elaborate so he let it drop, sticking close.

The server took their order and brought over a glass of wine for Maggie and a beer for Kyle. He held her hand, running his thumb back and forth over her knuckles. He couldn't get enough of touching her skin.

"So, you had a story to tell. I want to know about you. About your family."

She shook her head and put a hand up. "Oh no, we don't need to go there. Tell me about your family instead."

"Huh uh. It's your turn. We've already talked about Polly Chase. Let's hear about Cecelia Wright. Come on, please?" He fluttered his lashes at her making her laugh.

Sighing, she took a drink of her wine and a bolstering breath. "Okay, the truncated version, then. Cecelia Bradshaw was Miss Georgia. Before that Junior Miss Georgia. She was also homecoming queen two years running, the Magnolia Festival Queen, and a whole host of other titles that she'd be happy to tell you all about any old time you wish. When Cece was nineteen years old, she met the son of the man who owned the largest orchard in the county and of course, Tom Wright was immediately and forever in love with her. They married at twenty and moved into the house I live in now.

"Cece, has one tall, regal, golden haired daughter who is married to the quarterback and has two adorable children and they live in a brand new home over in Cherry Hill Estates. That daughter keeps a spotless home, always has perfect hair and makeup, and bakes cookies and embroiders. Butter would not, and never has, melted in Jane Marie's mouth. Janie, as you know, followed in Cece's footsteps and was homecoming queen and Magnolia Festival Queen and a host of other pageants that my mother would also be happy to talk to you about.

"Now poor Cece has another daughter. This one is not tall, is not beautiful and hated the very idea of pageants. No, poor Cece's youngest child liked—gasp—books! Not just books but history. Of course Cece's suffering went even deeper when her husband would brave her wrath to occasionally nurture this child's love of books and history.

"Luckily, this daughter went to college and graduate school out of town, only returning for holidays and continually disappointed her beautiful mother by not bringing home a quarterback, heck, not even a defensive end. Worse, said short, bookish daughter with the red hair—*Margaret, you can have a variety of hair colors these days, darling, why don't you let me make you an appointment at my salon*—became a teacher! Are you aware how much money teachers make? Are you aware that that daughter will never marry an appropriate man if she hangs around a school all day?

"Doesn't this all sound like I should be on some daytime talk show? It sounds bitter but honestly I'm not hindered by it. I've moved on and Cecelia Wright is a nice enough woman. I was just not what she expected. Anyway, now you know the whole sordid tale and you should feel free to run for your life."

Enraged and utterly shocked, Kyle's hands balled into tight fists. Why on earth would any mother act like that? Cece Wright should be proud to have a daughter as wonderful as Maggie. That she didn't treasure Maggie made him sad.

"Honey, I'm not running anywhere and you know what? Red hair—your red hair—is incredibly beautiful and downright sexy. Plus, I love history and my house was always filled with books. Heck, you'd probably know that working with my momma on the Historical Society Board. Oh and I voted for Amylynne Jessup for homecoming queen."

"Oh my, you flatterer you." She laughed. Relief moved through him as he saw the strain leave her face.

"I thought that was you," a female voice said. Kyle and Maggie both looked up to see Janie standing there.

"Hey, Janie."

"Maggie." Janie nodded her head at her sister and then looked to Kyle, her face breaking into a smile. "Hi Kyle. What are you doing here?" Janie looked at Kyle as if Maggie weren't even there.

"Are you asking me?" Kyle was surprised and appalled at the way she barely spoke to her own sister. Of course, given the history he just heard, he shouldn't have been.

"Yes of course. Who else would I be asking?"

"I'm here on a date with Maggie. We're having dinner. What else would I be doing?"

"On a date with Maggie?" She sounded incredulous.

"Why do you sound so surprised, Janie?" Maggie asked with an arch of her eyebrow.

"I, uh, well I just thought that Kyle was a bit out of, well, not from your crowd."

"My crowd?"

"You know, Kyle and I moved in different circles. You weren't exactly in the popular crowd."

"High school was ten years ago, Janie," Kyle gritted out, wanting very much to be done with her.

"She means to say that you're out of my league, Kyle. Isn't that right?" Maggie asked, eyes narrowed in a way that Kyle had come to notice meant she was getting hot under the collar. He liked it, made him want to bend her over something and fuck her.

"Of course not!" Janie's claim was utterly unbelievable, especially as she rolled her eyes.

"Well he is. But for some reason, he likes me, go figure."

Kyle put his arm around the back of Maggie's chair and looked up at Janie. "I do like Maggie very much. Moreover, Jane Marie Campbell, I had no idea you were such a snob, and toward your own sister. I'd have thought that out of all the people in Maggie's life, you'd certainly be a fan. Your sister is a beautiful, intelligent and strong woman. Hell, she's out of *my* league."

"Hardly. I'm sorry, I'm not trying to be mean or anything, but Maggie knows more than anyone what her limitations are. How she managed to go out with two Chase brothers in a few months, well, I can't begin to imagine." She made it sound like Maggie was some two bit whore.

"My limitations?" Maggie snorted, choosing to ignore the last comment for the moment.

"Well at least you're smart and pretty enough. And now look, you even have a good looking date. But you aren't pageant material and you weren't popular and this is not your kind of place. I'm just saying what's true."

Kyle's mouth dropped open in shock. "You are truly the rudest woman I've ever met and you've been shamelessly bitchy to your sister. I think *you're* jealous, Jane Marie. Now, if you'll excuse us, our food will be here any minute and you are ruining my appetite."

Janie spun around and stalked off without another word. He turned to Maggie and shook his head in disbelief. "My god, Maggie, has she always been like that?" No wonder she had issues about her looks.

"She comes by it honestly. It's nothing my mother hasn't said a thousand times."

He didn't even know how to respond to that. Their food came and luckily, he was able to joke, tease and coax her into a better mood and they ended up enjoying their dinner.

"Let's go, gorgeous. I can't wait to get you out on that floor and show you off."

She snorted, following him outside into the fresh, Janie-free air. Truthfully, she hadn't felt this good in a long time. She'd never stood up to Janie like that before. She knew she'd hear from her mother about it, but it was worth it to see Janie's face scrunch up like she'd sucked a lemon when Kyle sent her packing. Maggie hoped she got wrinkles from it.

The Honky Tonk was packed. Wednesday nights were buck beer and two dollar well drinks night. Cheap booze was always an incentive to get out and dance and listen to music. She and Kyle had a beer and a shot and hit the dance floor. He was really a good dancer and despite the height difference, they seemed to fit well together. He twirled her gracefully and even managed to sneak in a few quick kisses while they were dancing.

After six songs he pleaded exhaustion and dragged her to a table. Matt and Marc were there with some friends who all greeted them happily as they came over to join them.

Matt reached out and pulled a corkscrew curl straight and let go, watching it spring back into place. "I've wanted to do that since fourth grade," he said, laughing.

"I know, it's the bane of my existence. It's why I wear it in a bun so much."

"Bane? My god why? Your hair is incredible. I know women who go to the salon to get expensive perms and still can't get hair like yours." To underline his point, he pulled another curl with apparent delight.

Maggie grinned at him and Kyle slapped Marc's hand when he reached over to try it. "Hands off," he growled.

Maggie was stunned. He actually acted jealous.

"Hi, Kyle, let's dance," Lyndsay Cole sidled up to him, stopping just short of rubbing against him like a cat in heat.

Maggie shot her a look of annoyed anger. It was obvious that Kyle was there with her. Hell, he was sitting with her chair between his thighs, holding one of her hands.

"Lyndsay, do you know Maggie?" Kyle asked smoothly, moving away from her touch and even closer to Maggie.

Lyndsay looked over at Maggie for a quarter of a second and back to Kyle. "Yeah. So anyway, how about that dance?"

"Lyndsay, I'm here with Maggie. I'm *with* Maggie. She's my only dance partner."

"Her?"

Annoyed, Kyle sighed. What was with the women of this town anyway? He was beginning to get a very good understanding of Maggie's inferiority issues. He realized he had to find ways of working through them with her. "Of course her. Who else?" He turned his back to Lyndsay and kissed the nape of Maggie's neck but he felt her stiffness. "Darlin', shall we dance?"

"You know, I'm tired. I think I'd like to go home." Her voice was so small, it squeezed his heart.

He turned her face to his gently. "Don't let her get to you." He said it in no more than a murmur.

"I'm not. I really am tired," she lied. She realized then that it would be like this every time they went out. He'd gone out with a lot of women, all of them pretty and popular like Lyndsay and Jane Marie. Maggie was so far out of their league that she'd never find a way to fit into his life.

He narrowed his eyes at her. "Maggie, don't run off on me." He meant more than just her wanting to leave the Tonk. "We're having a good time. My brothers and friends are all happy to see you—to see us. To hell with what people like your sister and Lyndsay think." He could see she was skittish, probably thinking up reasons why they couldn't be a couple and he wasn't about to let that happen.

Standing up he grinned down at her. "Come on, it's a slow number, at least dance close with me before we go." He put on his best little boy pleading face and she relented, holding out her hand for him to take.

Once on the floor he pulled her tightly against his body. Head resting on his chest his heart beat for her. The citrusy scent of her hair wafted into his face, teasing his senses. Her body fit against his, soft against hard. His arms tightened around her and he smiled against the top of her head. It would take some work to get past her defenses but he knew she'd be worth it. He could kick Shane's ass for making things even worse. But then again, if Shane hadn't been such a fool, Maggie would be in his arms now instead of Kyle's.

The slow song faded and a fast number came on. Smoothly, Kyle kept his hold on her, easing her into a faster dance. Maggie hesitated a moment but relented and let him keep her on the floor.

"You're smooth, Chase." Her smirk of amusement made him chuckle and twirl her into a dip. He laid a series of kisses down her neck while he had her extended over his arm and delighted in her laugh.

"It's all been practice for the time when I had you to work on."

Grinning, she looked into his face. "Lord, you are so full of it." He righted her and clutched his heart in mock dismay.

Laughing, they walked back to their table where, thankfully, Lyndsay had left. "I really should be getting home. I have to be at school by nine tomorrow morning."

"Oh all right. I'll take you home but only if you promise to come to my house for dinner on Friday night. That is *after* your drink with the girls and my pitcher and pool with my brothers. I wouldn't want you to flout tradition, after all. We can leave from The Pumphouse for my house at eight thirty. That should be enough time for me to trounce them all at pool and for you to gossip with Liv and Dee."

"Oh all right," she said with mock annoyance, echoing his earlier words, but it was ruined by the grin she couldn't suppress. He made her happy.

"Good answer, now your carriage awaits, princess," he said, bowing.

"Night, Maggie," Matt said, kissing her cheek.

"Night guys." She waved at them. Marc stood up to give her a kiss too but she saw Kyle raise an eyebrow at him. Marc burst out laughing and blew her one instead.

"What was that all about?" she asked him as he drove her home.

"Marc's a skirt chaser, he likes your skirt."

"If you say so. I'll remind you that I've lived in this town my entire life and the only Chase brother who's ever really spoken to me before two months ago was Matt."

"Hey! I've talked to you here and there."

"Excuse me, miss, you dropped your book, doesn't count. We're from totally different worlds, Kyle. Surely you can see that."

"What I can see is that in high school—back ten years ago for me and what, eight for you? What I can see is that we ran in different crowds but heck, I was two years ahead of you anyway. You went to college right away and then grad school. I started my own landscaping business. If you'd yelled at my brother before that night I'd have surely noticed you. Okay, so I didn't really notice you before that night but once I did—once I got to know you a bit—I saw what I'd been missing."

She sighed, putting her forehead against the window.

"Maggie, stop trying so hard to find things wrong with being with me. I know you're skittish after Alex and then dumbass Shane, but I'm not them. Let me show you that."

She turned to him, giving him a small smile. "I'll try."

He took her hand and kissed the knuckles. "Good."

When they got back to her house she sat bolt upright. "What the hell?" She yanked open her door before the car had even come to a full stop, heading toward her front porch at a dead run.

"Wait! Damn it, Maggie, wait!" Kyle yelled as he put the car in park and jumped out to catch her and grab her arm.

She stared at the broken front window and "WHORE" written in red paint across her front door. "Who would do something like this?" Her voice was a taut whisper.

Kyle held her tightly against him. With his free hand, he pulled his cell phone out and called Shane who agreed to rush over immediately. But not before admonishing them not to go inside.

"Sweetheart, let's sit in the car out of the wind until Shane gets here," he said softly. With gentle hands, he guided her back down the driveway to his car, holding her while they waited for Shane.

"Jesus, Maggie, I'm sorry." Shane arrived shortly and walked up to her front door, surveying the damage with a wince. Another officer was there with him and appeared to set about looking for clues or evidence or whatever cops did.

"We're going to talk to your neighbors to see if anyone saw anything. Right now, I want to go into the house to make sure it's clear all right?" She nodded, handing him her keys and his eyes tangled on Kyle's arm wrapped around her shoulders.

"Maggie, why don't you stay with me tonight? I have a guest room and I'm near the high school. Your windows are broken out, it's not safe." Kyle brushed his lips over her temple.

Before she could say anything, Matt and Marc pulled up. Throwing the car into park, they rushed to where she and Kyle were standing. "Oh shit, Maggie! Are you all right?" Matt looked agog at the door and what was written on it.

"Alex," she said in a hoarse whisper.

Shane came back out of her house and spoke to the other officer before coming back to them. "Maggie, it's clear inside. There's no one there. There's a brick on your floor. It's probably what they used to break out your window.

It landed on your coffee table so the glass there is broken, too. Matt, can you and Marc get those windows boarded up?"

"You bet," Marc said.

"There's wood in my garage from when I was remodeling." Her voice was flat, emotionless, as she struggled to process it all.

Matt squeezed her arm and he and Marc walked past her and toward the garage. Before too long, they were hammering boards over the broken out window.

"Maggie, you think Alex did this?" Kyle asked.

"He called me a whore at The Pumphouse that night and he went off on Liv once at the market, saying the same thing. I've never been called a whore in my whole life other than by him." Tears rolled down her face, she bit her bottom lip to keep it from trembling.

"I'll go and check him out, ask him a few questions. Listen, can you stay with someone tonight? Even with the windows boarded up it isn't as safe as it could be." Concern was clear on Shane's face.

"She's going to stay with me," Kyle informed him.

"No. I'm not leaving. I will not let this chase me out of my own home," she said angrily before walking past them both and into her house.

Kyle looked at her, annoyed and Shane glowered. "You need to convince her to leave." Shane's voice was gruff.

She returned with a bucket of cleaning solvent and a big scrubbing sponge. She dragged on rubber gloves and set to scrubbing the horrible world off her door.

"Not gonna happen," Kyle said in an undertone. "Find who did this, Shane. We can't let her be terrorized like this."

"I will. If it's Parsons I'm gonna stomp him."

"Don't. Don't get fired. Arrest him, then I'll stomp him later."

Shane laughed with cruel promise and walked back up to the porch where she had succeeded in removing the W and most of the H. "Maggie, please call me. Any time day or night if you need anything." He lowered his voice. "I'm sorry I was such a jerk but please trust me to protect you right now. Let me be your friend as well as the sheriff, all right?"

She nodded her head, not taking her attention from the scrubbing. "Thank you, Shane."

"Why don't you let Matt and I do that, sweetheart? We've finished with your windows. Go on inside so that you can call the glass shop. They can get out here first thing to replace them." Marc gently took the gloves off her hands and put them on his own and took the sponge. "Go on, baby." And she nodded.

"Thank you."

Kyle squeezed Shane's arm and followed Maggie into the house. "Maggie? If you won't stay at my house, let me stay here. I promise my intentions are purely to help, no ulterior motives. Please? I'll be worried about you if you stay here alone."

Before she could answer, Polly Chase came through the door and pulled Maggie into her arms. Even at eleven on a Wednesday night, her hair was in its usual bouffant and her spiky heels were on those tiny feet. "Honey, you're coming over to my house right now. No arguments!"

Maggie looked at all of them—Shane talking to her neighbors across the street, Matt and Marc who had just finished scrubbing her front door and had boarded her windows, Kyle who stood there looking worried for her and now Polly. In the last half an hour she'd gotten more comfort and love from the Chase family than she'd had from her own over her entire life. It hit her like a blow to the chest and she began to sob in earnest.

Polly smoothed a hand over her hair, crooning motherly soft words. Kyle looked worried and helpless. His mother locked eyes with him. "Kyle, go upstairs and pack a bag for Margaret."

"I can't impose on you," Maggie choked out, shaking her head. "I'll be all right." She'd always been. She'd taken care of herself most of her life.

"Kyle, do as I say. Margaret, you aren't imposing. I'm a mother, it's my job. Let me help, sugar. Let us help." She didn't ask if Maggie wanted to stay with her parents. Polly had seen the way Cecelia Wright treated her youngest daughter and the father seemed pretty disinterested. She knew that Maggie had no one to help her other than her girlfriends and the Chases. "On second thought, Kyle, come take over for me. I'll go grab some clothes for Maggie. Goodness knows what you'd pick for the girl to wear to work tomorrow."

Kyle looked at his mother thankfully and pulled Maggie into his arms, rocking her slightly while his mother click clacked up the stairs.

"It's the last door on the left," Maggie called out.

"You see how useless it is to oppose her will?" Kyle asked with a smile on his face and was relieved to see Maggie smile back at him. "Resistance is futile, Maggie. My mother is tougher than any Borg."

Polly came back downstairs and led them all out the door. "Kyle, why don't you drive Maggie over to our house? I'll meet you all there."

Kyle nodded and helped Maggie into his car. He watched her carefully out of the corner of his eye on the way to his parents' house. "I won't ask if you're all right, I can see how not all right you are. I know my family is a bit overwhelming but we mean well. Let us in, let us help."

"I..." *don't know how.* "I'll do my best," she said instead.

He pulled up in front of the house and helped Maggie inside. "Come on, baby. I'll get you settled in the guest room. Which by the way, is my old room." He raised his eyebrows suggestively and she allowed herself a laugh.

He put her overnight bag on the bed. "Why don't you take a shower and get changed? Come down afterwards. There'll be hot cocoa and there's no saying no. My mother will only come and drag you down."

She nodded and walked into the bathroom at the end of the hall a dazed look on her face. He stayed there in the doorway until he heard the shower turn on.

ଔ ଔ ଔ

"Did you tell her to come down for cocoa?" Polly asked as he entered the kitchen, throwing himself in a chair with a heavy sigh. He watched his mother rattling around starting to heat the milk and took comfort from it.

Kyle grinned at Matt and Marc, already sitting at the table. "Yes, Momma. She's taking a shower first. I told her to come down and that you wouldn't take no for an answer." Standing quickly, he hugged her and kissed the top of her head. "Thanks for taking her in. She needed a momma tonight. I don't think the one she has fits the bill."

"Cecelia Wright is a cold fish to that girl. I never understood it," Polly said with heat.

Shane walked in as Maggie came down the stairs wearing sweats and a tee shirt. Polly saw her bare feet. "Oh no! Honey, I forgot to get you some slippers. Matthew, go and get her a pair of socks to keep her feet warm."

"It's okay, I'm fine." Maggie held out a hand to stay Matt.

Matt just laughed at her and jogged out of the room. He returned in less than two minutes. "Here, sugar, put 'em on or she'll do it for you."

"Thanks." Maggie looked up at Shane as she pulled the socks on. "Well? Any news?"

"We've arrested Alex Parsons. He had a bucket of red paint sitting on his back steps. The fool still had it under his fingernails."

Nausea roiled through her and she felt lightheaded in disbelief of the situation. "Why? I only went out with him three times! We never got more serious than a kiss. I don't understand why he hates me so much."

"Well, I don't think it's hate. It gets worse."

Kyle moved his chair closer to Maggie's, reaching out to grab her hand. Maggie paled. "What?"

Shane sighed. "He had pictures of you. *Hundreds* of pictures of you. Some of them were taken of you at the school, working in your yard, some were of you in the house. And there are ones he clearly used a telephoto lens with. You're, um, naked in some."

She put her head down on the table, rage, shame, and mortification fought within her. She wasn't sure she could even begin to process it all right then. "I've seen him in my neighborhood a lot. I just tried to ignore him."

"He had some of your stuff too, Maggie. He must have broken into your house to get it."

"Stuff? What stuff?" She looked up at him.

"Um." He scratched the back of his neck. "Underwear, bras, nightgowns."

She groaned. It just kept getting worse. "He snatched my panties? Naked pictures of me? The whole town is going to hear about this. I'm going to have to move."

"You'll do no such thing! You have nothing to be ashamed of, Margaret!" Polly said sharply. "Honey, he's the pervert. Why should you be embarrassed?"

"Are you kidding me? Jeez Louise! Not only does some freak totally violate me and my home but I'm going to look like a slut when this is all over. I'll probably lose my job."

"You look like no such thing, honey. How could you think so? He's the one who fixated on you. People know you. No one who knows you could ever believe such a thing."

Maggie scrubbed her hands over her face. "They're going to see one guy that I dated taking pictures of me naked. And that I've dated two other men since, both brothers. You don't think that makes me look a tad bit loose?" Just saying it made her want to dig a hole to crawl into.

"It makes you look like you have good taste! I'll tell you one thing, Shane and Kyle are two of the five best looking men in this town. Why shouldn't you have dated any of my boys?" Polly lowered her voice and pushed a curl out of Maggie's face. "I've known you since kindergarten, Margaret Wright. You're a good, honest, upstanding woman. There's nothing loose about you."

Kyle smiled at his mother over Maggie's head. She'd already taken Maggie into their family as one of their own. Whether Maggie liked it or not, Polly had extended her family's protection to her. No one would be making any cracks about Maggie in the presence of any Chase.

"What's going to happen to Alex?" Maggie asked Shane, still red-faced but looking slightly less mortified.

"He's being booked for vandalism. The window people will be out at your place first thing and if the cost of replacing the windows is over five hundred dollars we'll charge him second degree. After the underwear thing, we'll charge theft as well. I can't say that we'll be able to charge breaking and entering, depends on whether or not he admits to getting into your house to grab your stuff."

Edward Chase entered the room and patted Maggie's shoulder. "Hey, sugar. I sure wish our first meeting could be under better circumstances." He smiled gently before sitting down at the table. "I've heard most of the story. If you can believe it, Alex called and asked me to represent him! I declined of course, conflict of interest for me. Anyway, he's got Larry Dickerson from Riverton coming out. Larry's a decent sort. I think you should go first thing and see Judge Benson and request a temporary order of protection against Alex. I'll come with you. If you like, I can talk with the District Attorney and see if she'll make an order of no contact part of any sentence Alex gets. It's pretty standard in a case like this."

"You're all being so nice to me. I don't know what to say, thank you doesn't seem to be big enough." Her face heated and tears threatened to return.

"Don't say another word, Margaret. It's what you do for the people you care about. Now, get that hot chocolate into you. Are you hungry? I can make you a sandwich." Polly patted her shoulder.

"I'm hungry," Matt said.

"Me too," Marc echoed.

"Yeah, I could use a ham sandwich. Do we have any of that ham from dinner the other night left over?" Kyle asked.

"If we do, can I have extra mustard on mine?" Shane grinned.

Edward smiled at his wife and looked back at the tiny woman his sons had made part of their family. "I'll go out into the garage and grab some milk from the big fridge."

"I'm not hungry. I think I need to lie down. I have to be at work at nine."

"I think you should call the principal and let her know what's going on. Take a personal day. You have a busy morning ahead of you. You'll have to see the judge and make a statement and press charges down at the station."

"Good idea, Shane. Why don't you call now?" Kyle asked her.

She sighed. "I'll call from upstairs. I need to call my homeowner's insurance agent and make a claim too."

"I'll walk you up," Kyle said.

Maggie stood up and put a staying hand on his shoulder. "That's all right. I know the way." She looked at him and the rest of the family. "Thank you all so very much. Good night."

Kyle kissed her hand and looked up into her face. "Good night, sugar. I'll see you in the morning."

She nodded and went up the stairs into the guest room and closed the door behind her.

She called Ellis Mason, the principal of Petal Senior High and told her what happened and that she'd be out for the rest of the week. Mason was shocked and sympathetic, urging Maggie to take all the time she needed to and to call if she needed any help.

She called her insurance company and put them in contact with the glass company and gave them the case number as well.

She dialed Liv's number and dumped the whole story on her, sobbing.

"That perverted bastard!" Liv fumed. "Don't worry about the pictures, chances are this won't even go to trial. I'll even forgive you for not telling me—your best friend since the third day of kindergarten—that you were dating Kyle. Are you sure you don't want to stay here?"

Maggie laughed, wiping her face on the hem of her tee shirt. "Who knows if I'll be dating him after this whole mess. Jeezalou, this says *issues* from about five miles away. I appreciate the offer of a place to stay but I'm fine. I'm going back home tomorrow after my windows get replaced. Will you call Dee for me? I'd hate for her to drive by and see the boards and not know what was happening."

"You bet, dollface. Are you going to call your family?"

"No, what's the point? Anyway, I'll be hearing from my mother soon enough, I told Janie off tonight, or rather, Kyle did. She'll run straight to my mother with it."

"Okay, you must tell me the whole story very soon. I may be able to wait until our Pumphouse date but not a moment more. Now, go to sleep and call me if you need me."

Maggie hung up and snuggled down into the bed. It was indeed Kyle's old boyhood bedroom, the bed smelled of him. She drew it around her, letting herself be comforted by that.

Downstairs, Polly placed a platter of sandwiches on the table. "I can't believe all that girl has gone through."

"Well, I just hope Alex pleads out. A trial would suck for her. I'm not even sure the pictures would get out. They may not be admissible. But the scandal would hurt her. Doesn't matter that Alex is the one who did wrong." Shane spoke around his ham sandwich with extra mustard.

"Enough people saw the incident at The Pumphouse and I'm sure Liv would be happy to testify about his comments at the market, too. I'm betting that some of Maggie's neighbors saw Alex lurking around the neighborhood as well. I'm hoping that the evidence is such that Larry just advises him to take a deal. He most likely won't even do time, just a fine and anger management." Edward sighed.

"He won't even go to jail for that? After he terrorized her and broke her windows?" Marc said, outraged.

"I doubt it," Shane said. "Even if they did have a trial and he was found guilty, he'd still probably only do two or three weeks. The court will see it as he didn't hurt her physically. And of course he'll promise to never do it again. He's a librarian, they'll want to go easy on him. They'll see him as a positive influence in the community."

"Does he have any priors?" Edward asked. "I find it hard to believe that he would suddenly obsess over one woman like this. This kind of stalking behavior is usually a long term thing. I'll have one of the investigators I work with do a bit of checking with Alex's old girlfriends."

"Good idea, Dad. I know he doesn't have any priors here in Petal. I ran his information myself when we booked him."

"He went out of town to college. UGA if I recall," Matt said.

Shane picked up his cell and dialed the station. He spoke to the officer on duty, telling him to check to see if Alex had a criminal record either at the University through a grievance system or in other cities.

Chapter Six

The next morning Maggie woke up, getting ready quickly. Her hair up in a triple twist at the nape of her neck made her feel sleek and classy and a bit untouchable. She silently thanked Polly for packing professional looking clothing when she unzipped the garment bag. Choosing a black skirt and a cream colored blouse and some black pumps, she checked herself over in the mirror one last time before leaving the room. Chin up, she headed downstairs.

"Good morning, Red." Kyle came out of the kitchen to greet her. He kissed her quickly and gently on the lips and then placed another kiss on her forehead. "You look nice. Momma's got breakfast just about done. Come on into the dining room."

She walked into the dining room and saw that Edward was already there dressed in a suit and Matt was there too. "I thought you two lived on your own?" She asked Kyle.

Edward laughed and went back to his newspaper.

"We do. But I wanted to take the day off to help you, to be with you. My loser brothers are here all the time to scrounge free food from Mom."

Touched, she reached out and squeezed his hand. "You took the day off for me? You didn't have to do that."

He brought her hand to his lips. "I know I didn't have to, I wanted to. Now sit down. You want some coffee?"

"That would be nice, thank you." She sat, looking to Edward. "Mr. Chase, what time should I go to see the judge?"

"Edward please, darlin'. And I'll come with you. He does *ex parte* motions at ten thirty on Thursdays. I've had my assistant get the paperwork filled out—what parts you don't have to do that is—and we'll swing by my office to finish them first. We can leave here by nine thirty. You can ride in with Kyle. I'll need my car later."

"Don't I need to fill out a fee agreement or something?"

"Honey, this is not something I'd charge for. You're like a part of our family! I wouldn't dream of charging money for it."

She shook her head. "Edward, I can't let you do that. You're providing professional services and guidance to me. It wouldn't be right to take advantage of that."

Kyle narrowed his eyes at her as he put a mug of coffee in her hands. Damn but she was independent. He wasn't worried though, if Edward Chase could handle Polly, he could handle Red.

"I would be insulted if you pursued this any further." Edward looked down at her face, putting on his uber father mask, throwing in a bit of lawyer for effect.

Maggie didn't know what else to do or say. She didn't want to insult the people who'd helped her so much. When she got home she planned to make a huge batch of her lemon almond scones and some blueberry muffins and deliver them to Edward's office. She'd bring extras to the house as well. "Thank you for your kindness," she finally said, admitting defeat.

"Any time, sugar." Edward smiled and went back to reading the paper.

At the courthouse, the judge heard two minutes of her story before issuing the temporary order. It helped that one of the witnesses was the sheriff. "The papers will be served to Mr. Parsons at his home address. I understand he is currently out on bail."

"Thank you, Your Honor," Maggie said and they walked out into the hallway. Once out of the judge's hearing she turned to Edward. "He's free? They let him go?"

"I hadn't heard yet. Apparently so."

Shane stepped forward then. "He made bail a few minutes ago. He's home on his own recognizance. I'll have the papers served immediately. I need you to come to the station now so we can take more of your statement."

"How could they just let him out? He broke my windows! He wrote that stuff on my door. He has...pictures of me! The man is a panty thief!"

"I'm sorry, Maggie, it's not up to me," Shane said gently.

"Well this is just bullshit!" she hissed and the men around her were taken aback by her language but hid their amusement well.

"I'm sorry, sugar. This is the way of it, sometimes." Edward patted her shoulder. "I'm going to leave you in Kyle's able hands. I have a hearing to get to. I'm your attorney so if you need help, you call me right away, all right?"

"Thank you so much." He probably couldn't have any idea how much he'd helped her but she hoped she could make it up to him somehow. Even if it took her ten years.

He kissed the top of her head and was off with a wave to his sons.

"Kyle, you don't have to baby sit me. I know you have work to do."

"That's why it's so cool to be the boss. I'm not only going to stay with you, but when I take you back home, I'm going to install some motion controlled lights for you."

She thought about arguing but saw the set of his mouth and let the idea go. He was just as stubborn as she was. Instead she gave him her thanks and sent some silent thanks of her own out for having such good people in her life.

ল ল ল

Back at her house, Maggie cleaned up the inside while Kyle installed the motion detectors for the lights. From his vantage on the ladder, he saw a Lincoln pull up to the curb out front. A tall, blonde woman got out and stalked up the steps and into the house. An open window was right below where he was working and he heard the entire exchange.

"Margaret, where have you been?" the woman called out as she walked in through the door.

"Hello, Mother."

"I tried calling you all last night but you didn't answer. Nice girls don't stay out night, you know. Think of how the town will talk. Were you with some man? Oh never mind, silly question. Anyway, I got a call from Jane Marie about the deplorable way you treated her last night. Your jealousy of your sister has made you mean spirited. She can't help that she's prettier than you are and has a handsome man. You had no right to take it out on her."

"Oh, I see, so automatically, whatever Janie says is true? That's right, why even bother asking for my side of the story." Kyle heard the hurt in her words.

"You cannot be trusted over your sister."

Hearing all he could take, Kyle walked around and up the steps and into the house.

"For your information, Mrs. Wright, Maggie wasn't home because her house was vandalized and windows were broken out. She stayed with my mother and father until the glass could be replaced."

"Are you the contractor?" Cecelia looked at him haughtily until recognition lit her eyes and she sent him her thousand watt beauty queen smile. "Wait, you're a Chase aren't you?" Her eyelashes fluttered in the presence of such a handsome man and Maggie rolled her eyes.

"No, ma'am, not the contractor. I'm Maggie's boyfriend, Kyle Chase." He held his hand out to the vile woman.

"Boyfriend? *You?*" Cecelia started laughing as it if were the funniest joke she'd ever heard.

Kyle cut off her laughter. "Moreover, and I don't mean to tell tales out of school, but I think you should know that it was Jane Marie who was a very nasty woman last evening. Maggie and I were having dinner, minding our own business when she came over to our table and was deliberately hurtful to her sister. Maggie did nothing more than defend herself. I'm the one who asked Janie to leave us alone." He put his arm around Maggie's shoulders and wished he could toss Cecelia Wright right out of the house.

"Margaret has been jealous of her sister's superior looks her whole life. Margaret never ran in the popular crowd or got elected homecoming queen and she couldn't stand it that Jane Marie was. Jane Marie is simply superior and Margaret needs to accept that once and for all."

Fury and hurt coursed through Maggie. And then, clarity and calm. She was done letting herself get treated that way. By anyone. "That's a lie. I was happy for her. If she could actually stop being so nasty to me for a few days, she and I got on quite well. I'm still happy for her. I just no longer choose to be spoken to like I'm an ugly stepchild."

"What are you talking about?" Cecelia looked shocked that Maggie would dare to defend herself.

"The way you've spoken to me my whole life, Mother. As if I could never quite make the grade because I didn't look like you and Janie. It's quite an achievement to win pageants and I'm happy and proud of both of you. But there's more than one kind of achievement in life. I graduated second in my class at college and first in graduate school. I had full ride scholarships for all six years. I have a good job. I have nice friends, a good life. Mother, why can't you just accept me for Margaret and not as someone who isn't a carbon copy of you?"

"The boyfriend thing is new." She eyed Kyle up and down.

Leave it to Cecelia to focus on that instead of everything else. Maggie sighed. "First of all, I've dated since I came back to town to teach four years ago. If you had ever bothered to ask me about my life, you'd know that."

"A bit of a make-over I see. Now if you'd just go blonde you could really look good. Although I must admit that even Jane Marie never landed a Chase brother."

"Don't talk about him like he's a grade of meat."

"Darling, he's much better looking than you are. You must be doing something right. Maybe I underestimated you."

Kyle exhaled sharply. "Ma'am, I was raised by Polly Chase to never be rude to a woman but in the last day, between you and your oldest daughter, I've been put to the test something fierce. Maggie is beautiful. She's funny and smart as all get out. She's compassionate, strong and generous. How dare you talk to her like she's not?"

Cecelia Wright's eyes opened wide. "Margaret, are you going to let your young man speak to me like that?"

"Hell yes, Mother. Good bye. Oh and I do so appreciate you asking if I'm okay after my home was vandalized last night."

Cecelia Wright gasped and stormed out of the house.

"Oh my god, Kyle Chase." Maggie turned to him, lips in a tight line, hands on her hips.

"I'm sorry, Red. I didn't mean to be rude but I couldn't believe how she was talking to you."

Maggie threw her head back and laughed. She laughed and laughed until tears ran down her face and she had to sit down right in the middle of the floor. "Oh my lands! I've never seen her with that look on her face, I hope it freezes," she gasped out her laughter.

A smile cracked Kyle's worried face. He joined her on the floor and pulled her onto his lap. "Girl, you are something else," he murmured into her hair.

"Question is, what exactly is something else?" she asked, looking up into his face.

"Something special," he said softly, leaning down to kiss her upturned lips. "Something sweet," he added and nibbled on her chin. "Something sexy." She tipped her head back to give him access to her throat and he kissed down to the hollow there.

"Mmm. That's nice."

He looked down the line of her body, over the curve of her breasts, down her stomach, her small hands fisted in his shirt. "Yes, very nice." God he wanted to see her naked. To feel her bare flesh against his own. To taste her.

Maggie laughed then, a low, sexy sound. This woman was trouble. She made him want to jump inside her skin. Wanted every day memories like going camping and working in the yard. Yearned to hear her voice, smell her skin. See if she had freckles anywhere else.

For years he'd avoided such trouble, liking the single life very much. But Maggie Wright was the best kind of trouble he'd ever been in and he wanted to gorge himself with more.

Trailing the tips of his fingers down her belly he traced circles around her navel, slightly easing the hem of her blouse up. She shifted then and ran her fingers through his hair, dragging her fingernails lightly across his scalp. "Oh god, please touch me. I need your hands on me," she whispered.

"Hey, girl! You in there?" They both jumped at the sound and Kyle reluctantly sat Maggie up, smoothing her shirt down.

"I'm sorry," she whispered and he laughed and shrugged. "In here, Liv," Maggie called out, having to clear her voice.

Liv walked into the living room and saw them both getting up off the floor. "Whoops! Sorry. I can come back later."

"No, I need to finish installing those motion lights, anyway." He turned and kissed Maggie's nose and whispered, "I'll get back to where I was later on."

"You'd better." She smiled at him and watched him walk out of the room.

"Well," Liv said with a grin on her face.

"Yeah, turns out I had the wrong Chase brother to start with but now that I've corrected my mistake things are much better." She snorted, starting to laugh.

Liv tossed her bag into a chair and crossed her arms, looking at her friend. "So what happened with Alex? By the way, I'm parched. Can I get some tea?"

"Yeah, come on through." Maggie motioned her into the kitchen, giving her the basics on the way. "They let him out on bail today. He's home! I can't believe that. Oh, and they're charging him with possession of stolen property for having ten pairs of my underwear, three bras and a teddy, a bustier and a silk robe. It was my favorite robe, too! I thought it was at the dry cleaners. It's not like I can wear any of that stuff again, god only knows what he did with it all."

Both women shuddered in disgust. "Eww. What about the pictures?"

"What about them? Apparently he didn't do anything illegal. Any pervert can set up and using a telephoto lens, shoot you taking a shower. Ridiculous. You can bet I'll keep my curtains closed up tight. Hell, I even safety pinned them closed because a few of the pictures were shot between the gap where the two panels didn't quite meet. Though they do go toward making him look like the perverted stalker he is so we can use that in the protection order hearing."

"I feel guilty, he seemed so nice."

"Don't feel bad, Liv. How could you have known? He was a nice guy for a while."

"So tell me about the fracas with Janie last night." Liv's eyes lit up as she drank her tea.

Maggie spilled the entire story to Liv.

After first being shocked, Liv started laughing at Kyle's response. "I knew that boy was a keeper! Has hurricane Cece been here?"

"Of course. She starts in on how she's been trying to get a hold of me and how nice girls don't stay out all night. Kyle comes in and tells her I've been vandalized. She actually flirted with him and then he tells her he's my boyfriend and she laughed like it was a joke. Liv, she told me that my word couldn't be trusted over Janie's and that I was jealous because she was superior to me." That sliced into her gut.

Liv looked like she saw a pile of steaming dog doo. "Your mother is awful. She's a crime in thirty states."

"I stood my ground, Liv. For once in my life I defended myself and it felt great. Kyle defended me, too, which was very sweet. Poor ol' Cece ran for the door looking like she needed some more botox. I hope she and Janie get five new wrinkles from this."

Unashamedly listening from his ladder outside, Kyle nearly burst out laughing.

"You know, Liv, the Chase family showed me more love and concern in half an hour than my mother has my whole life. You should have seen them all here last night. Every single last one of them helped me. Matt and Marc boarded my windows and then finished scrubbing my door off. Polly showed up and ordered me to stay with them. At their house she made me hot chocolate and Edward appointed himself my attorney. Today he came to court with me. Shane took my report personally and has kept me updated on everything and Kyle has been with me the whole time. He took on my insane evil mother and sister."

She stopped for a moment, tears choking her voice. "It's just that I've been alone for a long time. I've had you and Dee and all but if my knee got scraped I got a lecture about being clumsy. Polly Chase is the kind of woman who would've cleaned it off and blown on the skin while she put hydrogen peroxide on it. They're all so wonderful and I'm horribly frightened that Kyle's feelings for me will wear off and I'll be alone again. Only after having been a part of their world, it'll be really lonely." Her voice had gone to nothing more than a whisper at the last admission.

Liv held back her own tears and hugged Maggie tight. "Girl, you always, always have me and Dee. And I think you should give Kyle a chance. By your description of his actions, he's in it for the long haul—the good, the bad and the ugly. Anyway, why quit now? You've already been in their world, it's not like you can erase it."

"Oh, Liv, last night it was so clear that I'm in way over my head. At The Oak Room everyone knew him. It was filled with people who never spoke a single word to me in high school. Everywhere we go women stare at him blatantly. Lyndsay Cole came onto him right in front of me! Even after he told her he was with me. How can I compete with that?"

"Maggie, you have got to stop this. You're nearly twenty-seven years old. How long are you going to let your mother and sister do a number on you? You don't need to compete with the Lyndsays of the world. You're better than they are anyway! Take a real look at yourself, please. You underestimate yourself so much! That's why you dated men like Sam for so long. You made a comment a while back about lowering your standards—sugar, raise them. You deserve it. Let yourself be happy. Let yourself be with Kyle Chase. You won't die if it doesn't work out. But imagine if it does."

Kyle leaned against the wall of the house, under the window, trying to process all he'd heard. He had to launch *Operation Make Margaret Wright Know What A Goddess She Was*, and he had to do it right away. Listening to her talk about her mother and sister, about how she felt last night among people he'd moved with for years, he felt bad. He needed to look at his own life a bit. He saw how shallow Jane Marie and Lyndsay were and wondered how many others in his circle were like that?

He pushed himself to standing and finished the last bit of installation for the lights and tested them. He was walking around the front of the house when Shane pulled up.

"Hey, Shane." He walked over to meet his brother's approach.

"Hey. Listen to this, Alex Parsons has four prior no contact orders on file. Seems that he had quite the way with the ladies back in college. I also talked with Dad's investigator who spoke with two women here in Petal who've had such bad experiences with Alex they were afraid to file police reports."

"Well, well, well. What a bastard. What does this mean then, for his case?"

"I passed it all on to the Prosecutor's Office. They contacted Alex's attorney. He's going to plead out."

"At least she won't have to testify or face him in court," Kyle said. "Let's go and tell her."

Shane nodded and they went in. Liv gave Shane a dirty look but smiled at Kyle.

"What's happening with the case?" Maggie asked, handing each of them a mug of hot tea and pointing their attention to the platter of scones.

"He has a criminal history of stalking women, Maggie. He's got four protection orders taken out by women at the UGA. He also apparently has a bad history here in town. He made a plea deal today. He'll officially sign it in court next Wednesday if the judge agrees, which he will. He's agreed to a permanent no contact order—he has to stay five hundred feet away from you at all times, can't contact you, and he's promised to not take any pictures of you. He'll have to pay for your windows and take anger management classes and have counseling."

"And how much time will he have to serve?"

"He won't be serving any time at all."

She froze, blinking quickly. "*What?* The man broke into my house and stole my panties…for god's sake! My favorite robe—I bought that robe in Milan and I can't ever bear to touch any of it again. He took pictures of me without my knowledge or consent, he manhandled me, broke my windows out and wrote an offensive word on my door and he doesn't serve any time? Worse, he's got a history of this and he gets away with it again? It's no wonder those other women didn't come forward. But oh well, I suppose I got what I deserved and all, being a woman who dared to go out with him and then you, oh and don't forget Kyle too."

"I'm sorry, Maggie. If it were up to me he'd be in prison for years, you know that. But the court doesn't view his crime as that serious and they'd rather take a plea agreement than prosecute because it's cheaper and easier. If he violates the protection order—which you'll have granted as a permanent order because he's agreed to that as well as the no contact order—you'll have double protection."

"Oh well, I'm sure that piece of paper will do a fine job! Oh and now I can't even use the library because he's there."

"This conviction will go on his record. He'll have to get help. Maybe he'll truly get the help he needs."

"Oh, his permanent record, I'm sure he's shaking in his boots! And help? Bully for him. But. What. The. Fuck. About. Me? Huh? What do I get out of this except for broken windows and a twitch every time the wind blows a branch against a window?"

Liv gasped, not because she found the word so horrifying but that she'd never ever heard Maggie use it. Kyle had an amused look on his face.

Shane looked at his brother, annoyed. "What?"

Kyle turned and looked at Maggie. "Get mad, Red! Who is this asshole to terrorize you? Who are these judges and attorneys who're going to let this guy off? Who is your mother to treat you like crap? Who is Jane Marie to treat you so badly when she's a nasty cheating liar? Aren't you sick and tired of it all? Don't you deserve better than that?"

"*Yes*! Damn it, I do! I'm a good person. I volunteer. I'm a teacher. I treat people right and look at what happens."

"Look what happens when you don't accept anything less than the respect you deserve, Maggie," he said softly, running the backs of his fingers down her cheek.

Realization dawned. "You trying to teach me a lesson, Kyle Chase?"

"Sure am." He folded his arms over his chest with an aura of authority. "You may not be able to make the court system punish Alex for this. Not in the way you want, but damn it you can make sure that everyone else in your life treats you with respect and on your own terms."

"Like my mother."

"Yeah, and your sister."

"And women like Lyndsay," Liv added.

"Definitely," Maggie added, looking dangerous.

"And me," Shane said. He sat down on the couch and looked up at her. "I owe you a big apology. I'm sorry I didn't just have the decency to say I couldn't see you any more to your face. You deserved better than me shoving Kendra at you like that."

Maggie looked at Shane for a long silent moment. Panic ate at Kyle when he understood that he was falling hard for little Miss Red. If she still had feelings for Shane he didn't know what he'd do.

She took a deep breath. "Apology accepted. Shane, you know, I didn't expect you to propose or anything. I understand you've been hurt badly but not every woman is like your ex. There's someone out there who you can make a future with. But if you keep running and closing yourself off at the first thought of actually having feelings for someone, you'll die lonely. Don't do that. Underneath that gruff exterior, there's a really special man."

Maggie looked over at Kyle. Smiling, she held out her hand for his. Relief rushed through him but he pretended that he'd never been worried at all.

"In the mean time, Shane, if you ever hurt a friend the way you hurt Maggie, I'll kick you right in the junk." Liv's eyes were ferocious as she said it and Shane crossed his legs.

Maggie's phone rang and she grabbed it. It was Polly.

"Hi, honey. Are any of my boys over there with you now?"

"Yep, Shane and Kyle. You need them?"

"I just wanted to invite you to dinner. You can tell them to come too. I'm making smothered pork chops, mashed potatoes, salad, corn bread and I wasn't gonna bother baking after you sent those delicious scones and muffins over."

"Thanks, Polly, that's so kind. I don't want to impose on you two nights in a row."

Kyle narrowed his eyes at her. "Is that my momma?"

"Yes, she's inviting me to dinner and she says you two can come, too."

"What's she making?" Shane asked.

"Smothered pork chops."

"Tell her I'll be there," he said immediately.

"You and I will be there in half an hour." Kyle's expression didn't leave room for argument. "Oh, and wait, let me talk to her." Kyle grabbed the phone she held out. "Momma, you got room for one more?"

"Of course I do. Who else is coming?"

"Olivia Davis, the Mayor's secretary. She's Maggie's best friend and she's here right now."

"Good, she's a pretty one. I'll put her between Matt and Shane. See y'all soon then."

Kyle hung up and looked back at them all. "Olivia, my mother would love for you to come as well. I promise you an excellent meal. Plus, well my family can be a bit overwhelming so it'll help Maggie to have you there."

"That and there's never an objection at our house to another beautiful woman," Shane added.

"Flattery and pork chops when all I was gonna do was eat a Lean Cuisine? Hmm, I think I'll have to choose the pork chops."

"Okay, but let me change. I have dust and glass shards on this skirt." Maggie bounded up the stairs to her room.

She changed into a pair of soft jeans and a fleece pullover and came back downstairs. "I sure like watching you go up and down stairs," Kyle murmured as he captured her waist, pulling her to him.

Smirking, she kissed him quickly as they headed out to the car. "Glad to be entertaining."

ରେ ରେ ରେ

Maggie felt immediately at home when she walked inside the Chase's home. Within moments she'd garnered hugs and kisses from everyone, although Kyle scowled at Marc who just laughed.

"You all know Olivia?" Maggie introduced her friend.

"Yes," Matt answered immediately. "You'll be sitting next to me tonight."

Maggie smiled. It looked like with a little help from Polly, Maggie was able to get Matt and Liv together after all.

"You got any other hot friends, Maggie?" Marc asked.

"Sorry, Marc. You've dated most every woman in Petal. Dee is lovely but she's engaged. Everyone else you've probably gone out with."

Kyle laughed at that one until Marc took her hand and kissed it. "Except for you, sugar." He winked.

"My goodness, you boys are a menace." Maggie blushed and Edward laughed as he led them all into the dining room.

The food was, as advertised, completely delicious. Maggie watched, amused as Matt and Liv hit it off. The brothers argued about the Braves' chances for the next season while Polly and Maggie talked about the upcoming auction for the Historical Society.

After they'd eaten and cleaned up, Kyle put his arm around Maggie. "Well folks, I'm going to get Maggie home. Matt, can you please give Liv a ride home? She rode over with us and I want to stop by my place for a minute to pick something up."

Matt perked up. "Of course, no problem. I was hoping to stay for dessert though. Liv?"

"Are those Maggie's lemon almond scones I see?"

"Oh, yes. She brought them over earlier today."

"Then I'll definitely stay for dessert." Liv got up and hugged Maggie and whispered, "Tell Kyle I owe him one."

Once they were driving, Kyle reached out and grabbed Maggie's hand. "I wasn't trying to get rid of you, Red. I was trying to get rid of them. I thought that it might be nice to stop by my condo to get some coffee ice cream. Maybe watch a movie. What do you say?"

"I say, I love coffee ice cream!"

Kyle's condo complex was on the south side of town and had a series of small streams that led into a large man-made lake at the center. Kyle's two story townhouse was on a little spit of land that looked out over the water.

He pulled into the attached garage and took her inside through a side door. Maggie had to admit she was impressed. The living room and kitchen opened up to the second floor. Pretty maple hardwood floors gleamed and ceiling fans circled lazily, moving the air. It was tastefully furnished and reasonably neat.

"This is really nice, Kyle."

"Want the grand tour?"

"Sure."

He showed her through the first floor, through his office and the living room and nice sized kitchen.

The upstairs featured a guest bedroom and attached bath and a large master suite with windows overlooking the stream and lake. Hues of sage green and sand gave the space a cool and relaxed feeling. His bed, on a low platform, dominated the room. Maggie couldn't help but stare at it for long moments.

"Wow, this is beautiful. Puts my bedroom to shame."

"I thought the same thing when I saw your bedroom. It's so warm, so you."

She turned to him and he looked at her without saying anything for several long moments.

"Red, we should probably go downstairs now."

"Yeah."

Neither of them moved.

Reaching up, Maggie unzipped the front of her pullover. It exposed her skin to just above her belly button. *Oh my god, did I actually just do that?* She panicked but then realized that it was done and she may as well ride it, or him, out. It was time to take her life into her own hands and live it.

His lips parted and he looked at the small vertical slash of skin exposed through the open zipper.

Maggie turned and walked into the hallway, leaving her pullover unzipped. She went down the stairs and heard him follow her. Calmly, she sat down on his couch, turning to look at him when he joined her. His pupils were huge, his breathing shallow.

He pulled her close. "What are you up to, Red?" His voice was a lazy purr and suddenly, she felt a bit like prey.

"Nothing, it's just a bit warm," she said breathily. His nearness affected her, sped her heart. Warmed her from the inside out.

The corners of his mouth tugged up. "Are you teasing me, Red?"

She shook her head slowly. "I'm promising you."

"Good lord, woman. You trying to kill me?" He nuzzled her neck.

"Huh uh." It came out slow and soft as her head lolled back to give him more access. "I'll need you later. Or now."

"Are you saying what I think you are saying?"

She sat up and laughed. "Sheesh, Kyle, I know you've slept with like a hundred women. Haven't any of them teased you? Or am I doing so poorly at it that you don't get it?"

"There's the Red of my dreams. I love it when you go all sassy on me." He pushed his face into her cleavage and breathed her in. His goatee tickled the sensitive skin there and shivers of delight and anticipation broke over her.

"I was hoping you meant you wanted to make love. But I wanted to be sure because I respect you so much. I just don't want to push past where you're willing to go."

She leaned over and pressed her lips to his ear. "Kyle, can you respect me while you're inside me? Because I really—and I mean really—need you to fuck me." She knew she was blushing but it felt so good to say what she'd been thinking.

She saw the shiver run down his skin and he moved to look into her face. "Do you know how sexy you are? I don't know that I've ever wanted anything as badly as I want to make love to you." Standing up, he held out his hand to her and she took it. Hand in hand, he led her up the stairs to his bedroom.

Closing the door behind them, the rest of the world felt far away. While she stood and watched him, he pulled out some matches and lit the candles that ringed the room.

"They're new. I bought them thinking about how you'd look with the candlelight flickering off your skin."

"Dude, you say the best stuff. You're so getting lucky." Smiling, she grabbed hold of the bottom of her pullover and yanked it over her head.

He blinked a few times. "Damn it, woman, you're gonna kill me. Just full of surprises, aren't you?" With a grin, he reached to turn off the overhead light. "Yeah, just what I thought. You and candlelight—a very sexy combination."

"*I'm* sexy? Kyle Chase, do you look in the mirror very often?" Maggie went to him, reaching out to slowly unbutton his shirt. She gloried in the feel of his skin as she slid the shirt down his arms and off. The warmth of his body and the scent of him hit her face. She closed her eyes, leaning in to take a deep hit of him.

Drowning in hormones she stepped back to take a long look at him. His upper body had the long lean muscle of a runner or a cyclist. He was hard and packed but not bulked.

"Dear lord, you're beautiful." Leaning back toward him, she flicked her tongue over one of his nipples, delighting in his hungry moan. The heated salt of his taste set her taste buds on fire. She wanted more of him. All of him.

Needing to touch him, she slid her palms down the muscled plane of his abdomen. Her fingers tucked just inside the waistband of his jeans, tracing around the edge and the sensitive skin there. Getting down to business, she unsnapped each of the seven buttons there. Every pop seemed so loud— vibrating off her spine as she uncovered a bit more of his body.

Kneeling to help him step out of his jeans and socks, she looked up, thrilled when she saw the inescapable evidence of just how much he wanted her—how much Kyle Chase wanted Margaret Wright.

"Now there's a picture to last me many a cold and lonely night," he murmured, looking down at her kneeling. Heart hammering in his chest, he reached down to caress her face. Every nerve ending in his body lit when she rubbed a velvety cheek along his thighs. Her fingers and nails grazed down the backs of his legs, kneading the muscles of his calves.

Her caresses came back up his legs and into his boxer-briefs to cup the hard muscle of his ass. Grabbing the material, she pulled them down, leaving him totally naked to her view. He should have felt exposed. But instead heat spread through him at the sight of the greed in her gaze.

She'd intended to stand back to look at all of him but the heated velvet of his cock called to her and she didn't want to resist. Instead, she grabbed him in her hands, holding him so that she could take him into her mouth. Her tongue slid over the bead of semen that pearled at the head and his taste burst through her.

"Holy shit, Red," Kyle stuttered as his hands fisted in her hair.

She hummed her appreciation around his cock and continued to taste him. Her nails lightly scored over his balls and he sucked in a breath. "This is going to end before it begins. Come on, Red, stop for a minute."

She sat back with a kiss to the head of his cock. And then one more because she needed him so much. With a sigh of longing she took his hand

and let him help her stand. She stepped back so that she could look her fill at him. And she could have done it for ages, he was so handsome.

"Red, come here. You undo me with the way you look at me. I want to look at you now." Kyle's voice had gone husky and she heard the strain in it.

Taking the two steps to get to him, she put her hand on his stomach and slid it down, taking his cock into her fist. Moaning, he arched into her hold. She looked down at him, hot and hard, avarice on her face and he laughed.

"You're good for my ego, Red." He ran the tip of his index finger down her skin and over a pouty pink nipple. The material of the bra was sheer and embroidered with leaves of all colors. "Pretty." He popped the catch between her breasts and slid the bra down her arms. "I love front closure bras. Best. Invention. Ever."

She looked up at him with a smirk. "Seen your fair share of them have you?"

"Oh no." He put his hands up in surrender and shook his head. "That's not a question I'm even going near. It's an unwinnable woman dead end question like, does my butt look fat in this."

"No way! The answer to that question is always no. Anyway, you brought it up." A grin won over her face.

"My answer is it doesn't matter. No other woman in the universe matters but you."

"Good one. More than enough to get me into your bed."

"We do try," he murmured. "Now, I was in the middle of something before you interrupted me, Red."

"My apologies, sirrah. Pray do continue." She bowed in a mock curtsy.

He laughed, picked her up and laid her on his bed, putting her hands up above her head. "That makes a lovely picture." Leaning down over her, he placed a reverent kiss on the tip of each nipple. She sighed happily.

He smiled while his clever hands made quick work of her jeans. The underwear was a match to the bra. "You had this sexy stuff on under all of those conservative clothes all the time didn't you?"

"Pretty underwear is an addiction. Some people buy shoes, some people buy expensive wines. I buy lingerie and books."

"That's an addiction that I am fully willing to enable, Red." He gave her a lascivious smile, pulling the small scrap of material down her legs. When she was totally naked, he paused to slowly drag his gaze up the length of her body. "You are so beautiful, Maggie."

And she was. Hair spread out over the coverlet, a flush of passion on her face, breasts heaving, long legs moving a bit restlessly under his gaze—amazing. "Oh," he whispered, moving his face closer to her. "Look at this. It looks like someone shook powdered cinnamon here." He ran the flat of his tongue across the dusting of freckles on her shoulders. "Tastes better than cinnamon though," he murmured.

She squeaked at the contact of his warm tongue. He chuckled and flicked the point of his tongue on a path south to her breasts. "Now these, Red." One of his eyebrows rose as he snuck a quick look up at her and then back to her breasts. "I had no idea that breasts so pretty existed under those blouses you wore buttoned up to your chin. Not that I haven't spent a lot of time in the last few months thinking about them." He circled a pebbled nipple slowly with one hand and mimicked that with his tongue at the other.

Arching her back, she pressed her breasts closer to his mouth. She tried to reach for him but he was too long-waisted. Moaning in frustration, she shoved at him, pushing him onto his back.

Moving to kneel between his thighs, she ran her hands across the muscles there, down his calves and back up again. His stomach was flat and she traced the bands of muscle up to his chest, which also bore a mat of blond-brown hair.

His nipples were cinnamon and deliciously sensitive. Moving her mouth to him, she licked over the flat ridge of each. Shuddering, his hands fisted in the blankets as she followed the licks with the edge of her teeth.

Sitting up, she looked at him some more, trying to decide what to touch next. His face was masculine and defined but still beautiful, the kind of face that still looked handsome at seventy. He watched her through gorgeous green eyes fringed with lashes any woman would love to have.

After raising her finger to her lips, tapping it as if she were trying to make a decision she moved to slide her hands over work-hard biceps and powerful forearms. Her lips kissed the tips of each finger on his large hands. His neck was long, chin bearing a cleft covered in that sexy goatee. She traced the tip of her tongue over his lips across to his jaw and up to his earlobe for a quick nibble.

"You're killing me," he groaned out and she laughed.

"Let me see what I can do about that," she murmured, kissing her way south. And then he heard nothing but the blood rushing in his ears as she lowered her mouth over him. His body jerked at the intensity of the sensation. He whispered her name and his hands went to her head, caressing her scalp.

Looking down and seeing the mass of red curls spread over his stomach and her sweet ass swaying in the air as she went down on him nearly drove him over the edge.

"Baby, please, stop, I want to be inside of you. I want to look up at you as you ride me, Maggie," he whispered hoarsely. The smile she sent him made his cock jump in anticipation. "There's a condom in my pants pocket. Over there on the chair near the foot of the bed." She nodded and crawled down to the end of the bed and reached out, grabbing the pants and rifling through his pockets until she found it.

"I won't comment on the fact that you had one in your pocket, Kyle." She smirked as she ripped the foil packet open and rolled it on him. She moved up to straddle his thighs, smiling sexily down at him.

"And I won't comment on how spectacular you looked bent over getting my pants—except to tell you that your pussy is so pretty and to promise you that I will be getting that view again soon. Only with my cock deep inside you. As for the condom, a guy is dead without hope. What if we'd been driving out by the lake or something and we'd wanted to make love? Badda bing, badda boom, I had a condom and we could have done it. Oh dear god...." His words ended on a gasp as she slowly slid down onto him, encasing him in her very tight, very hot pussy.

She moved, taking him into her body inch by inch and pleasure drove up his spine. He looked up at her, surprised at himself. Woman on top had never been a real favorite position for him for sex. But watching her—lips slightly parted and wet from her licking them in concentration and desire, her eyes glazed, lids at half mast, breasts gently moving as she did, the patch of auburn curls meeting his brown-blond one—he reconsidered. She was so amazing that it made his stomach hurt. He grabbed her hips, his own rising to meet hers and he slid in that last inch or two. A sigh broke from both of them as he seated himself fully inside of her.

The embrace of her pussy, the way she squeezed him and fluttered around his cock was fantastic. So much so, he needed to still for several moments to rein himself in. "Sweet heaven, your pussy feels amazing, Maggie. I don't think I want to leave it."

His words shook her down to her very core. The raw need in them, the way he'd laid himself so open and vulnerable to her got to her in ways she'd never even imagined.

She had to take a deep, steadying breath. Orgasm was very close and it felt like every single nerve in her body was firing and shouting with joy. This was something more than great sex. More than physical. This was deeper. She swiveled her hips experimentally and his eyes flew open wide and he groaned.

"Oh, I see you like that." A throaty laugh bubbled from her and she did it again, this time tightening her inner muscles around him.

The truth was that at almost twenty-seven, Maggie had only had sex—well, intercourse—with three men. Now four. She wasn't very experienced. Adding up even the four men, she'd actually only done it ten times total and it'd been a year since the last time. Although if the other times had felt this good, she didn't think she could have withstood a year-long break. She felt vastly inexperienced next to Kyle but he made her feel like it didn't matter to him at all.

"I like everything you do, but that was quite exceptional. Do it again," he said in a hoarse voice as he brought his hands up to cup her breasts, kneading them and rolling her nipples between agile fingers.

Her head lolled back, arching her back, bringing a change in her angle over him. This brought his thrusts even deeper into her. Swiveling at the same time he rose to press into her brought a gasp from both of them. The intensity of the contact was immense. One of his hands slid down her belly to her pussy where he gathered her honey up to her clit, slowly circling it as she rode him.

Suddenly her back went straight as electric pleasure rode through her, bringing climax in its wake. She moaned his name once before losing speech as the erotic assault pulled her under.

The rippling and pulsing of her pussy around him, combined with her cries of pleasure pushed Kyle over with her. The muscles on his arms corded with exertion as he moved her body over his own while the flush of her climax crept over her skin.

After what had to be one of the most intense orgasms of her life, she went boneless, collapsing onto him, utterly unable to move. Gently, he rolled her to the side and pulled out of her and she whimpered at the loss of contact.

"I need to deal with the condom, Red. I'll be right back." He jumped up to run into his bathroom and came back quickly, sliding into the bed next to her, pulling her into him.

છ છ છ

They must have fallen asleep because the candles were almost burned down completely when Maggie opened her eyes. One of Kyle's legs was thrown over her thighs and his arm was curled around her. She lay there for a few minutes, enjoying the way he felt against her body, his breathing against her hair, the anchoring sweetness of his fingers threaded through her own. She felt totally satisfied. Physically and emotionally.

After some time, she craned her neck to look at the clock. Seeing the time, she sighed.

"Hey, Red." Kyle stirred as he awoke and kissed her thoroughly.

"Hey. Sorry I woke you. It's after two. I should probably go home."

He tightened his grip and burrowed his face into her neck. "Why? I like you right where you are. You're so warm and sweet. You smell so good. Plus, it'll be a lot easier to have sex with you again if you're actually here. Naked."

She smiled. "Well isn't it against the rules to have me stay over?"

"Which rules are those? Is this from the mysterious hot guy rule book you referenced the other day? I must tell you, Red, you need to stop worrying about all these supposed rules."

She socked him playfully. "Don't make fun! I'm not good at this. I don't know how to do it."

He looked at her, his lascivious grin back in place. "I don't know about that, Red. It felt like you knew how to do it pretty darn well to me."

"That's not what I was talking about and well, if you must know, that was only the eleventh time I've ever done it. I know it seems like I'm easy, but that isn't the case."

"You're a natural then. And I've told you before, you don't seem easy, not by a long shot. You're wonderful." He chuckled but his soul roared with satisfaction. Only eleven times? He loved that about her. That she was a natural sex bomb turned him on immensely.

"Easy for you to laugh, you're an ace at this."

"Thanks for the compliment. I'm glad you think so."

She sighed in frustration. "You're deliberately trying to confuse me and yank my chain."

"No, I want you to yank mine." He wiggled his eyebrows and she dissolved into laughter and he kissed the tip of her nose. "Maggie, I *want* you to stay the night. I *want* to wake up with you in the morning. I don't have a rule book. I just go by what I feel. This is all new to me too, you know. You're the first woman who's ever slept in this bed. I'm not normally a spend-the-night-with-me kind of guy. I told you, I'm wooing you, Margaret Wright."

She snorted and snuggled back into him. "In that case, I've got to tell you that wooing has totally exceeded my expectations. By the way, I have the day off tomorrow. Are you going back to work?"

"You temptress! I do have to work, but I can do it from my office downstairs. Why? Are you actually opening up enough to spend the day with me?"

"I thought we could at least have a nice breakfast."

"And lunch and don't forget I'm making you dinner. You did already agree to have dinner with me. I think you should just stay in my bed all day, naked. I'll bring you anything you need, including me."

She cracked a smile. "I like you, Kyle Chase."

He sobered and kissed her, a bare brush of his lips across hers. "Oh good, 'cause I like you too, Maggie. A whole hell of a lot."

"Enough to cough up that coffee ice cream you lured me over here with?"

He burst out laughing. "For a tiny little thing, you sure eat a lot."

"I have a fast metabolism."

He sat up. "It sounds good. Let's go." He pulled on a pair of sweats and she grabbed what she thought was her shirt but it was his. Moving to put it down and look for her own shirt, he startled her when he put a hand on her arm. "No, put it on."

She pulled on his shirt and buttoned it up. Of course, she had to roll the sleeves a few times and the hem came to her knees but shivers ran down her spine when she caught him watching her with that lazy cat look of his.

"Damn, this will change the way I feel every time I hear Keith Urban sing, 'You Look Good In My Shirt'. You look so good that I want to throw you right back down on the mattress and climb between those thighs of yours."

"Later, I want ice cream," she said and it ended on a squeal because he lunged at her. She ran past him and down the stairs laughing.

He dished up two bowls of ice cream and they spread out a blanket on the living room floor, watching a movie while they ate. Or they watched the beginning of a movie anyway.

Kyle took her bowl and put it aside. "Done eating?"

She cocked her head at him. "Well, since I allowed you to take my bowl without protest, I'd say yes."

"Good. Because I'm not done eating." His lips curved up and she gasped as he pushed her back onto the blanket. Making quick work of the buttons on her shirt, he pushed it off. She looked up at him, watching his eyes as he devoured her with his gaze. Smiling like the Cheshire Cat, he reached out and brought his bowl over.

With a yelp, she nearly shot up off the floor as he drizzled ice cream over her breasts. But soon that yelp became a moan as he licked up the sweet liquid with the flat of his tongue. The cold ice cream followed by the heat of his tongue gave her goose flesh.

"Hmmm, where else would this ice cream taste good?" He raised an eyebrow as he spooned it down her belly and over her thighs.

She watched him as he licked his way down her belly and over her thighs. He pushed them open. "I need my hands, Red. Hold yourself open for me so I can lick all of you."

Her breath caught but she did as he asked.

His cold tongue licked up through the folds of her pussy and around her clit and she couldn't resist rolling her hips.

"Sweeter than ice cream and I can eat it in any weather," he murmured against her.

Her hips raised up involuntarily and she whispered his name. "You like that, Maggie?" he murmured and flicked his tongue over her clit. "Damn, but your pussy is sweet. Sweet and wet." He pressed a finger deep into her and shuddered as the walls of her pussy gripped him. "I like that you're so slick for me."

She was beyond a place where she could form the words to tell him how good he felt there between her thighs. All she had were whimpers and breathless sighs as her head slowly moved from side to side. The muscles in her thighs and abdomen began to tremble as orgasm approached.

When he hooked his fingers inside her and found her sweet spot she rolled her hips and cried out. The pleasure was sharp edged, nearly too much to bear.

"Yes, Maggie. Come for me, honey," he said just before he slowly sucked her clit into his mouth, grazing his teeth over it just slightly.

In a rush of intense sensation, her climax drowned her as her very cells exploded in heat and light and pleasure. Wave after wave shuddered through her in a seemingly endless pattern. Wringing her out, flooding her mind and body.

He continued, not stopping until he'd pushed her into another aftershock orgasm and she sobbed with pleasure and the intensity of feeling, finally pushing his head away and begging him to stop.

Afterwards, his lips on hers tasted of sugar and ice cream and her.

Chapter Seven

The next morning, Maggie opened her eyes and saw that she and Kyle were laying on his living room floor with a blanket thrown over them. She stretched with a wince. Man, that was some work out. Each of those aches was well earned and she planned to enjoy the memory of the night before with each and every protest of her muscles.

She sat up slowly and finally noticed that he'd been watching her. She made a mental shrug. It was too late to be embarrassed now, he'd seen her, *had her*, in many combinations just a few hours before.

He pulled on a corkscrew curl and let it go as his brother had done. "Matt was right. That is fun." He did it a few times more.

She raised an eyebrow at him. "Finished? I need a shower and all of my stuff is at my house."

"You're not leaving here. At least not yet. You can wear my shirt with your jeans until you go home to change. I'll even lend you a pair of my underwear."

"Which will hang to my knees." She snorted and then remembered what had happened to her own favorite pairs of underwear and shuddered with revulsion.

"Why the shudder? Do I disgust you?"

"It's not you. I was just thinking about underwear and then about my underwear that got stolen. And that's just icky. I feel the need for some retail therapy."

"Retail therapy?"

She turned to him, eyes widened. "You don't know what retail therapy is? I thought you were an expert on women?"

He threw back his head and laughed. "I thought so until I met you. Now I think that I was an expert on bimbos and I'm woefully uneducated about real women. So teach me."

She gave him a smug smile. "Good answer. Anyway, retail therapy is shopping. It's what some women do as a pick me up when they're down. Although in this case, I'm not down in the traditional sense, things are going pretty well for me right at the moment." She looked at him and fluttered her lashes. "No, I need to exorcise a demon. A nasty perverted rat bastard demon named Alex who came into my house and pawed through my panties and stole every single pair of my favorite ones."

"Let me do the work I need to, it should take me about an hour and a half or so. Go home, get showered and changed, bring us back some breakfast and coffee and then you and I are going panty shopping."

"You? A man? Wants to come shopping with a woman? For clothes?"

"Ah, but not for clothes, not for skirts or shoes." He shuddered. "For lingerie. And that, my love, is a whole different story. Any time you want to shop for silky underwear, I'll gladly accompany you." *Did I just call her, my love?* He thought about it for a second and realized he wasn't panicked about it the way he would have been if he'd said it to any other woman. Of course, he never had said it to another woman.

Ohmigod, did he just call me, my love? She panicked and then realized, after a moment that it felt totally natural. "I'll warn you, I have very discriminating tastes with respect to lingerie. I go to Atlanta for it."

"Good, we can get lunch there." He stood and helped her up, swatting her behind as she went up the stairs to grab her pants and the rest of her clothes.

"I can't wear your shirt, it's cold out. My pullover is much warmer." She pulled on her jeans without underwear and a slow sexy smile broke over his face.

Grabbing the pullover from her hands, he turned and pulled something out of his closet, tossing it at her. "There. It's wool. Very warm."

She pulled it on, without a bra and had to fold the sleeves up a few times. It smelled like him and felt heavenly against her skin. It was huge on her but it was warm and he looked like he was going to devour her.

"My sweater and no bra, I feel like it's Christmas morning! I just want to bend you over something. All those alpha male instincts are aroused."

Of course, that wasn't the only thing aroused. The man could really talk a good game. He made her tingly just listening to him and he wasn't even really trying.

Grinning, he walked her out. "Oh, you don't have your car. I drove." He reached over and grabbed his keys off the table at the entry hallway. "Take my car. That's my house key, just let yourself back in when you're finished. I'll get to work now. Don't forget to bring back coffee and breakfast."

He kissed her silly and fought a smile as she got into his car and had to adjust the seat forward. He opened the garage door for her and stood there as she pulled away.

Maggie's house was fine when she got home. No broken windows, nothing taken that she could see. Checking the locks one last time, she headed up to take a long hot shower to work out the kinks in her muscles from the repeat performances on the living room floor at two thirty in the morning. Catching sight of what looked like carpet burn on her ass, she giggled as she toweled off. Who'd have ever thought that she, Maggie Wright, would get rug burn from oral sex on Kyle Chase's floor!

Quickly drying her hair, she got dressed, put on a minimal amount of makeup and went down to check her messages and with a smile, got back on her way.

She stopped off at the café and placed an order for two deluxe breakfasts with pancakes and smoked ham to go and headed back to Kyle's place. When she unlocked the door and turned back to grab the food she'd set down, he was there, smiling at her. Taking the bags from her hands he dropped a kiss on her forehead.

"Hey, Red, set the coffee on the table. I'll bring the food, plates are already out." He started opening containers and popping things in his mouth.

"Knock it off. Sheesh, you're a hound dog in more than one way. I don't take kindly to my potatoes being purloined."

"Me? A hound dog?" He grinned as he sat down next to her and she started filling their plates with the huge amount of food she'd brought.

"I got two deluxes with ham. I hope you like ham." She knew he did of course, remembering his request for a ham sandwich from his mother a few nights before.

"I love ham, and eggs, and potatoes and toast and pancakes. This is perfect." He put three small chunks of potato back on her plate. "To replace what I stole."

Snorting, she speared them on a fork and ate them. "Don't think I'm too proud not to eat them. I love potatoes."

He laughed. "Roger that. You were gone two hours."

"You said you had about an hour and half of work to do. I thought I'd leave you alone to do it."

A woman who willingly gave him space? "I missed you. I thought you could help me in the shower." He grinned wolfishly.

"Maybe later," she said dryly and tore into her breakfast.

"I'm beginning to see that it's dangerous to come between you and your plate."

She gave him an annoyed look and took a bite of his toast.

ଓ ଓ ଓ

The hour and a half drive to Atlanta and back with Maggie was quite enjoyable. Kyle couldn't get over how funny and vivacious she was. How he could have had a woman like that right under his nose all these years and not noticed was beyond him.

And there was no denying how enjoyable it was to sit and watch her finger lacy and silky panties and bras for the better part of an hour either.

He'd sat in the store, a pile of lingerie on his lap, hiding his erection as he thought of taking each piece off her. With his teeth. The thought of all of those silky scraps laying against her bare skin made him so hard he had to move a few times to keep from injuring himself. As it was, he was sure there would be imprints of the rivets from his button fly on his cock.

He dropped her off at her place with several bags of things he couldn't wait to see her wearing. Running inside, he checked to be sure the place was okay and made plans to meet her at The Pumphouse later on.

CR CR CR

She walked in the front door of The Pumphouse at precisely seven to find Dee and Liv already there with a pitcher and chili cheese fries. After some quick hugs and kisses they got down to gossip.

"So? You were going to tell me about last night with Kyle?" Liv sipped her beer.

"Oh my lands! You know, I go for a year without any sex and when I break the dry spell it's with Kyle. The man is so unbelievably sexy that I'm all fluttery just thinking about it. Thing is, with Kyle, it's so much more than sex. I mean, we laugh all the time. He's so smart and kind. It just feels like we've known each other for a very long time. The sex was astounding. I'm talking ice cream coffee in the, um, small of my back at two in the morning, astounding."

"You go! Speak of the stud himself, he just walked in with Matt," Dee said, and Liv and Maggie both turned around.

Kyle saw her and a big grin spread over his face. It mirrored the happiness that spread, warm, through his chest. He promptly went to her side, bending to kiss her. And it wasn't a quick peck either. He couldn't just take a small taste. He pulled her into his body and set his mouth to hers in a kiss that stole her breath. He wanted to mark her, take up her every thought the way she did his.

When she put her arm up to go around his neck, he saw a flash of the lace edging the pink bra. Oh yeah, the one with the teeny matching thong. His cock throbbed at the memory. And at the memory he'd be making with her later on.

"Hey, Red. See, pink does work on redheads," he said softly as he pulled away and kissed the knuckles of the hand that had been around his neck.

"Hey, Kyle." Her blush matched the tremor in her voice. He loved that he made her feel that way.

"Hi, Matt," Liv said with a grin.

Matt smiled sexy at Liv. "Hi, Liv. Dee. I'd ask how you were, Maggie, but since Kyle hasn't shut up about you since he picked me up from work, I already have a good idea."

Maggie blushed. "We've got more gossip to dish here and Shane is scowling and tapping his watch at you so you'd better get over there. I'll see you at eight thirty."

"You bet, Red." He kissed her again and sauntered back to the pool room with a wave at her.

"Oh my god. You two give off more heat than a transfer station. Holy cow!" Liv fanned herself with her hand.

"How did the night end with Matt, anyway?" Maggie asked Liv to change the subject.

Liv sighed. "He's a perfect damned gentleman! He took me home and we talked in my driveway. I asked him in for coffee and he told me he had to work!"

Maggie wrinkled her nose. "He did? Well, I know he's sweet on you. Maybe he really did have to work. I'll do a bit of snooping. Totally subtle, I swear!"

"So how are things with Arthur the stud?" Blushing furiously, it was Liv's turn to change the subject.

"Good. He put new floors in the hall bathroom and the pantry, they look so nice. We had sex on our deck, outside!" Dee said the last bit in a whisper.

"No way!"

"Well it was dark and we were under a blanket on the glider but still, it felt naughty."

"Woo, Arthur," Liv said grinning. "I'm glad you two are getting some. I haven't had any in a month. Since my last date with Shaun."

"A month! How do you survive?" Maggie said sarcastically.

"Hey, I like it regular! When I was with Charlie, we had sex at least once a day. Since he and I broke it off, it's been catch as catch can. I tell you, Matt Chase looks so good I could eat him with a spoon." She looked wistfully back at the pool table where the Chase brothers were playing.

"They're so beautiful," Maggie said, smiling.

"Yeah huh," Dee agreed.

"Oh, is that Lyndsay?" Liv asked.

Maggie looked and saw that indeed Lyndsay Cole was undulating her way over to Kyle. "No way, girlfriend. Kyle wanted me to get mad and demand respect? This is day one." Standing up, she made her way back to the pool room.

"Hi, Kyle. Why don't you buy me a drink? I promise you'll get lucky." Lyndsay sidled up to him.

He stepped away. "Hi, Lyndsay. No thanks. I told you, I'm with Maggie." He took his shot and missed as he saw Maggie stalk over looking like a gloriously angry fairy.

"Maggie?" Lyndsay looked confused.

"Yeah, Maggie Wright. As in me."

Lyndsay turned around and made a big show about looking down at her but Maggie stood her ground and narrowed her eyes at the other woman.

"You must be joking. Did you lose a bet or something, Kyle?"

Maggie just looked at the other woman, her arms crossed over her chest. Kyle took his shot and made it. Kissing Maggie's neck, he took his next shot, sinking it as well. He totally ignored Lyndsay. He normally would have hated any kind of showdown between women over him but he was utterly turned on by watching Maggie mark her territory. And it was good for Maggie to stand up for herself.

"Be on your way, Lyndsay, he's not interested." Maggie made shooing motions with her hands and Matt laughed.

Lyndsay snorted. "Please. You think you can hold a man like Kyle?"

"Seeing as how you never had him to begin with and I have him now? Yeah. In any case, if things do go bad and we break up, you're free to take a shot at him then. Unless and until that day comes, back off. Kyle is taken and your feelings about that are irrelevant."

Kyle put his arm around Maggie and pulled her into his side.

"Whatever. You can't hold him for long." Lyndsay flounced off in a huff.

Maggie said something unladylike under her breath and Kyle threw back his head and laughed. He kissed her until she was breathless and led her back to her table. "Thanks for defending my honor, Red."

"Mmmm," she replied and he walked back to the pool room chuckling.

"Way to go, Maggie!" Dee and Liv grinned at her.

"I have to confess, being an uppity woman is really fun. I can't believe I've missed out all these years. I do have a lot of ground to make up!"

Liv laughed and gave her a thumbs up.

"So, Arthur and I are hosting Thanksgiving dinner at our house this year. My parents and his are coming over, as well as his brothers and their wives and my sister and her husband and kids. You two are welcome to come."

"I'm going to go to my sister's in Crawford. I promised last year."

"I don't know what I'll do. Usually, I'd let myself be guilted into a day of agony at Cece's house of pain but I think I'm going to decline this year. I'd rather eat a frozen turkey dinner than subject myself to any more from them."

"Well, as long as you know you're welcome at ours. But from the looks of it, you'll be eating turkey and watching bowl games at the Chase household." Dee seemed convinced but Maggie looked dubious.

At eight thirty the pool game broke up and Kyle stopped at their table. He held out his hand with a bow. "Are you ready, darlin'?"

She smiled and took it. Turning around she leaned down and hugged her friends as she said her goodbyes.

"Oh hey, you coming to the Grange tomorrow?" Dee called out as they got to the door.

"Oh, is that tomorrow night?"

Every year, the weekend before Thanksgiving, Petal had a community dance at the Grange that also served as a fundraiser and food drive for the local food pantry and soup kitchen.

"You aren't going to any dance without me, Red. I have two tickets already. In fact, the whole Chase family does it every year. Please do me the honor and come as my date?"

"Well, when you put it like that." She kissed his nose. "I guess I'll see y'all there," she said to Liv and Dee.

When Kyle got into the car he turned to her. "I told my momma that I'd bring her over some milk and butter. Is that all right with you?"

"Do I mind if you do a sweet helpful son thing? Of course not."

Kyle laughed. "You don't understand Polly Jean Chase, Red. She's probably got three gallons of milk in the giant refrigerator in the garage and at least two extra boxes of butter as well but she wants to see you. To monitor this thing between us."

"Ah, to make sure I'm treating you right?"

He laughed again. "No, sugar. To make sure *I'm* treating *you* right."

They stopped by the Piggly Wiggly and took the groceries over to the house. Polly pulled them both into a big hug and stuffed a cookie into Kyle's hand.

"Momma, I'm taking Maggie back to my house to make her dinner, I don't need this."

"Eat it, Kyle Maurice Chase. You need your strength." Polly looked to Maggie and smiled. "Oh and, Margaret, I wanted to let you know we expect you at noon."

"Noon? For what, Mrs. Chase?"

"Polly, honey. And for Thanksgiving dinner of course. In fact, if you want to come earlier, we have breakfast at eight."

Kyle looked amused as he devoured the cookie he'd protested so vigorously minutes before.

"Um, are you sure I won't be imposing?"

Polly put her hands on her hips and squared her shoulders. Kyle, recognizing the stance, took a step back and watched. "Honey, you're dating Kyle. That makes you one of us. I'll be cooking a turkey and a ham, it's not like a bitty scrap of a girl like you eats that much." Kyle wisely kept his snort to himself.

"You're the first steady girlfriend that we've had in this family since that bitch Sandra broke Shane's heart. You don't think I need another woman here in this sea of testosterone? Besides, I like your company."

"Thank you. I'm sorry if I seem ungrateful. I'm happy to be invited, I like being here." How could she say, *It's just that I didn't grow up in the most normal of households and I'm only learning now how to interact with families that aren't as messed up as my own?* It was just too embarrassing so she just smiled. "Can I help cook?"

"Oh no, honey. My sister will get here the night before. She and I'll get up early to start everything. Just come when you want. I take it you'll be coming, then?"

"Yes. Thanks so much for inviting me. I insist on bringing dessert, though."

"I can't argue with that. I've been eating your baked goodies for years."

"Good!"

"Have we passed inspection yet? It's getting late and I want to get Maggie fed."

"Of course! I'll see you both on Thursday then."

"You'll see us tomorrow at the Grange," Kyle said.

"I forgot that was tomorrow night. Well, I'll see you both then. Night, sugar." She kissed Kyle and then Maggie.

Kyle chuckled the whole way to his place. After trying to ignore him, she finally gave in. "What are you laughing about?"

"You, trying to fight off my momma. She's determined to make you one of our own. You can't fight it. I don't want you to either."

Back at his condo she sat and drank a beer while she watched him prepare the salad that would go with the lemon chicken he'd popped into the oven. He looked good there. Proficient and able.

She hadn't said much since his last declaration in the car. In her mind she'd gone back and forth but she couldn't deny it anymore and she didn't want to. Screwing up her courage at last she put her beer down and took a deep breath. "I'm not going to, you know."

"Not going to do what, Red?" He turned to look at her, a smile on his face.

"I'm not going to fight it anymore. I like your family. If you're truly comfortable with me at events and dinners, I'll come when I'm invited."

Putting his knife on the cutting board, he came to kneel at her feet. "I love for you to be with me and my family. This is all rather new for me you understand. I've never, ever had a steady girlfriend but I'm not freaked out like I thought I might be. I don't know, it just seems," he paused, searching for the right word, "right. Being with you seems right. My family loves you." He stopped and swallowed. "And I'm well…quite frankly, on my way to loving you, Margaret Elizabeth." He shrugged. "Now if six months ago someone had said that I'd say that to any woman without a gun to my head or without feeling faint, I'd have laughed. But you seem so right to me. I hope I'm not freaking you out."

She reached out and pushed a lock of his hair out of his eye. "I'm not freaked out. I have my moments of insecurity where I wonder why a man who looks like you is interested in me." She shrugged. "But I've decided that I don't care. And okay, so there's a bit of residual strangeness about the whole Shane thing. But I love being with you. You make me happy. You make me laugh. You accept me on my own terms. It feels right to me, too."

"I thought the Shane thing might bother me but last night, when we were together, it didn't. And anyway, I get to see you naked and sweaty. He never did. I shouldn't feel smug about that but I do."

Unsuccessfully stifling a smile, she shook her head in amusement. "Well, sick as I am, I'm sort of flattered by that. I suppose we're made for each other then, huh? Look, the thing with Shane was totally dumb. It wasn't anything and it wouldn't have been a blip on my life radar if he hadn't acted like such an ass at the end. But it's over and done and I don't sit around and wish things had gone differently. You don't hold yourself back, I don't hold myself back. This is more. Intense and deep, special."

"I'm sorry he hurt you. Thing is, if he hadn't messed up, you'd be with him right now instead of me so I can't feel bad so much about the outcome. As for how it is between you and me? Yep, it's special." He leaned forward and kissed her lips. "Can you spend the night tonight?"

She nodded. "I like waking up with you. I've never woken up with anyone before, it's very nice."

"Me either. Before you, Red, I was the guy who left. Not the moment I came or anything so crass. But shortly afterwards. I like having you here. I like hearing your voice and smelling you in my bedroom."

Maggie liked that very much. "I like being here, too. I do need to do some yard work tomorrow though, so I need to go home in the morning."

"Well, you know that your boyfriend's a landscaper right?"

"I'd heard something about that, yeah." She laughed.

"Well, why don't I help you? We can go over to your place and do whatever yard work you need doing. I can spend tomorrow night at your house. That is, if I'm not rushing."

"You aren't and yes, I'd like that."

Dinner was excellent, Kyle was a very good cook. After they'd cleaned up the kitchen together he turned and her pulse sped to see the look in his eyes.

"Maggie, I need you. Right now." Her mouth dried up as she watched him stalk toward her. He was overwhelming in that moment and it thrilled her. One handed, he pulled the fly of his jeans open and hers with the other hand.

Making quick work out of getting naked, she stood there frozen against the force of his needy gaze. She found herself backed against the wall in the dining room. He dropped to his knees and her stomach clenched.

"I want to taste you," he murmured and spread her open with his thumbs. "Thigh on my shoulder." It wasn't a request. Complying, she leaned back, putting her weight against the wall. A gasp ripped from her lips as his mouth closed over her pussy.

One of her hands gripped the doorjamb and the other sifted through his hair. She cried out when two of his fingers pressed deep into her and turned to hook, stroking her sweet spot. A gasp of his name when his teeth scraped gently over her swollen clit.

"Mmmm. You like that." He couldn't see her enthusiastic nod so she pushed his head back into place and ignored his chuckle.

The tip of his tongue drew circles around her clit over and over until her legs shook so hard she could barely hold herself up.

"Oh god, please. Kyle, please."

"Please what?" He looked up at her and one eyebrow slid high.

"Pleasemakemecome!"

A third finger joined the other two inside her and he moved back into place. His tongue drew through her pussy, sliding back and forth through her folds until he got back to her clit. And he stayed there. Insistently, relentlessly flicking over her with a feather light but consistent stroke. On and on until her climax bloomed and exploded over her with such force she flung her head back, smacking it against the wall behind her.

Muscles still jumping she found herself bent over the table. She heard the crinkle of the condom wrapper as he widened her thighs. Gripping the side of the table, she braced herself as he thrust into her to the root in one long stroke.

"Told you, you made me want you bend you over something. Holy smoke you're so hot it drives me crazy," he murmured and began to thrust deep, over and over. Her nipples hardened against the cool, unyielding surface of the table.

She'd never been taken in such a spontaneous, raw way and it thrilled her to her very core. That she made him feel so out of control that he had to bend her over the kitchen table and have her right at that very moment was wildly exciting. His desire of her elevated her. Made her feel like a goddess. To be the focus of such regard, such intensity, made her tremble and sweat.

Kyle looked down at the feminine curve of her spine, before arching back to watch his cock disappear into her body only to withdraw, covered in her honey. Damn but he wanted her. In every way, in every place he could imagine. He'd never desired a woman so deeply before. She affected him on such a primal level that it should have scared him. But all he could feel was the way the hot, wet flesh of her pussy embraced him. Sucked at him even as he pulled out and welcomed him again as he thrust back deep.

"Damn it, Maggie, you feel so good." His head fell back as orgasm took over his muscles and he came deep inside her.

He pressed a kiss to the back of her neck and carried her upstairs to his bed. He went to sleep knowing that the woman curved against his body would be that way for the rest of his life.

¨ ¨ ¨

By the time they arrived at the Grange the next night, most the Chase family was there and had scored a table. Her heart warmed at the genuine enthusiasm they greeted her with. All the brothers told her to save them a dance and Kyle scowled and rolled his eyes at them.

"You know, Liv should be here too." Maggie's tone with Matt was casual and she was delighted to see his face light up. "I knew it!"

"What?"

"You *are* interested in her!"

He sighed and then grinned in resignation. "Yeah, I've had a crush on Olivia since high school."

"For heaven's sake, why didn't you kiss her the other night? Or at least go inside?"

"I've been kicking myself for that ever since then. I really did have an early seminar that next morning. I want to give her the time and attention she deserves."

"Oh good! I'm relieved to hear it. Of course, she's my best friend and has been since the third day of kindergarten, so I'm totally biased," she gulped in a deep breath before continuing, "but I can still tell you that she's just the most wonderful woman on the planet."

"I doubt it, Red. I know the most wonderful woman on the planet and she's not Liv Davis." Kyle kissed her freckles and heat bloomed as she blushed.

"Lord. I hope that's not catching," Marc said of the two of them. "It's nice for you two and all. But Kyle has been a happy go lucky bachelor all of this time and he's so obviously gone over you, sugar, it scares me."

"It'll happen to you too, you know. When it's supposed to." Kyle's smile was smug.

"Maggie, fancy seeing you here."

Maggie turned in the direction of the cold voice and saw Janie and her husband Rick, and their parents, Cece and Tom Wright.

"Janie, Rick, Mother, Daddy. Hello," Maggie said tightly. The look on her mother's face told her it wasn't going to be a pleasant conversation.

"Hey, honey." Her father bent down to kiss her cheek. "Sorry," he whispered into her ear. She braced herself for what was coming next.

"I had no idea you'd actually have a date for this but as you're here I'll go ahead. Since you've decided to be so mean and jealous of your sister, you're no longer invited to Thanksgiving dinner. Perhaps if you spend the day thinking about how you can be a better sister, you can come to Christmas dinner." Her mother's voice was so cold it hit Maggie like a slap and she winced.

Rick looked distinctly uncomfortable as did Tom but neither man said anything.

Maggie just sat there for a moment as she pushed the pain away and gathered her strength and self respect. Inhaling deeply she looked her mother straight on. "If that's how you feel, Mother. Have a nice evening."

"Wait just a darned minute, Cece Wright!" Polly stood up and came over to Maggie, putting a hand on her shoulder. Kyle held her hand on the other side.

"Yes, Polly? I suppose you're going to butt in?"

"You can keep your snotty comments to yourself. Maggie's coming to dinner with our family on Thanksgiving, where she's loved and appreciated. Christmas, too. If you refuse to see what an exceptional daughter you have, well, you know, I've always wanted a daughter, what with four boys and all. You should be ashamed of yourself."

Maggie could feel the Chases build a protective wall around her. Shane stood on the other side of Polly, Matt on the other side of Kyle. Edward and Marc were on the other side of the table but had stood as well.

"Margaret should recognize her betters. She needs to accept that her sister is prettier and more successful than she is and stop being so bitter about it," Cecelia snapped.

Maggie had had enough. She stood up. "Mother, you don't know anything about it. I am *not* bitter that Jane Marie is pretty! I don't know why you keep saying that, it simply isn't true. But pretty isn't everything! You treated me, my whole life like nothing else mattered but pretty. Well what about when pretty goes away? What about when pretty only is on the surface? What about when she's like you? Pretty on the outside but cold and heartless on the inside?

"I told myself that if I could just do well in school that you'd appreciate me. That if I behaved and never got in trouble you'd love me, but it never happened. When I was nine and you told me that you wished you'd never had me because I left you with a C-section scar, I tried to tell myself that you didn't mean it that way but you did. And I understand that now. I accept you for the monster you are, Mother."

Kyle looked at his family and they all bore the horrified look he had. This woman told her child she wished she'd never had her, because of a scar? She'd just told her child in front of others that she wasn't as good as her sister because she wasn't as pretty?

"How dare you talk to Mom like that!" Jane Marie spat out. "You're jealous of us both. Jealous of what we have!"

"This is so ridiculous I wish I could laugh. Janie, I'm not jealous of you. I am happy you are lovely and have a nice husband and a good life. I won't, however, let you or anyone else make me feel inferior anymore. I'm done with being the family scapegoat. You all enjoy your night and Thanksgiving dinner."

Janie grabbed Maggie's arm then and towered over her. "You think you can hold a man like Kyle Chase just by opening your legs for him? I was a virgin on my wedding night. Too bad you can't say the same thing." The ugly words came out in a hiss.

Maggie looked at her sister, shock clear on her face. And then she narrowed her eyes. Kyle knew what was coming so he sat back and waited.

"How dare you say that to me, Jane Marie? You of all people. You sure you want to go down that road? Rick isn't the only one of us who knows that's a lie," she said in a voice so quiet and low that it made the hair on Kyle's arms stand up.

"How dare you say that! I was a virgin. You are just, again, jealous that you can't get a man to marry you or even to date you without putting out."

Maggie sighed. "Okay then, why don't we give old Charles a call, shall we? You remember him right? My old grad school advisor who was also my boyfriend? You know, the man who rucked your precious pleated Anne Klein skirt up around your waist and fucked you on my couch while you thought I was out on a walk? Don't sell your bullshit about being a virgin to me, Jane Marie. I saw your legs wide open, *to my boyfriend,* so I know the truth."

Jane Marie paled. "You...you, saw? You knew and never said anything?"

"What could I have said, Janie? How could I have conveyed how betrayed I felt? I mean, my whole life people told me how much prettier you were, I convinced myself that you were. That I couldn't hold a man if you were after him too. I know a lot better these days. I'm a different person now."

"What is she talking about?" Rick asked.

"Now all of you go on and have a nice evening. I've said all I needed to say and I feel ever so much better. Just think, now you can have the family you always wanted, Cecelia. Since you already pretend I don't exist, it shouldn't be hard."

Maggie turned her back and sat back down between Kyle and Polly, who both hugged her tightly.

"Don't come crawling back when he dumps you," Cecelia spat out and they all moved off.

"Oh good lord. Who needs a drink?" Edward drawled.

Maggie raised a hand and he took it and kissed it. "You got it, baby girl. One stiff bourbon. Be back in two shakes."

Shane sat down as did Marc. Liv, Dee and Arthur, who had heard the whole thing, came over as well. Liv and Dee pushed in and each hugged her tightly. Polly looked over them at Kyle and her eyes were shining with unshed tears.

"Good for you, Maggie. You should have said all of that a long time ago. I'm proud of you. By the way, how could you not tell me that Janie slept with your boyfriend?" Liv said.

"I don't want to talk about it anymore. Not for a while. I can't or I'll lose it and I don't want to. More and more people are showing up and I just can't face being the focus of yet another town drama."

"I'm sorry, sweetie," Liv sat down in an empty chair, conveniently next to Matt. Dee and Arthur sat across from them on Marc's other side.

"Here you go, sugar." Edward put the bourbon in her hand and she downed it in three big gulps. His eyes widened for a moment and he laughed and put the one he got for himself in her hand as he exchanged it for the empty glass.

"I think you and I need a dance, Red," Kyle said.

She stood up, knocked back the second bourbon and sat the glass down, looking back over her shoulder at Edward. "Thanks. I feel much better now." He winked at her and watched as his son took her out to the dance floor, wrapping himself around her protectively.

"Our boy is falling in love with that little spitfire," he said to his wife, who'd come to sit next to him.

"Yes, I think so too. It's nice. She's special. I can't believe her family. My goodness, how awful to tell a child you didn't want her. To compare her to the other child and say she's lacking."

Kyle looked down at Maggie and felt a protectiveness he'd never felt toward anyone other than his family. He felt possessive and full of admiration for the woman in his arms. "Baby, I'm sorry about all of that."

Maggie was snuggled into his body and she just shook her head, not wanting to talk. When the slow number ended he led her back to the table where luckily everyone had moved on to another topic.

"You hungry, Red? Wait, stupid question. You want me to grab you a plate?" Kyle teased.

"No, I'll come with. You'll steal my food if I don't guard it," she said.

"Never come between Red and her food," he told his family.

Despite the beginning of the evening, the rest of it was quite enjoyable. Maggie danced with every male Chase including hers, at least twice. She laughed with her friends and ate at least three platefuls of food. She saw Kyle talking to the DJ and then come back toward her, looking like the cat that ate the cream.

"What are you up to, Kyle Maurice Chase?"

"You know my darkest secret now." He gave a quick look toward his mother. "My great grandfather was named Maurice. I narrowly escaped it as a first name."

She chuckled and then cocked her head as a slow number came on. One that she and Kyle had danced to at the Honky Tonk and later, had made love to. "Raining on Sunday" by Keith Urban.

"I'm beginning to think of this as our song. Care to dance with me, Red?"

She nodded and he led her out to the floor, pulling her snug against him. With a satisfied sigh, he kissed the top of her head before laying his cheek there.

ৎ ৎ ৎ

Back at her house he drew her up the stairs to her room. "Let me love you, Maggie. Let me show you how special and beautiful you are," he murmured.

"I'm yours, Kyle."

He grinned. "I'm a lucky man." He picked her up, gently putting her on the bathroom counter.

Watching her in the mirror he reached around to unzip the back of her dress. She shrugged out of the top of it while he pulled the rest of it off. Her nearly bare ass sat against the cool counter, her nipples tightened in her sheer bra.

"You look good, Red." He popped the catch on the front of the bra and her breasts came free. He chuckled. "Now you look even better."

She grinned at him, looking into his face. "What is it about being nearly naked when you're fully dressed that turns me on so much?"

"That's a coincidence. It turns me on, too." One handed, he pulled his pants open and his cock sprang free.

A gasp broke from her lips as he pulled her ass to the edge of the counter and she caught a glimpse of the flutter of colorful silk as he tossed her panties over his shoulder. The crinkle of the condom wrapper made her body tighten in response.

His fingertips brushed through the folds of her pussy, making sure she was ready. "God damn, so wet. Always so wet and ready for me."

"Yes. Oh god, pleasepleaseplease, I need you, Kyle."

"Yes, Red. On the way." The fingers at her hip dug into her skin as he entered her hard, in one thrust. "Yesssss," he hissed softly.

She wrapped her legs around his waist and turned her head, watching them in the mirrors. Saw a woman she didn't recognize, small and sexy as a fully clothed man fucked into her. Watched that woman arch to take him in deeper. Listened to her pleas and orders.

"So beautiful. You're so damned beautiful, Red. Look at yourself. See what I see every time I make love to you." He met her eyes in the mirror. "Sexy. Those long legs wrapped around me. Your eyes, hazy with pleasure. Lips, shiny wet." He leaned in and nipped her bottom lip between his teeth, causing her to gasp. "I love the way your breasts move when I'm inside you. Love the way your pussy is so tight that it hugs my cock. You have no idea how hot you are deep inside. It drives me crazy. Sometimes during the day I'll be working and it'll come over me suddenly—the sense memory of your pussy, clutching me, fluttering around my cock like it's doing right now, just before you come."

He wet his fingers in her mouth and reached between them to find her clit, swollen and slick. "I want your orgasm, Red. Show me how gorgeous you are when you come."

Her eyes blurred as her breath caught. Endorphins flooded her as she came, eyes still locked with his in the mirror.

"Oh, yes. That's the way." He groaned as his own climax shot from the balls of his feet straight into her body in wave after wave until he could no longer stand. They stumbled back into the bedroom together, collapsing on the bed.

She fell asleep fairly soon and he covered her with a blanket before getting up to take his clothes off. He watched the easy in and out of her breath and wanted to kick the crap out of anyone who hurt her or made her feel lacking in any way.

જી જી જી

The next morning they made time for breakfast together before each left for the day.

"Your mother invited me to your family dinner tonight, Kyle," Maggie said as she put a mug of coffee in front of him.

"Good. I'll see you at six then." He flashed that sexy smile.

"Are you sure? I don't want to barge in or anything. And I…well, I don't want you to get tired of me, seeing me every day."

"Red." He hooked an arm around her waist, pulling her to his lap. "I am not going to get tired of you. I like seeing you with my family, they like you. I enjoy being with you. We talked about this. I thought you were okay with it."

"I thought I was. Are *you* sure? There's an awful lot of drama in my life these days. It annoys me, it must really annoy you."

He sighed. "Sugar, I know how much of a number your mother did on you but you have to stop letting her influence you. Believe me, if I want some space I'll say so. But I want to be with you. Do you want to be with me?"

Silently, she nodded her head. Afraid to say anything because if she did, she knew she'd blurt out that she loved him.

"That settles it then. I'll see you at six tonight."

That night, she stopped by the grocery store to buy pecans and corn syrup for the pecan pies she was going to make for Thanksgiving and some lemons for the tartlets she wanted to try. On her way out she saw Alex Parsons come in and fear gnawed at her. He watched her warily and when it was clear she was leaving, he went back toward the dairy section.

She ran home and put away her groceries and changed, putting her hair back with a loose clip. Once she'd arrived at the Chase's, Marc came out as he saw she was walking up the front steps. "Thought I'd grab my hug and some sugar out here. Kyle's crazy jealous." He gave her a kiss on the temple as he chuckled.

Grinning, she shook her head at his cheek. Once inside, Kyle saw her and got up to give her a hello kiss. "I saw that brother of mine out there, I suppose he accosted you."

"A girl doesn't tell tales," she said before going into the kitchen to say hello to Polly where she helped set out the food on the dining room table.

"Boys! Dinner is ready," Polly called out and they all came in rapidly. Edward held out Polly's chair and Kyle held out Maggie's. He settled in next to her and within minutes, plates were filled and people had eaten enough to take the edge off and begin talking.

"I saw Alex today," Maggie said quietly.

Shane looked up at her with serious eyes. "Where?"

"At the market. I was leaving. He was coming in. He waited to see which way I'd go and then went in the opposite direction. I hope that means he's going to obey the court order."

"Did he say anything to you?" Kyle asked.

"No. He barely even looked at me, thank god."

"If you see him again and he doesn't leave or it looks like he's come to bother you, call the cops immediately. I assume you have the order with you? We'll get you the permanent ones after Tuesday when he'll be back in court," Shane explained.

"Yes, I keep it in my purse. I have one in my car, at work and at my house like you said. By the way, I'm coming to court on Tuesday."

"Why?" Kyle asked.

"Because, I want to see it. To be able to speak if I can and to be sure that nothing else happens. It's bad enough he's getting away with it, I want to be sure he has to do all of the stuff I was told he was going to."

"Maggie, honey, why don't you let me go instead? I'm your attorney. I'll speak on your behalf if necessary." Edward looked concerned.

"Listen, I know I'm small and all but darn it, I won't hide from this. It happened to *me*. I want to witness it to its conclusion. I want those pictures back, with the negatives, so I can destroy them myself. I want my clothes back, too."

Shane sighed and looked wearily at Kyle, who just rolled his eyes and shrugged. "Fine, Maggie. But, Dad, I think you should be there too, just in case."

"I'll be there as well," Matt and Marc said at the same time.

"Me too," Polly said.

"Of course I will," Kyle added, squeezing Maggie's hand.

She tried not to cry—she'd been doing it so much lately—but she failed. "I'm sorry! I swear to y'all that I'm not usually so weepy. Anyway, thank you all so much. Honestly, I just don't have words to express just how much I appreciate all you've done for me."

"Well, certainly a bit of cherry cobbler will cheer you up!" Polly winked and passed the large pan around the table.

At nine that night, a very weary Maggie said her good-byes and Kyle walked her to her car. "Red, do you want to stay the night at my place?"

"I do but I shouldn't. I have to go into work early tomorrow to get some more work done. I want to have all sixty-eight of my students' term papers read and graded by Tuesday because we have Wednesday, Thursday and Friday off school. If I go back to your place, I doubt I'll get much sleep." She grinned at him.

"Okay, but have dinner with me tomorrow then. I'll pick you up at your house at six and we can grab a pizza."

"You drive a hard bargain, Kyle. I'll see you then."

He bent down and captured her lips and as always, after one of his kisses, she felt slightly woozy, like she was drunk from his touch.

Chapter Eight

She'd finished the papers by the end of the day and put them in her locked cabinet and went home. Only to find her father waiting for her on the porch.

"Daddy, what are you doing here?" she asked, unlocking the door and letting him inside. "I have a date, he'll be here in half an hour."

"Oh, honey, I failed you," he said.

"Yes, you did," she answered honestly. She gestured to the sofa and they both sat. "You see, I used to think that you did your best. That you tried to make up for how she was with our trips and the small indulgences you gave me but now I think that you just tried to duck your guilt. It's not right, but it's over."

"I'd like to say that I had no idea that she was that bad or that she didn't mean to be as harsh as she was but I'd be lying. I made bad choices. I loved your mother something fierce. I loved her beauty and I made a choice—her over you. It was wrong and that love I had for her has slowly tarnished and died over the years. I don't even recognize myself anymore, Maggie. I used to be such a strong man. I used to be a leader. I've run our family business for my entire adult life! People look up to me, trust me to take care of them and their families and they shouldn't because I couldn't even take care of my own."

She sighed. "Listen, Daddy, if anyone can trust you to take care of them, it's your employees. You've always done right by them. As for what you've become as Cecelia Wright's husband, I can't say. That's yours to deal with."

"I'm filing for divorce, Maggie."

Shock froze her in place. "What?"

"I stood there and watched your mother and sister castigate you in front of a room full of people. I said nothing. When I heard you say your mother told you she wished you were never born, I felt the last bit of love I had for her die. I failed you but I cannot stay with that woman another day. I've moved out. Edward Chase's brother is handling the divorce. The papers have been served."

"I don't know what to say."

"Don't say anything. Just let me try and prove that from now on, I can be a better father. Let me take you to dinner. I know you can't on Thanksgiving because you'll be with the Chases. How about Friday?"

Words escaped her as she thought about it. She should kick him out and never speak to him again but she couldn't. She loved him. The part of her that was the little lonely bookish girl whose daddy took her to Philadelphia for her birthday because she so loved history—that part of her wanted to recognize what a big step he was taking. "All right. Let's do it early though. I have a longstanding thing with Liv and Dee and I meet them at seven every Friday night."

He smiled and squeezed her hands. "Thank you so much, sweetheart. How about you and I meet up at El Cid at five?"

"All right. What are you going to do for Thanksgiving?"

"Darlin', you're such a sweet girl. Thank god you take after my mother. I'm going to your Aunt Delia's for the day. You enjoy your beau and his family. I'd like to get to know him better, he seems like he cares for you."

"I do, Mr. Wright and I worry that you might hurt Maggie."

Maggie and her father turned to see Kyle walking into the room. He leaned down to kiss the top of her head and sat on the arm of the couch next to her. "I knocked but you didn't hear me. I was worried so I let myself in," he told her.

"Kyle, this is my daddy, Tom Wright. Daddy, this is Kyle Chase."

Tom Wright stood and held his hand out to Kyle. "Young man, I'm here to beg my daughter to give me another chance to be a better father. I've left my wife. Your uncle has taken the case. I'm fortunate, because Maggie has agreed to let me try, starting with having dinner with me on Friday. Would you like to come as well?"

Kyle shook his hand and nodded solemnly. "I would, sir. If Maggie is willing to give you another chance, I can as well."

"I'm staying with your aunt and uncle for a while, until I find a place. You call me there if you need me. I'll see you on Friday." He nodded and walked out.

"Are you all right?" Kyle sank down next to her on the couch.

"I think so. I'm just stunned. My father adored my mother, literally. He said that the way she acted Saturday killed the last bit of love he had for her. My mother is going to be insanely angry about this."

"Who cares what your bitch of a mother thinks, sweetheart? Don't give her the power to hurt you ever again."

"I won't. I'm done. Now, I need to change. I'm sorry that I'm not ready." She jumped up and ran upstairs and changed quickly and came back down.

"You're quick. I don't have to ask if you're hungry." He grinned.

She socked him in the arm and he laughed, pushing her out the door and to his car.

 og og og

After dinner, leaning against the car, Maggie smiled up at Kyle as he rubbed a wayward curl between his fingers. "By the way, one of my students said you were hot and gave me a way to go today."

He chuckled. "That so? Well I'm glad we're on the gossip circuit, it should stop anyone from trying to poach you."

"Me? Okay, buster, if you say so." She snorted and turned to kiss the fingers holding her hair. When she turned back to face him, his eyes had gone a much deeper shade of green, almost the color of pine trees. Her breath caught.

"Maggie, let's go back to my house. Or your house I don't care which. I want to touch you, make love to you."

She felt the heat pool in her belly and she nodded—rendered speechless by the want in his eyes.

They were closer to his house and so they went there. Once inside, he grabbed her hand, leading her to his room. Moving to him, she pressed her face into the flesh of his neck, his warmth and scent lulling her. He picked her up and carried her over to the bed, gently laying her down.

Quickly kicking off her sneakers and yanking her sweater off, she was unzipping her jeans when she looked up to see Kyle already naked and looking down at her with intense heat.

"Oh," she whispered when he pinned her in his gaze.

He gently moved her hands and pulled the rest of her clothing off himself before lying down beside her. They both let out a gasp when bare skin caressed bare skin.

"You feel so damned good, Maggie. I've never wanted anything this much in my life," he whispered as he strummed his fingers through her pussy, making her even wetter than she already was. "I feel that every damned time I touch you. Keep thinking that it has to mellow a bit but each time I see you, I want you so bad it hurts. And when my fingers or my cock finds your pussy, you're ready for me, always so ready for me. It turns me on so much that you want me so badly." His voice was hoarse.

Her heart pounded in her chest. She reached back for the box of condoms he'd put in the drawer underneath his bed and grabbed one.

"Stay there," he murmured and she stopped, her head hanging off the bed. Pleasure rocked through her when his mouth reached the humid flesh of her pussy. Closing her eyes, her hands hung above her head, touching the carpet beneath the bed, still holding the condom.

The blood rushed to her head as the sensation built. His tongue speared into her and then up and around her clit. Over and over as his hands at her hips held her steady. She barely recognized the sounds coming from deep inside her as he slowly devastated her with his mouth, loved her. He built her up slowly and gave her no place to hide as the climax slammed into her.

He dragged her limp body back up onto the bed and took the condom from her hands. Dimly she heard it rip and her eyes opened in time to see him roll it on his cock.

"I need you, Red." And without any delay, slid into her welcoming body and shuddered at the intensity of it. "Man oh man do you feel good," he murmured, his lips against her neck.

Wrapping her legs around his waist, she rolled her hips up to meet his thrusts. The heated flesh of her pussy parted around him and then grasped, pulling him back into her body just milliseconds after he'd pulled out. Each thrust into her body felt like homecoming.

He moaned her name and braced his weight on his elbows to look down into her face. She gazed back up at him, open, totally open. Nothing existed but the delicious friction of their joining, of her silky thighs cradling his hips, of her heels digging into the flesh of the small of his back. Her eyes deep and luminous, like amber in candlelight—held only him. In that moment Kyle realized he was no longer falling in love with Maggie, he was already there. She owned his heart.

At that realization he came, waves of pleasure rolled through him as he poured into her. He put his face into the crook of her neck and breathed her in. "I love you, Maggie." he whispered as the last of his pleasure flagged and he slumped beside her.

She turned onto her side and peered into his face. "What did you just say?"

"I said I love you, Margaret Elizabeth Wright." He looked into her eyes seriously.

"Oh, that's what I thought you said," she replied and then got silent.

"Is that all you have to say?" he demanded sulkily. He'd never said the words to a woman he wasn't related to and she had nothing to say back?

"No."

"What?" He knew he sounded sullen but he was worried.

Noticing her fine tremble, he felt bad for upsetting her. But then she finally spoke. "Oh god, I'm so glad. I love you, too. I was so scared that it was all just me." The words came out in a gasp as if she'd been holding it inside desperately.

Relief flooded him as he hugged her close. "Thank god! I've never told a woman that before and here I was thinking that my first time out I'd totally bombed. God, Maggie, I love you so much it makes my chest hurt. I think about you all day and when you aren't with me, all night. I can't get enough of you. Not just the naked sweaty writhing you but the total package."

"I thought I'd die after I left you last night. I just wanted to give you some space but then I couldn't sleep. I tossed and turned all night long."

"I *told* you I'd tell you if I needed space, Maggie. I need *you*, silly woman."

She snuggled into his body and smiled against his flesh. "I actually should go home, I have no clothes here and I need to work tomorrow."

"No way, Red. I'll come with you and sleep at your place. I have a job at the Bluebird Inn, it's closer to your house anyway. I've realized I hate sleeping without you. I love that little body tucked into mine. I tried putting a pillow there last night but it was no good."

"It's nice to know I'm better than a bag of feathers," she commented dryly.

"Oh yeah," he agreed and rolled out of bed to grab a change of clothes and some toiletries.

Maggie watched him gather his things with a smile. So damned handsome and he loved her. She sighed happily. "You know, you could bring an extra few changes of clothes and leave them at my place, just in case."

He looked around at her. "Yeah? That would be all right?"

"More than all right," she said and he came back over to her, dropping a kiss on her lips.

"Okay. You should do that too. I mean, bring some stuff over here."

"I like the idea of my panties in your drawer and some of my clothes in your closet, just in case a skank like Lyndsay comes over."

He rolled his eyes. "I told you, I rarely brought women over here, Red. But I like the idea of your panties in my drawer, too."

"Better in yours than Alex's," she commented with a grin.

He looked at her askance and then laughed. "I'm glad you can laugh about it."

"What else can I do? I'm all cried out. Anyway, you make me feel like laughing instead of crying."

"Good. Now let's get over to your place and I'll make you moan instead."

"You've got a deal!"

ᘓ ᘓ ᘓ

They promised to meet at the courthouse at later that afternoon as they'd left the house.

When she got there, her nervousness abated when she saw Kyle and Edward waiting for her on the front steps. Waving, she climbed the stairs to meet them. Kyle stiffened up and a red flush broke over his face. Edward reached out to hold his arm, shaking his head once. Alarmed, Maggie turned around to see what he was so angry about and saw Alex walking up the steps behind them. His attorney put himself between them and Alex and ushered him inside.

"Kyle, cool down boy or I'll make you wait out here. Maggie, darlin', are you all right?"

Taking a deep breath to brace herself, she nodded. "Yes. Let's go in, I'm ready."

Kyle took her hand and they followed Edward into the courtroom where the rest of the Chases, Liv and Dee were already seated. Smiling at them all gratefully, she and Edward moved past them to a more forward row. Kyle stayed at her side, her hand still tucked in his even as they sat down. Shane came in through an interior door and sat down away from them all. Of course he was there as Sheriff but he caught Maggie's eye and smiled at her reassuringly.

The judge addressed the prosecutor and Alex's attorney before approving the plea agreement. Alex asked permission to address Maggie and the judge looked at her. "Ms. Wright, do you assent to Mr. Parsons addressing you?"

She leaned over and asked Edward if it would affect the protection order, which the judge had just made permanent and the no contact order and he shook his head no.

"Yes, Your Honor, he may address me."

Alex stood up and turned toward her and Kyle squeezed her hand.

"Maggie, I'm truly sorry for frightening you and for the damage I did to your home. I won't bother you again. I'm getting help in my counseling and I hope that someday we can be friends again." He sat down and looked at his attorney.

Maggie just sat there. Be friends with him? Was he out of his mind?

"Very well, is that everything?" The judge asked.

"No, Your Honor, there is the matter of the stolen property belonging to Ms. Wright, and the photographs and negatives that he agreed to turn over. We have not received these items." Edward stood and addressed the judge, back straight and Maggie felt in good hands.

The judge turned a steely gaze to Alex and his attorney. "Well?"

The attorney whispered to Alex, who began to argue with him. "Your Honor, Mr. Parsons has left these items at home and will forward them to Ms. Wright by the end of the week."

"*No!*" Maggie said urgently to Edward. "I want those pictures and my underthings back today! He promised."

"Your Honor, Mr. Parsons has known he had to turn over these items since he made this agreement last Thursday. My client is understandably upset. Not only has Mr. Parsons terrorized her and vandalized her home but he possesses intimate items belonging to her and has taken photographs of her, without her knowledge or permission. We are prepared to wait while a police officer escorts Mr. Parsons to his home to retrieve these items posthaste," Edward said calmly but firmly.

The judge looked at Alex and then to Shane. "Sheriff Chase, can you or one of your men escort Mr. Parsons to his home to retrieve these items? Which, by the way—I have difficulty understanding why he was given them back after he was arrested to begin with?"

"Yes, Your Honor. I can send Officer Spence right now. The items were given back to Mr. Parsons by mistake, included in the inventory of his personal items when he was released from jail."

"Do it then. Mr. Parsons. You have half an hour to produce *each and every one* of the items you agreed to in the plea agreement. If a single item is missing—a single photograph or negative—I will send you to jail for a week on contempt charges. Do I make myself clear? We will recess until two fifteen, at such time you had better be back here and in full compliance or I'll toss your butt in jail."

Alex nodded and Shane spoke quietly to his officer and he escorted Alex outside. Maggie shook with anger. When the judge walked out she turned to Edward. "He did that on purpose! He was going to try and get away with keeping all of that stuff. He's not sorry at all."

"I'm going to wring that bastard's neck," Kyle ground out.

Maggie put a restraining hand on his arm. "No. It's what he wants. It's better if we just get on with our lives and pretend he doesn't exist."

"Maggie's right, Kyle. He'd press charges and you'd be the one in jail," Matt said, having come to join them once the judge had left the courtroom.

"Then you all can protect Maggie." Fury still coursed through him.

"I don't need protection, Kyle, I need you. I don't want him to win anything else. Please."

Shane approached. "Hypothetically speaking and all, if I were, as the sheriff, to hear any threats against another citizen, I'd have to get involved." He looked directly at Kyle. Kyle nodded at him quickly, scowling. "You did a good job, Maggie."

"You sure did. You kept focused and remembered to address me instead of the court directly. The judge is on your side here," Edward said, patting her shoulder.

They sat and waited for Alex to come back and twenty-eight minutes later he did, holding a large box that Shane took possession of. "Let me do the inventory, Maggie. You don't need to see it."

She rolled her eyes at him and grabbed the box. "No, let me." She shooed them all away and asked to use the jury room. She wouldn't give Alex the satisfaction of seeing her upset.

"Sweetheart, please let me come in and help you." Kyle's words were softly spoken as he brushed a lock of hair out of her face.

"No," she whispered back, caressing his cheek. "I appreciate you wanting to be with me, I really do. But this is just too much for me to share with you. I plan to burn all of the pictures in my fireplace tonight but I want to make sure everything, is here. I can't wonder whether he's got copies or not or I'll go mad."

Kyle nodded and kissed her forehead.

"Liv, Dee, can you help me please?" she asked and both women nodded and went with her into the jury room.

All of her underwear and other lingerie were there and they moved it with a pencil rather than touch it and put it back into the plastic bag. The pictures were deeply upsetting. She counted each one and then Dee and Liv matched with a negative. Maggie knew how bad it was when Liv didn't even make a crack. She was horrified knowing her most intimate moments were most likely seen by half the police force. The other ones were just creepy, knowing that Alex had watched her do her laundry and go grocery shopping.

"They're all here. Let's go out and tell the judge." She put the lid back on the box and her head up high and they all went back out where the judge was waiting.

"Is everything there to your satisfaction, Ms. Wright?"

"Yes, Your Honor."

"Mr. Parsons, if copies of any pictures you took of Ms. Wright show up, I'll throw you in jail. You're lucky that you haven't had to beat off the concerned men of Ms. Wright's life over this incident. I am going to be keeping an eye on you due to your prior history of harassing and stalking women. Keep your nose clean and keep away from Ms. Wright. Do I make myself clear? If she is somewhere that you come upon, it is up to *you* to leave. If she comes into a place you are, other than your workplace or your home, it is still up to *you* to leave."

Alex nodded, keeping his eyes down.

"Then get out of my sight." The judge banged his gavel and the doors were unlocked for the next case.

"I have to go back out to my jobsite, Red. Why don't you go home with Momma? I'll pick you up there when I'm done."

"No, thank you. I need to get rid of all of these pictures and the other stuff. I can't bear knowing it's out there."

"I don't want you home alone."

"Listen, I have to get back to my life. I can't be afraid. I won't be afraid of being in my own home."

He sighed and kissed her gently. "I love you, Red. I'll come by after work. Please lock your doors."

"I love you, too. See you later, thanks for being here."

She turned to the rest of her friends and family who were dumbstruck at hearing Kyle say he loved her.

Kyle laughed. "What's the matter? You think she's too good for me?"

"Hell yes," Matt said and Marc laughed.

Polly started sniffling and gave Maggie a big hug. "Honey, you call if you need anything all right? You are a brave, strong girl."

"I'll have someone drive by every once in a while, Maggie, just to check." Shane said. He patted her on the shoulder and she smiled back at everyone.

"Thanks all. I'll see you later." She kissed Edward on the cheek and Kyle walked her to her car and watched her drive away.

Shane walked up behind him. "That should be me, but if it can't be, I'm glad it's you."

"You don't have the guts to let yourself love, Shane. You'd better find them or you'll end up alone. I'm sorry, Shane. I love her and she's mine. That you fucked up and she fell into my lap is a sad thing because I love you and you're my brother and all. But man, a woman like her, she's what I've been waiting for my entire life." He turned and looked at his older brother. "Deal with it, Shane. I don't want you to be alone. You deserve what I've got." He squeezed his brother's shoulder and walked away.

Maggie went home, took the box straight out to her back porch and loaded a pile of pictures into the fireplace and set them aflame. It took her the better part of an hour to get it all burned, including her beautiful lingerie, which she tossed in with a broken branch from the yard. She sat back and watched the flames of a regular fire that was incidental to the immolation of her nasty relationship with Alex Parsons.

Two hours later, she drank Jack Daniels straight out of the bottle as she looked up and saw Kyle standing at the back door.

"Hi," he said quietly, fighting a smile.

She got up a bit unsteadily to unlock the door and let him in. "Hi."

Taking the bottle from her hand he looked into her face and lost his battle to hide his grin. "Hmm, had a wee bit of whiskey I see."

"Just a bit," she said defensively but had to laugh when she heard how badly she slurred her words. 'Course once she started it was a bit hard to stop.

Continuing to grin, he led her to the couch and sat her down. "Feel any better?"

"I do now that you're here." Giggles finally dying, she climbed into his lap.

"Good answer, Red." He sounded amused. He stroked a hand over her hair. "Let's get something to eat, okay? Looks like you could use it."

"Okay. Your mother came by earlier and brought me three casseroles. Want some chicken noodle casserole, ham casserole or tuna?"

"I knew she couldn't stay away," he said with a snort.

"She didn't stay long. She just brought enough food to last me through a nuclear winter and left again. She's a good person."

"She likes you a whole lot." Which was an understatement.

"The feeling is entirely mutual." She stood up and held onto him as they walked into her kitchen and she put the casserole into the oven.

After eating a quiet dinner, they went up to bed. They didn't make love, instead, Kyle held her tight against him and she slept, feeling safe and protected.

Chapter Nine

Thanksgiving Day with the Chase family was quite an experience. There were the normal players, Matt, Marc, Shane, Kyle, Polly and Edward. But they were also joined by Polly's sister, Georgette and her husband Paul. Kyle's maternal grandparents Ellen and Andrew were also there. Maggie was overwhelmed as she came through the door holding three pies, a platter of lemon tartlets and a container of brownies.

"Good lord, honey! You must have been baking all day yesterday!" Matt kissed her cheek as he took some of the goodies from her arms. She followed him into the dining room and put the food down.

"No big deal, I had yesterday off."

He hugged her and grabbed her arm. "You ready? Come on through, the family's in the living room and they're all dying to meet you."

Taking a fortifying breath she nodded and let him lead her through the door. Immediately, she was greeted by the din of a family at holiday. There was a football game on and plenty of arguing about politics and sports. The noise stopped totally as they noticed she'd walked in.

Kyle jumped up and came over and kissed her cheeks and put his arm around her and introduced her to his grandparents who took to her right away.

"Is that Maggie?" Polly called from the kitchen.

"Yeah, Momma!" Shane called back.

Maggie stood up. "Oh for goodness sake, Shane, don't bellow at your mother." She looked down at their grandparents. "I'll just go in and say hello to Polly. I'll be back in a few minutes, I'm enjoying getting to know you."

Kyle walked with her down the hall to the kitchen. Polly was inside with her sister Georgette and lit up when she saw her. "Hi, honey! I'm glad you're here. This is my sister, Georgette."

A tall woman in purple stretch pants and a gold metallic sweater stepped from around the refrigerator and enfolded her into a bear hug. Maggie tried not to panic as her face got trapped between two enormous breasts.

"My goodness but you're a bitty thing! Just adorable. I'm glad to meet a woman who can take another Chase man off the bachelor market. You should have seen Edward when he first met Polly. He was the stuff around these parts, he and his brother. All the women of Petal wanted Edward Chase and he had his share of most of them. Until Polly let her hair grow and she suddenly got breasts."

Kyle looked as if he wanted the earth to swallow him whole but his aunt kept on with the story and Maggie struggled not to laugh.

"Oh my goodness, when we walked into the grange for a dance, lordy he fell apart. Tripped over his feet to get to her. From that night there was no other woman in Petal that could get his eye again."

Maggie smiled, thinking about what a looker Polly must have been at twenty years old. Polly smiled back at her. "Oh, honey, they may take forever to fall, but when they do, it's hard and it's forever."

Kyle rolled his eyes discreetly and Maggie pinched him. "Okay, Momma, I'm in the room."

Polly reached up and patted his cheek. "I know, darlin'. Honey, your uncle and your daddy are out back, chipping balls. Get them in here please. It's time to eat."

Kyle nodded and went out the door looking relieved to escape.

"He's so cute when you're around." Polly's smile was bright.

"He's always cute, Polly. You and Edward sure do make gorgeous boys."

"Yes, we did, didn't we? Now, let's get this food out there!"

Maggie sat in between Marc and Kyle and the constant carping between the two of them made her laugh. Marc was a shameless, but totally harmless, flirt and he did it partly just to needle Kyle. Finally, Polly leaned over and rapped Marc across the knuckles with her fork and told him to stop harassing his brother and Maggie laughed even harder.

The family was so wonderful and welcoming, she felt like she'd never truly even had a holiday dinner before. She helped clear up the dishes but then the men took over, sending the women out to sit and drink coffee and brandy.

"Ah…this is the life," Polly said, kicking off her spike heeled shoes and wriggling her toes. "Too bad they don't do this more often. Maggie, darlin', you must raise my grandsons to do the dishes. I came from a different generation, it wasn't done very often. I admit I spoiled them a bit."

"Just a bit," Maggie said dryly. "It is mighty difficult to not want to take care of Kyle. Luckily, he can cook and his condo is quite clean. As for grandchildren, well, let's just take this one step at a time."

Georgette laughed. "You're the sacrificial lamb, sugar. The first real woman who's caught a Chase boy this generation. Just think about how much easier it will be for the next three after she's broken you in."

Polly threw her sister a dirty look. "Don't you go scaring this little peach away! She's the best thing that ever happened to Kyle. Have you ever seen him so, I don't know, happy? Calm, satisfied looking? No, this little girl, she's so wonderful that Kyle's brothers can now see just how worthwhile love truly is. Not a sacrificial anything, an angel."

Maggie snorted. She wouldn't think Maggie was so angelic if she knew *why* her son looked so satisfied lately.

The doorbell rang and Polly started to put her shoes back on and groaned. Maggie put a staying hand on her knee and stood up. "I'll get it, just put those feet up."

She walked into the foyer and opened the door, only to come face to face with none other than Lyndsay Cole and her bimbo partner in crime, Stefanie Peterson. Maggie stared at them. "Yes?"

"We brought some pie by."

"That so?"

"We did it to be neighborly of course. We're very close to the Chase family, you know," Stefanie snapped.

"Oh really? Funny, no one's ever mentioned you."

"Lyndsay is close to the Chase family, or at least one of them in particular."

Maggie snorted and nearly jumped out of her skin when Polly came into the hallway, in her bare stocking feet. She turned and gestured to Lyndsay and Stefanie. "Apparently, they wanted to be *neighborly* and bring over a pie."

"Why would we want their pie when yours were so good?" Polly said with a smile that slid into a glare when she turned her gaze at Stefanie and Lyndsay. "Cut the crap, girls. What are you really doing here?"

"Hello, Mrs. Chase. How are you today? Momma just had an extra pie and wanted me to bring it over," Lyndsay cooed. Maggie had to admire the girl's steel for not quailing in the face of Polly's scorn.

Polly took the pie, looked at it and handed it back. She just stared at Lyndsay for some moments before speaking. "You say your momma made that pie?"

"Yes, ma'am."

"She working over at Kroger's bakery these days?" Polly jerked her head, indicating the Kroger's stamp on the bottom of the pie tin.

Lyndsay's face colored and then she brightened. Kyle walked into the hall and approached, putting an arm around his mother and Maggie. "What's going on here?"

"Apparently, Kyle, Lyndsay's momma is working at Kroger's bakery now and wanted her to bring over a pie. Also, Stefanie thought she'd come by as well, to be neighborly and all," Maggie said sounding quite dangerous.

Polly, hearing a tone similar to her own in Maggie smiled in her own dangerous way. "Apparently, honey, she forgot to wear a bra, too."

Maggie burst out laughing and Kyle smiled down at his mother and then looked at Lyndsay—from the neck up, he wasn't a fool. "You two need to go on home. My family is having a nice day and I don't want you to ruin it."

"She's not your family," Lyndsay said.

"Of course she is. You see, family is about more than genetics. It's about love," Polly said, taking Maggie's hand.

"And I love Maggie very much, as does the rest of my family," Kyle added.

"Yeah, well she's a home wrecker! You'll see! She doesn't deserve you!" Lyndsay spat out venomously.

"Go home, Lyndsay. You're embarrassing yourself. Kyle. Isn't. Interested." Maggie sounded bored but still looked dangerous.

"How do you know that? If he's not interested, where was he last night?" Lyndsay tossed that out with a smirk.

Maggie met that with a smug smirk of her own and leaned in close to the other woman. "With me. All night. Where he is *every* night. Believe me when I tell you he'd have been too tired to go anywhere else."

Kyle chuckled. "Very true, sugar."

"You broke up your own parents' marriage!" She looked around Maggie to Polly, who'd moved back a bit to lean against the doorjamb. "On top of that, do you know, Mrs. Chase, that she went out with Shane and dumped him to go out with Kyle? Kyle and I were in a relationship before she came along and wrecked it."

Kyle burst out laughing. "A what? I shared an ice cream cone with you. I kissed you a few times. That's not a relationship. As for the Wrights' marriage, the blame for that mess of a family lies at the feet of Cecelia and Tom. Lastly, I'd be pretty flattered if Maggie here dumped Shane for me but that's not what happened, not that it's any of your business. Now, Maggie is right, you're embarrassing yourself, go home and leave us alone."

Maggie waggled her fingers at them and Kyle slammed the door in their faces.

"You're perfect for this family, Maggie." Polly chuckled and walked into the living room.

"I'm really sorry about Lyndsay, sugar. Honestly, I never even took the girl out. I don't know what her deal is."

Maggie pulled him to her by the waist of his chinos. "Her deal is that you're the sexiest, most handsome man around and she lost her chance and can't deal. Too bad, 'cause I'm not letting you get away."

"Good." He kissed her quickly before anyone could come out.

ଓ ଓ ଓ

By the time Christmas approached, Maggie had pretty much moved into Kyle's condo. Her house meant a lot to her but also held a lot of ugly childhood memories. The less time there, the easier it was to deal with the fact that her mother had pretty much never wanted her. She'd bought the place, thinking if she'd made it hers, she could finally put the memories in perspective. But she realized now she had to jettison that house and move forward, making new memories and accepting her childhood for what it was.

Thankfully, she slowly built a relationship with her father. They had dinner every once in a while and spoke on the phone often.

She'd become a regular in the Chase household. They treated her like one of their own and she truly felt like it. Winter had brought a bit of a lull in Kyle's business and Maggie was off school for winter break so they had a lot time to spend together.

Kyle woke up one morning about two weeks before Christmas in a hyper mood. "Let's go and get a tree today," he begged. Maggie had decorated the condo but they'd held back on a tree until they both had the time off.

She stretched and pulled him back down to her. "Convince me."

"Gladly," he murmured and with a grin, disappeared beneath the covers.

"Oh, yes, that's the way to convince a girl of just about anything."

He chuckled as his mouth descended and sent shivers over her flesh.

സ സ സ

They went to the Christmas tree farm and chose a nice noble fir for the living room. She made mulled cider while he put the tree up and got it watered. Afterward, they decorated it with ornaments of their own and a few they'd bought together.

When they finished, they sat on the couch together and watched the lights on the tree, drinking the cider. "This is the best Christmas I've ever had," Maggie said with a satisfied sigh.

"Me too, Red." He loved the way they were building a life together. Loved to watch her in his kitchen—*their* kitchen. Loved to see her shampoo in the bathroom. Loved the way that her side of the bed smelled of oranges. He'd always thought having a relationship would be another person taking up his life, taking away space from him. Instead she added to his life, made it bigger, brighter.

"I need to finish my shopping. I'm not quite done. I'm going to meet Dee at three and we're actually going to brave the mall in Crawford. I'll meet you at your parents' for dinner tonight."

He nodded and kissed her as she got up to leave. "I told Daddy that I'd help with the tree in the side yard. Not that he's old or anything but I don't want him up in a ladder with a saw. Shall I take the presents in the hall closet over with me?"

They were going to have Christmas at the Chase household. They'd spend Christmas Eve there with the rest of the family and then open presents the next day. Her father was even going to come over for the gift exchange. He and Edward had become fast friends since Tom was using Edward's firm to represent him in the divorce with Cecelia.

She hugged him and bit his ear gently. "Thanks, hon, I'd appreciate that."

ØR ØR ØR

Kyle and Matt worked in the yard, dealing with the tree together and laughing. Kyle felt so relaxed. More than he'd ever felt. He'd always had a good relationship with his family but having Maggie in his life made him feel settled in a way he'd never imagined.

"You pick up the ring yet?" Matt asked as they put away the tools in the shed out back.

Kyle had decided to ask Maggie to marry him on Christmas Day. He'd have the ring wrapped up and waiting for her under the tree. "Yep. It's in Mom's jewelry box. She's going to wrap it and put it in a larger box. I wrote out the card for the inside already."

"I can't believe you're going to ask someone to marry you. Not that Maggie isn't great—she really is and the two of you give me hope that someday I'll meet someone who I fall that hard for. But still, this is big, Kyle. Forever and ever big."

"She's my whole life, Matt," Kyle answered simply.

From his spot across the road and behind a hedge, Alex ground his teeth. Of course the bastard was laughing, he'd stolen Maggie right from under Alex's nose. This should have been *his* Christmas with Maggie. It was their tree that should have been decorated and presents piled beneath.

Instead, all he had was an empty house and his memories of their time together. But that was about to change.

ର ର ର

Dee and Maggie had a great time shopping despite the horrible crowds at the mall just two weeks before Christmas. Maggie bought a beautiful watch for Kyle and the engraving was finished so she picked that up first. Dee bought some sexy silk boxers for Arthur and Maggie got the last item on her list for Kyle, the new golf club he'd been drooling over. She had everything wrapped and drove over to the Chase's for dinner.

"Hello all!" she called out as she let herself in with the packages she'd purchased that day. She put them under the gigantic tree in the formal living room and saw that the mound of presents had mutated and wondered what it would look like by Christmas day when everyone in the family had added theirs. She smiled when she saw that Polly had knitted her a stocking and it was hanging next to Kyle's over the fireplace. A rush of warmth stole over her, she felt like she truly belonged. She had a place for the first time in her life.

"Hi, baby," Kyle said as he came into the room.

"Mmmm. What did I do to deserve that?" she asked dreamily after he'd kissed her thoroughly.

"You simply exist, Red. There's plenty more where that came from after we get home." He waggled his eyebrows. "Did you buy me lots and lots of presents?" He grinned, looking around her at the boxes she'd just put under the tree.

"You're bad, Kyle Chase. Spoiled rotten bad." She laughed. "By the way, speaking of always getting what you want—I must have bumped into a dozen women who all pretended to care about me in order to ask about you. Checking on your availability." She snorted.

"I'm taken. Too bad for them. They'll have to deal with it."

She sure did. Kyle knew it'd been a hard thing to deal with how women looked at him every time they were out but she'd done it. He showed her every day how much he loved her and wanted her and her only. She was finally in a place where she felt secure. That made him proud. And glad she knew she could always trust his commitment to her.

"Maggie, honey? Did I hear you come in?" Polly called out as she came around the corner.

"Hey, Mom, what's happening?" Maggie asked, getting up to hug her.

Polly shot her son a huge grin. Kyle knew it tickled her to no end that Maggie had started calling her mom. She was also over the moon about Kyle's plans to ask Maggie to marry him. Edward had asked Polly to marry him on Christmas Day. In fact, several Chase and Landry marriages started with a Christmas Day proposal.

Polly told them of the complicated chess game of organization of who slept where on Christmas Eve and Maggie volunteered her air mattress and trundle bed to help. She also offered to sleep in separate rooms from Kyle but he vetoed it and Polly refused, saying she was just fine with them in together. Polly wanted them both there together to celebrate her first Christmas with them.

It would be a stretch, but everyone would fit somehow and it would be lovely to share the morning together.

ଓ ଓ ଓ

On Christmas Eve morning, Maggie woke up and stretched. Taking her time, she looked at the long naked lines of Kyle's body with a lazy smile. He was all hers. She got up quietly to run down and turn on the coffee maker before coming back up to shower.

"Hey, I think you missed a spot," Kyle said, stepping into the shower stall behind her. He took the sponge from her and soaped her back and down over the curves of her ass. He licked the cinnamon freckles of her shoulders and up her neck to her ear. He brought the sponge around and abraded her nipples with it, while tonguing her ear. Her eyes closed and she leaned back into him.

In her life she'd never felt so cherished and loved. His hands on her, his words in her ear wrapped around her heart. To belong to someone like Kyle had just never entered her imagination. Being loved like that was the finest gift life had ever granted her.

Rinsing herself off, she moved him around into the spray so she could do a bit of pampering herself. Stepping on the edge of the tub so she could reach him well, she washed his hair, gently massaging his scalp as she did. He held an arm wrapped around her waist to keep her steady. Afterwards she scrubbed his back and legs and everything in between. And the in between seemed quite pleased with the attention.

Her soap slicked hands wrapped around his cock. Gaze locked with his, she watched his lips part and his pupils dilate as he thrust, unashamedly into her grip. His free and easy acceptance of his sexuality turned her on immensely. He never hesitated to voice what he wanted or take what he needed.

Hot water rushed over them both, over her hands and arms and his cock until suddenly he picked her up and plunged inside of her. She cried out at the slice of sensation as he filled her up. He placed a foot on the edge of the tub to support her ass. Needing more of him, Maggie wrapped her thighs around his waist, opening herself up for him.

He slid in and out of her and she lost words for long moments. Her body arched, hands clutched his shoulders.

"I. Love. You." He spoke each word succinctly with his thrusts.

"Ohmigod. Iloveyoutoo," she rushed out in a gust of breath.

She looked into the sea green depths of his eyes and he felt like he was falling into her whiskey colored ones. She opened herself to him, made herself vulnerable. It was raw then, tender and ferocious and what she was to him clutched his insides. He snaked a hand between them to find her clit, pressing a thumb over it in the way he knew she liked so much.

"Oh yes," she moaned out, her hips arching, moving on him. While he watched her face, he saw her eyes glass over. Her pussy rippled then, clutched him in that slick-hot embrace and climax hit, quicksilver from the base of his spine. He thrust and thrust and thrust as he poured into her, his forehead resting against her collarbone.

He stood there, muscles twitching, breathing hard and not noticing the passage of time until he felt the water run cold. Reluctantly, he pulled out and put her down.

"Oh god." He realized why she'd felt so good, so hot and tight.

"What?" she asked, turning off the water and grabbing a towel and drying his skin.

"I didn't put a condom on. I forgot. I brought one in here. It's on the counter. It's just when you ran your slick, soapy hands over me, I just lost it. I'm so sorry." He searched her face expecting her to be upset.

She sighed and smiled at him, slapping his ass. "It's all right. I wanted to make it a Christmas present but I went on the pill three weeks ago. It takes two weeks to work so I didn't want to say anything until the time was up. We both got tested for STDs, it's okay."

He exhaled in relief. "Oh god, you feel so good without a condom. I'm so glad we won't have to use them anymore. I wasn't sure how I could bear to go back to being covered while inside of you once I'd been there bare."

She kissed his chest and quickly dried herself off. "You do say the most unique but wonderful stuff, baby."

Laughing, he took the lotion bottle from her hands and applied it to her skin himself. "I won't be able to share a shower with you until we come back home so let me do this to tide myself over."

"It's just one night, Kyle. Sheesh."

He backed her into their bedroom. "But not being able to hear you scream out my name is going to be hard to live without. Even for just one night." His eyebrow went up and a frisson of lust twisted through her.

They ended up back in their bed for another forty-five minutes before stumbling up to get dressed.

The crowd at Polly and Edward's was insane. Kyle took their bag upstairs to their room while she headed into the family room where people covered every possible surface. They were all going to a Christmas Eve service at church and then coming back for dinner.

Nan and Pop were gushing over their new great grandbaby and looking at Maggie and Kyle with sly smiles of expectation. Nan and Pop were Edward's parents. Pop was something of a local legend. A war hero in the

Pacific who lost an eye, there were no less than three buildings and a street named after him. They took to Maggie right away. Pop was a terrible flirt and Nan just grinned at her and made unsubtle hints about great grandchildren until Kyle just burst out laughing.

After the service, they laid out a huge buffet dinner of cold cuts and salads and then got down to the very serious business of game playing.

They cleared the dining room and set up some card tables in the family room. Two fast and furious games of canasta started. Kyle and Maggie were partners and their unspoken communication enabled them to kick butt. She saw that the Chase boys were as competitive at cards as they were in billiards.

In the end, after Kyle and Maggie won every round, Shane and Matt made a rule that they weren't ever to be on the same team at cards again.

ભ ભ ભ

Christmas morning was total chaos. Despite the fact that everyone there was in their mid-twenties or older, the rush to the tree was reminiscent of a bunch of seven year olds. Maggie's dad came over and settled in on the couch while Pop played Santa and handed out presents. The process took well over three hours as they waited while each person opened their present until the next one got distributed.

"This one is for Maggie, from Kyle." He bought a large box and sat it before her.

She ripped it open only to find another, slightly smaller box inside. Unwrapping that one, she saw yet another smaller box inside that one. She did it five more times until a small box remained. She looked down at it and saw the card tied to it. *"Open Me First."* She read it to herself.

Maggie, my heart never truly beat until the first time I touched your lips with my own. You are my everything. The air I breathe, the blood in my veins. You are my heart and my soul and I love you.

With tears welling up in her eyes she unwrapped the final package and saw the black velvet ring box. Stilling for a moment, she cracked it open with trembling hands, exposing a pear cut solitaire diamond that was at least a carat. Her eyes widened and the room remained totally silent.

Kyle, who was already sitting at her feet came up on one knee and took her ring from the box and then her left hand. "Margaret Elizabeth Wright, my sweet Red, will you do me the honor of marrying me?"

Her hands shook as she looked into his face and saw everything she'd ever wanted and dreamed of, sitting right there.

She nodded, tears running down her face. "Yes. Oh definitely," she said and he slid the ring on her left ring finger and a whoop of joy sprang up from several people around the room. Kyle hugged her to him tight and she saw he was crying, too.

"I love you so much, Kyle," she said into his ear.

"Ditto, sugar," he answered with a grin.

"Hot damn!" Matt exclaimed, a goofy smile on his face. "I've got the loveliest sister-in-law to be in the entire state of Georgia."

"Polly and I couldn't ask for a better daughter-in-law. You make our boy the happiest we've ever seen him. Thank you, sugar." Edward kissed her cheek and Polly, who stood at his side, weepy, nodded mutely.

She was on cloud nine for the rest of the day. Kyle loved the watch as well as his new golf club and the clothes and music she'd gotten him. She couldn't stop looking at how her ring sparkled on her hand as she sat outside on the porch after dinner watching the guys play a very rough game of football in the yard.

Shane came and sat beside her on the glider swing. The game had gentled a bit as they all had a few aches and pains. Many of the others had gone for an after dinner walk.

Shane reached out and squeezed her hand. "Hey, Maggie, congratulations. I hope you and Kyle will be very happy together. He's a very lucky man to have a woman like you. I'm jealous."

"I think she's out there. The one for you. Waiting for you. When you find her, I hope you can open your heart enough to let her in."

"You think?"

"I really do."

He smiled and kissed her cheek and then yelped when the football Kyle had been throwing hit him in the head. "HEY!" He came up off the glider and headed down the steps.

"Hey yourself, loverboy. Keep your lips off my woman," Kyle taunted and then got tackled.

"Excuse me! What am I? A chew toy or something? Shane get up off of him. Kyle…oh nevermind!" she snapped and turned and stomped back into the house.

"You're in trouble," Marc taunted and got tackled in turn.

She was shoving her clothes into the overnight bag when he came upstairs. "Hey, are you really mad at me?"

"Last night you made that crack to Shane when we were playing cards. And I know you and your brothers joke a lot but the whole history between Shane and me is uncomfortable enough. When you make comments like, 'you had your chance' or you tell him to keep his lips off me—when, by the way, he was congratulating me on our engagement—it just makes me feel like a thing instead of a person. You guys are competitive enough. I don't want to feel like I'm something to be fought over. And I don't want you disregarding what I have to say because you feel like you need to get even. It's not fair and it's not respectful."

He was quiet for a few moments, thinking over what she'd said. "I'm sorry, Red, I hadn't thought of it that way. I don't mean it like that. Although I do suppose I like to rub his nose in the fact that I could see you for the fabulous woman you are when he acted like a dick. I'll try hard not to do it any more."

She looked at him and let go of the smile she's been holding back. It was nearly impossible to stay mad at him. "Fine. See that you don't. Now, I was thinking that I'd go and swing by my house. I haven't been there in a week or so and I want to make sure everything is all right. We've had such cold temperatures that I want to be sure the pipes are okay."

"Maggie, you and I need to have a discussion about the house and our living situation. I'd like to set a date for the wedding, too."

"Okay. But not here." She held up her hands to quiet him. "No, it's not negotiable. I love your family but this is something I want to talk with you about *alone*. Why don't we talk about it tonight at your place."

"*Our* place. Move in with me, Maggie. You're practically living with me now. Sell your house and we can buy a place together. It's silly to have that great big house just sitting there empty and my place is going to be too small for us in the long run. We could live in your house but you seem to be a lot happier when you don't live there."

"It's true. I suppose that house has a lot of bad memories lurking around inside of it. Let's talk about this later all right? Honestly, you know someone is bound to come in here within the next three minutes and I don't want this to be a discussion by committee."

"Okay, sugar. Take my car over to your place and come back by to get me when you're done. I've got a game to finish with my brothers. Unless you want me to come to your place with you?"

"No, it's no big deal. I'm three minutes away, for goodness sake. I need to grab some more clothes and check the pipes. I'll be there and back in less than an hour."

"Okay, Red." He kissed her and they walked out to the car.

Chapter Ten

She whipped into her driveway and gave a quick look around the outside of the house. The pipes looked fine but she got the insulation out of the garage and wrapped them, anyway. Especially as she'd already made the decision to accept Kyle's invitation and move in to his place so she wouldn't be around.

That done, she went inside and ran upstairs to grab some more clothes. She was zipping the garment bag when she heard steps behind her.

"Jeez, it's only been half an hour, couldn't live without me?" she teased and turned around. Only it wasn't Kyle, it was Alex standing there and a chill of dread slid through her gut.

"I can't live without you, Maggie. You're mine and I'm yours. Can't you see that? Why aren't you home anymore?"

"What the hell are you doing here! Get out of my house now or I'll call the police." She tried to edge her way closer to the phone on the bedside table.

"I'm here to take back what's mine," he said in a strange sing song voice, inching toward her. "What is that?" He grabbed her hand and stared at the ring. "NO!" He pulled it off and threw it on the bed.

"Stop that!" She reached for her ring and the world went black for a moment. When she came to he was dragging her out of the room. A surge of strength and will to survive surged through her and she grabbed the wall near the door and tried to hold on but he yanked her loose. He half dragged her, half carried her down the stairs. Reaching down he slapped her across her face, hard, when she kept grabbing the spindles on the banister to stop him. Her head hit each stair, and her world hovered gray as she fought to keep conscious. She tried to yell but all she could do was moan and hoarsely whisper at him to stop.

"I'm taking you away from here, away from those meddling Chase boys. Now be a good girl and walk out of here. I don't want anyone getting suspicious." He yanked her upright and held her by the hair and she tried to kick him but got the leg of the table instead and knocked it over. Weeping now, she tried to grab at the doorway to hold on but he elbowed her in the face and the darkness fell over her again.

ଓ ଓ ଓ

After two hours Kyle began to really get worried. "What could be taking so long? She said she'd be back in less than an hour and it's been nearly two." Kyle grumbled to Matt and Shane. Most likely she'd bumped into Liv and they were chatting about the engagement and he was worrying over nothing. Still, he had a strange feeling about it that only got worse as the minutes passed.

"Why don't we take a drive over there? Maybe she had problems with the pipes. If so, you know how she is, she's probably trying to do it all herself," Matt said laughing.

"Yeah, let's. It's not like her to not call if she's going to be held up."

They pulled up and saw the Saturn in the drive. "She's still here."

"Stay here," Shane said and was out of the car before it had stopped. Kyle, sensing that something was wrong got out too, following his brother. The front door was wide open and the table near the entry was on its side, the glass vase and bowl that sat upon it, broken, pieces all over the place.

There was blood on the doorjamb. A bloody handprint. "Jesus. Where is she?" Kyle meant to yell but it came out as a whisper. He was suddenly cold.

"Go back to Matt's car. Call the station on your cell phone and tell them I said to send out a car with two officers. On the double." Reaching back, he took his gun out of the shoulder holster he had on.

"No, I'm coming in."

Shane turned and shoved Kyle, hard. "No you are not, damn it. This is my job, Kyle. Do what I tell you and do it now. You're endangering me and her by not listening." He turned away, closing the discussion and slowly walked into the house.

Matt approached and Kyle turned and ran to him. "Call the station now! Tell them that Shane said to send out a car with two officers, on the double." Matt nodded and got on his cell phone. Kyle began to pace.

Back in the house, Shane walked up the stairs. The sight of the blood on the light colored carpet runner sped his heart. He crept along, listening for any sound but heard none. Entering Maggie's bedroom and saw the bedside table had been overturned and blood on the floor and then on the wall near the door, as if someone had grabbed it to hold on and pull away from someone dragging them. He walked in carefully, not wanting to disturb evidence and he saw Maggie's engagement ring on the center of the bed. He swept the rest of the room and the upstairs but found nothing. By the time he came downstairs, the other officers had arrived and had gone through the first floor.

Kyle couldn't seem to stop shaking as he waited out on the front lawn. Matt was with him, an arm around his shoulder. Seeing Shane come out of the house broke Kyle's stillness and he ran over. "Where is she, Shane? Is she all right?"

"She's not here. Kyle, I'm going to tell you what I saw in there but I need you to hold it together, okay?" Stunned, Kyle nodded and Shane exhaled before continuing. "There's blood in several places. Her ring is on the bed. There was a garment bag of clothes but it's on the floor like she dropped it. Kyle, it looks like there was a struggle. There's a blood trail from the bedroom, down the stairs and to the front door. The officers are taking blood samples so that we can run a match. Thank goodness we got that grant money to have better lab equipment here, but it will still take time to identify the blood and the bloody handprints at the doorway. Kyle, the handprints are very small though. I'm guessing they're Maggie's. I think she was attacked and taken."

Kyle's eyes went wild, his heart threatened to burst through his chest in terror for her. "No! Damn it, Shane, find her!"

Shane grabbed Kyle's upper arms and got in his face. "Keep it together, Kyle. She was still alive when he got her to the door. That handprint shows she tried to fight. She won't give up, Kyle, remember that."

"It's Alex, you know that! Find him."

"I think so, too. I've called the judge and asked for a warrant to search Alex's apartment and he granted it. We're going to go over there now."

"Okay, let's go."

"No, Kyle, you can't. This is police business. I can't take the risk of you losing it and messing with evidence. Go back to the condo or to Mom and Dad's. Heck, raise a search party. But *do not* to go Alex Parsons' house." He paused. "We will find her, Kyle."

He turned and stalked off, getting into the squad car he took with another officer recently arrived.

Matt hugged his brother tightly. "Let's go back to Mom and Dad's to get people out looking. We'll drive Nan and Pop to your place in case she shows up and Grammy and Gramps can stay at Mom's in case she comes there."

Polly was beside herself but Edward and Peter helped by organizing everyone. Polly stayed back with her parents and Nan and Pop went over to the condo to wait there. They split up and took opposite sides of town to search. They all had cell phones with them and a description of Alex's car.

Shane called in to tell Kyle that Alex had taken a suitcase and some clothes. Dee was at the bank, checking the records to see if he'd pulled any large amounts of cash out of his account recently.

"Kyle, it's bad. There are more pictures here. Of the two of you. His walls are covered with pictures of her and there are stacks of letters everywhere that he'd written to her but never sent. His obsession with her has grown."

Kyle hung up, shaking with rage, terror burning the backs of his eyes. He looked at Matt who was there with him. "If that bastard hurts her in any way, I'll kill him."

"I'll help you. But she's going to be all right." Matt said, hoping he wasn't lying.

ର ର ର

Maggie woke up in a strange room, disoriented. Her head hurt like hell. Blinking to try and clear her vision so she could figure out where she was, she quailed when Alex came into her line of sight. Suddenly, memory of what happened earlier rushed back, filling her with terror.

"Alex, please, let me go. This is crazy. Let me go and I won't call the cops, I promise." She desperately tried to recall the advice from the self defense course she'd taken the year before.

He laughed and kissed her forehead and she tried not so show her revulsion. "Oh sweetheart, I'm not letting you go. You're mine, silly. I'm sorry I had to hit you. Is your head all right?" Maggie tried not to panic as she listened to him. His voice was so odd, dreamy and high pitched. It frightened her, filled her with dread. He was obviously insane.

"What do you think, Alex? Can you untie my hands at least? My shoulders really hurt and this angle is making my back twist."

"No, I can't risk it. But I'll help you sit up and get you some Tylenol for your head." He gently moved her into a sitting position and left the room, coming back with a glass of water and two tablets. "Here. Open your mouth and I'll help you."

She clamped her lips shut tight and shook her head. God only knew whether or not he'd drugged or poisoned the water or even if the pills were actually Tylenol.

"Maggie, why are you being so difficult? Look." He held the pill up so she could see the factory stamp and he brought the bottle in as well. "See, here's the bottle. The water is from the tap. It's well water. The cabin is on a well. I wouldn't hurt you, Maggie. You can trust me."

She narrowed her eyes at that ridiculous statement.

"Suit yourself, then," he said with a sigh. He sat the glass and the pills down. "Let me know if you change your mind. Seems silly to hurt out of spite."

She snorted but didn't say anything else.

When he reached out to caress her face, she shrank back as far as she could go until she hit the wall. Nausea and revulsion roiled in her gut, fear threatened to drown her. She gave herself a mental slap. She had to keep it together if she was going to get out of this mess.

"I love you, Maggie. I just want to touch you."

"Alex, get away from me. This has gone far enough. Take me home."

"You are home. Our home." He smiled dreamily and got up.

"Where are we?"

"This is our cabin. Our honeymoon cabin," he answered and walked out of the room.

She felt woozy and her world became fuzzier and fuzzier until at last, she lost consciousness again.

ଔ ଔ ଔ

It was three in the morning and many of the Chase household slept on couches and sitting up in chairs. Kyle, his brothers, father, his uncle and Maggie's father were in the dining room sitting at the table, looking at pictures.

"Damn it! Where is she!" Kyle raged. They'd stayed out searching for hours and had found nothing.

Shane had come back to report on the situation. They had surveillance camera footage from the ATM machine at the bank. Alex took the maximum two thousand dollar withdrawal. In the background, after they'd blown it up, Maggie was clearly lying against the front seat, her eyes closed, a bloody trickle from her scalp down her face.

"Kyle, this was at five twelve, about forty-five minutes after she'd left here. We've narrowed the time frame down considerably. At least we know roundabout when she was taken."

"But she could be d-dead by that time. Her eyes are closed," he replied, barely containing a sob. Edward moved to hold his son, bracing him with his arm around his shoulders, lending him strength.

"Son, if he'd killed her, he'd have gotten rid of the body. She was probably unconscious. She was alive then, we have every reason to think she's alive now. Alex is obsessed with her. He doesn't want to kill her. He wants to possess her. She's a smart cookie, she'll do what she has to to stay alive."

"And what will that be, Daddy? What will he do to my girl?" Kyle whispered. "We have to find her. Where could he have taken her? God, I never should have let her go over there alone. We were talking about buying a house together. About her moving into my condo and selling her place and buying our own."

"That's it," Shane said, looking up at Edward. "Daddy, can you run a title search? See if Alex has bought any property in this and the surrounding few counties since September?"

Peter stood up. "I can. Let me run into the office and check," he said, looking relieved to be able to help in some way and Shane followed him out the door.

Polly came into the room. "Honey, it's three in the morning, why don't you get some sleep? We'll wake you if anything changes." She stroked a hand over his hair, trying to comfort him.

Kyle stood up. "I can't sleep while Maggie is out there being held by that sick bastard!" he shouted and Edward hugged him tightly and Kyle broke down and wept.

Tom went to him. "Listen to me, son. My little girl has been on her own, out of necessity, for most of her life. She's independent and she will not quit. I promise you that. She's strong, my baby. She won't let herself be killed, boy. Not without a fight. You keep that ring for her because she will be back here and she'll want it back."

Pulling himself together, Kyle took a deep breath and looked at the engagement ring he'd been wearing on his pinkie finger. He locked eyes with his father-in-law to be and nodded.

ભ ભ ભ

When Maggie woke up again, the throbbing in her head had subsided to a dull ache. She opened her eyes carefully but it was still dark. Judging by the position of the moon that she could see through the window, it was sometime between midnight and about four a.m. Alex lay next to her on the bed, his arm curled around her thighs. She shuddered in disgust.

Think Maggie! How can you get out of this? She tried pulling at the ropes that held her hands but that just made them tighter and her movement roused Alex.

"Maggie, honey? Are you all right?"

"I have to go to the bathroom."

"Oh of course! Let me help."

He got up and helped her to stand and led her to the bathroom. The cabin was large and modern. That was a hopeful sign that they weren't out too far into the middle of nowhere, Georgia. He opened the door and started to undo her pants.

"No! Jesus. Get off me. Untie my hands, Alex and wait for me out there. The window in here is too small and too high up, I couldn't get through it even if I could get up there. Let me have some dignity."

Alex sighed. "I'll untie you, Maggie. But I have a gun and if you try anything funny I will shoot you. Do you understand?"

"Yes. Now untie me."

He did and stepped back, looking at his watch. "You have two minutes and I'm coming in."

She moved her fingers a bit, getting the blood back into them and went to the bathroom quickly. Not knowing when he'd decide to barge in, she got re-dressed and washed her hands and then her face, which had bloodstains all down the left side. She had a bump the size of a softball on the back of her head and another smaller one on her upper forehead, just at the hairline.

She noticed that he seemed to take it all right when she was a bit bossy but she knew he wouldn't take too much. She had to bide her time. The longer that she was there, the more time she had to think and plan. And hopefully, the more time Kyle would have to find her. She decided to be extra obedient. She wouldn't try to run just yet, she had to get her bearings back but she needed him to let her stay untied. She called out to him. "I'm done and I'm going to open the door now."

She did, slowly and held her hands up for Alex to see.

"You cleaned off your face. I'm sorry, I meant to do it for you but I fell asleep. Let's go back to bed. I'm tired and you need to rest your head."

"All right," she agreed meekly and hoped he forgot about the ropes.

He didn't. "Maggie, I need to retie you."

"Please don't. My wrists are all raw and it hurts my back, neck and shoulders to have to sit that way." She tried very hard not to beg.

"I can't trust you not to run."

"Then tie me in the front and wrap something around my wrists to go between my skin and the rope. Please."

She wanted to seem reasonable but not have a turn about of behavior that would be unbelievable either. She had to gain control of the situation.

He studied her. "Fine." He got out some face cloths and put them around the abrasions on her wrists and then binding her wrists in front. The price was that she had to lie down beside him. It took every bit of her will to survive not to scream in terror and revulsion as he put his face in the nape of her neck and his breath skated across her skin.

Kyle, where are you?

ರ ರ ರ

"We got it!" Shane burst in through the door. "He bought a cabin about two hours east of here six weeks ago. I've called the judge. It's still in this county, and he's issued a warrant for arrest and a search warrant. It's in an unincorporated area, no local police force so I'm taking my men out with me. We'll meet the cops from the nearest jurisdiction to make a joint raid on the house."

"I'm coming, too," Kyle said and Shane started to disagree until he saw the set of Kyle's mouth.

"You may wait outside the police line if you promise not to get involved. I mean it, Kyle. You can't interfere, you could get her or yourself or one of my men killed if you don't obey me."

Kyle nodded.

"I'll drive him," Matt said and Edward grabbed his keys and he and Tom got into the back seat of Matt's Bronco. Soon they all tore out of the driveway, heading east.

They drove at eighty miles an hour and made the two hour drive in under an hour and a half. Shane and his officers met with the local sheriff. Kyle watched, tense as his brother and his men all donned body armor and began their silent creep through the woods. They'd stopped their vehicles about a mile away from the cabin so they could approach it unseen.

ल ल ल

Maggie was laying in bed, trying to think up a plan. Her muscles ached from holding still but she didn't want any movement to wake him up. The sun was rising and Maggie figured it was about seven or seven thirty. She sighed without meaning to and Alex stirred.

His eyes opened and stared into hers with an eerie light. He brought his hand up and cupped her breast and she screamed.

He hit her in the face. "Shut up, you whore! Why are you acting so afraid? It's not like you haven't fucked half the town already. Everyone but me. You led me on and I can't have that. You're mine, Maggie." He squeezed her breast hard and she bit back a whimper.

"Get off me, you bastard. I don't want you, damn it! There are plenty of other women in town. Date them and leave me alone!" She looked around the room for a weapon, anything she could use to stop him.

"I don't think so," he snarled and ripped at her shirt, sending buttons flying and exposing her bra and her bare stomach. "I mean to have what's mine."

"No! NO, ALEX!" Struggling and screaming, she turned her head and saw a face in the window. He held his finger up to his lips, indicating she should stay quiet about his presence.

Alex ripped at the fastenings of her pants and she kicked at him and tried to raise her hands but her wrists were still bound and he had them pinned with one hand, while the other was pulling at her clothes.

"*Get off me, you bastard!*" She screamed. She screamed and she screamed and he slapped her again, so hard she tasted blood. He ripped at the front of her bra and it came open, baring her breasts and she began to weep. "Stop it, damn it! I don't want this."

"Doesn't matter," he muttered and unzipped his pants and started to pull himself out.

Suddenly, the door slammed open and several large men in body armor poured in pointing guns and screaming, "GET DOWN! GET OFF THE WOMAN NOW!"

Shane stepped forward and yanked Alex off of her and threw him across the room. Another officer came to her and gently pulled the sheet from the bed around her, covering her nakedness.

"Are you all right, ma'am?" the officer asked softly.

She started to tremble, shaking so hard her teeth chattered.

"Did he rape you?"

"N-n-no. He-he tried b-b-b-but you s-s-s-topped h-h-im," she stuttered out.

Shane came forward looked her over. "Maggie, honey? I just need to look at you. Make sure you aren't injured." He gently opened the sheet and winced as he saw the hand and finger shaped bruise on her left breast but he felt relief seeing that her panties were still on. "Honey, we don't have any female officers here but I want to get pictures taken of you and your injuries. Will you let me do it? Officer Jeffries here will stay in the room but he won't look at you when I have to take the pictures of your breasts. I'm sorry to even ask it of you but it's necessary for the case."

Tears running down her face, she nodded, still trembling. She went into another place in her head as he took pictures of her face, neck and her wrists and then of her torn clothes and the bruise on her breast.

Shane did it as quickly and methodically as he could but he couldn't fight the rising bile, the anguish over what she'd gone through.

"All done, honey. I'm going to wrap you in this blanket here. It's a blanket from my car, not his. I'm going to take you out to where Kyle's waiting for you. He's been so worried. And then we're going to take you to a hospital." He spoke to her calmly and softly as he touched her carefully.

Sobs tore through her stomach. "Kyle's here?"

"Of course he is, Maggie. He threatened to kneecap me if I didn't let him come with me. Come on, honey, let's get you taken care of."

Nodding, she stood still while he gently put the blanket around her and picked her up. He held her against his body and carried her the mile back to where the cars were.

Her eyes were closed but she heard hear Kyle say, "thank you, God," and come moving toward her.

"Thank you for saving me," she said softly to Shane and he nodded and handed her over to Kyle.

"We need to get her to a hospital. Kyle, you ride in the back with her. Dad, you all follow us."

Maggie opened her eyes but one of them was pretty near swollen shut and she had to close that one. "Kyle, he...oh god," she whispered and began to cry.

"I'm here, Red. Always here. God, I love you so much. Hell, I'm so damned thankful you're okay. We'll get through this, baby." He stroked gentle fingers over her hair.

They checked her into the hospital. She had a concussion and they wanted to monitor her at least for the next twenty-four hours.

છ છ છ

Alex had been transported to jail and awaited arraignment on kidnapping, false imprisonment, attempted rape and assault charges in addition to violating the two orders of no contact.

Maggie slept but they woke her up every hour to check on the concussion. She was feeling loopy from the lack of REM sleep and the rush of adrenaline her body had produced over the last day.

Kyle never left her side and he looked almost as bad as she did. The whole Chase clan was splayed across every available surface in the waiting room as were Maggie's father and her friends. Maggie's father had called her mother to tell her what had happened but she'd expressed disinterest in the whole situation.

Finally, after twenty-four hours, the hospital discharged Maggie and Kyle carefully loaded her into Matt's Bronco and they drove back home.

She stared out the window and he looked at his father with a worried expression. When they neared Petal, Matt asked, "Where to, sweetheart? Momma wanted me to tell you that you're welcome to stay with her and Daddy until you felt better. I figure you and Kyle might like some time alone. I can take you to your house, too. Just tell me where and I'll go."

"Not my house, not ever," she said, panic at the edges of her voice. "Take me to the condo please, Matt. If that's okay with you, Kyle."

"Of course it is, Red. Whatever you want, baby." Kyle looked back at Edward and his father's eyes softened at the sound of anguish in Maggie's voice.

All three men helped her into the house, even though she was perfectly capable of walking. She let them fuss over her a bit and thanked Matt and Edward for their help. She turned to Edward as he was leaving. "They won't let him go will they?"

"Honey, I want you to know I am on the prosecutor's ass about this. He was denied bail at his arraignment. I don't foresee that changing. Alex will do time. They'll charge him with everything they can, I promise you. Oh baby, I'm sorry," he said and swept her into an embrace.

She nodded up at him and blinked back tears. "Thanks, Dad," she whispered and his heart nearly broke in half.

She looked at Kyle and kissed the hand holding hers. "I'm going to take a shower and change. I'll be down in a few minutes."

"Hey, Red, afterwards we'll get tucked up on the couch. I'll order in Chinese and we'll get pay-per-view. Holler if you need me all right?" Kyle asked gently and she nodded and walked up the stairs.

"Daddy, I know Momma wants to come over but can we hold off for at least a day? I can't see that she's got much reserve left to go on right now."

"Yes, I'll talk to her. You take care of my future daughter-in-law you hear? And yourself, too. You look like hell. I love you, son." Edward hugged Kyle tightly.

"I want to kill him, Daddy. She has a bruise in the shape of his hand on her breast. He gave her a concussion. He tried to rape her. Damn it, I want his blood!"

Matt grabbed his brother's arm. "She needs you, Kyle. I know you're angry. We all are. But you have to deal with this so you can help her through. We'll do all we can to be sure he does time but you can't go off half cocked because she needs you. Now, do you have to work tomorrow? Marc, Shane and I will do shifts here with her around your schedule if you need us."

"No, I don't have anything until next week. She's due back in class on the third, we'll see how it goes. I want to wait to talk with her until she's had a chance to settle in. Thank you, though."

"We'll go and leave you two be."

Kyle watched them drive away and then called and ordered dinner, built a fire and went to change his own clothes. Worried that she still wasn't out of the bathroom, he went and knocked softly on the door. "Honey? Can I help you with anything?"

"No." She sniffed and pulled herself together. She'd scrubbed her skin for the last fifteen minutes and she still couldn't get the feeling of his hands off her skin.

"Maggie, I'm going to come in now," Kyle said seriously and slowly opened the door to see her sitting in the shower, the water still on. "Honey, let's get you out of there," he said gently and turned the water off. He hadn't seen her naked and the sight of all of the bruises she bore made his stomach tighten with rage. He dried her carefully and helped her get her clothes on and led her downstairs.

They ate from the cartons and watched a comedy and he massaged her temples as she lay tucked into his body. She looked at her ring, back safely on her finger. "You know, you don't have to marry me if you don't want to."

He moved so that she was facing him. "What? Why on earth wouldn't I want to marry you?"

"Well, I mean, I'm trouble. I can sense that you feel differently about my body. You're angry with me. I swear that I didn't do anything to lead him on."

"Oh my god, Maggie, how could you think that I'd ever imagine that what happened to you was your fault? Of course you didn't do a damned thing to deserve what he did to you! No woman who's been raped ever does. And I don't feel differently about you or your body. I just want to kill him when I see what he's done to you. I love you—god, I love you so much. I thought I'd die when I saw the bloody handprint that you left on your front door. I failed you. Maybe you don't want me because I didn't protect you. I should have gone with you to your house that night. I could have protected you." He started crying.

"I want to kill him, too," she whispered and kissed his tears away. "You didn't fail me. You didn't give up. You saved me. I love you, too."

He led her upstairs and sheltered her with his body and she slept, the first time in several days, she slept feeling safe.

Chapter Eleven

Maggie walked into the conference room at City Hall and total silence fell. "Hi, everyone. I brought the spreadsheets from last year's auction, I thought they might be helpful," she said, trying to keep a professional tone in her voice.

Kyle took a seat away from the table and pulled out a book. He attempted to pretend he didn't want to run interference for her with the Historical Society members seated around the table. All of whom looked at her with shock and pity.

"I'm glad you're here, honey," Maude Sheckley said and got up to hug her. "I'm glad you're all right."

"Thank you, Maude. I am too." Maggie said softly.

In the following moments, every member of the Society got up and gave Maggie a hug and the tension was broken. People were laughing and joking around when the click clack of high heels on the wood hallway greeted their ears. Suddenly, the talking stopped. Polly swept into the room, gave Maggie a quick kiss and went to her seat at the head of the table, gave her hair a fluff and threw her massive purse down.

"Evenin' all. Did Maggie tell you that she's now engaged to my son, Kyle?"

The room once again erupted in chatter and Maggie smiled as she showed off the ring. Kyle gave them all a wave and went back to his book.

They discussed the auction and other Society business and finally adjourned at eight. Kyle accepted hugs and congratulations from everyone and finally reached Maggie and his mother. "You ladies hungry? I'd love to take my two best girls to dinner."

Maggie froze up. She hadn't been out of the condo much in the last two weeks. She worried about facing the townspeople.

"Honey, this is your home. People here love you. I'm starving, let's go to The Sands and get some food," Polly said gently.

"All right," Maggie said taking a bracing breath.

It was late enough that the place wasn't full to the seams with patrons but still had plenty of folks inside. Ronnie Sands, the owner, got them into a booth and squeezed Maggie's hand. "Hi, honey, good to see you." She looked down and saw the ring. "Oh my! Is this what I think it is?"

"Ronnie, this lovely woman has agreed to marry me. Am I lucky or what?"

"Isn't that wonderful! Congratulations you two. When's the day?"

"He only asked me on Christmas and then…well, anyway. We haven't even discussed it yet," Maggie said and Ronnie's face softened.

"I was hoping that we could do it in late spring," Kyle said.

"Ooh! Good idea, the weather will be so pretty." Ronnie grinned and looked to Maggie. "Shall I get you all the usual?"

"Sounds good. Make my fries extra crispy, please."

"Of course, girl. I've been serving you fries for a long time. Be back in a bit with your food and teas." She winked and headed back to the kitchen.

"Where should we have the ceremony?" Kyle asked.

Maggie narrowed her eyes at Kyle. She did not want to do this with an audience. But he was just so damned excited about it, she couldn't really be mad at him. "If we do it in late spring, say after Mother's Day, we could easily do it outside." Maggie hoped Polly would rein in her impulse to take over.

"Hmm, yes that could be nice. We could do tents for the reception. Where though? We could use the park I suppose." He had the sense to look a bit chastened as he saw her narrowed eyes.

Oh well, in for a penny, may as well be in for a pound. Maggie took a deep breath. "Or your parents' back yard. It's over an acre." She looked to Polly. "That is, if it would be all right with them."

"Honey, you're too good to be true!" Polly exclaimed, clapping her hands.

"But, Momma, remember that this is *our* wedding, yeah? So we'd love your *help* and appreciate your *advice* but Maggie and I need to make a lot of decisions for ourselves." Kyle squeezed Maggie's hand beneath the table.

Polly snorted. "Of course! I won't try and take over."

It was Maggie's turn to snort and she tried to pretend she didn't and Polly just laughed. "Okay, so you know me well, dear heart, but I promise, I do know what it is like to be a bride and I'd never want to take that joy from you. But I do want to tell you that I consider you a daughter. And well, I know that your own momma is a fool so please come to me whenever you need a hand all right?"

"Thanks, Mom, I appreciate that so much."

"So the Saturday after Mother's Day at Mom and Dad's house. We have a date and a place," Kyle said.

"I'd like to get my dress made, which doesn't leave much time seeing as how it's already January. Dee's mom just finished making her dress and it's amazing. I wonder if she'd make mine? I'll have to talk to her about it. We need to talk guest lists and color schemes and flowers and food. We need to deal with the invitations and the rentals for the tents as well. Oh my, so much to do." Maggie broke out a pad and a pen and Kyle watched smiling as she and his mother started talking all of the details over.

Я Я Я

Kyle and his brothers moved all of Maggie's belongings out of her house and she put it on the market. In the meantime, he and Maggie looked for a place of their own and soon found a four bedroom near the river that they fell in love with.

Maggie went to counseling both alone and with Kyle for a while to deal with what happened with Alex. It helped a great deal.

The invitations went out in March and Alex's trial approached. Maggie prepared her students for finals and decided on a caterer, she had dress fittings and chose flowers. Kyle converted the first floor bedroom into an office space for both of them. He chose tuxedos with his brothers and asked Shane to be his best man. Maggie asked Edward to walk her down the aisle with her own father. She wanted them both to give her away. Cecelia and Janie were not invited.

The trial happened to fall on the week of spring break so Maggie planned to be there every day. Kyle also took time off and the entire Chase clan and Tom Wright were there to support her although Maggie couldn't attend until after she testified, the same with the others.

Testifying was awful. It was fine when the prosecution was examining her but when Alex's attorney got up it was just horrible. He tried to twist her words, to make it seem like she'd led Alex on and that she'd run away with him on her own instead of being kidnapped. He also tried to make it seem like the bruises were due to rough sex and not assault. Thank goodness Edward and Peter had helped her by doing a little role play and showing her what it would be like before the trial. She managed to keep on task and to not let herself get too riled up. The other women that Alex had stalked when he was a student at the University of Georgia testified to his behavior.

Alex did not testify in his own defense as Edward told her he probably wouldn't. The defense case was relatively short and was essentially an argument that everything that happened was consensual. Which—in light of the testimony from the women who'd been stalked by Alex, her own testimony, the pictures and medical testimony of her injuries, signs of struggle at her home, and the testimony of the police who came to the cabin and saw her screaming and trying to fight him off — seemed ridiculous.

It only took the jury forty-five minutes to come back with a guilty verdict and Maggie sobbed in relief. Liv and Dee and a great many other people from Petal had come out to the trial and they all burst into applause and the judge had to pound his gavel to shut them all up.

The sentencing phase would be decided by the judge and he scheduled a hearing the following week to hand down his decision. When they returned, Alex was sentenced to seven years in prison. Edward explained that was pretty good considering but Maggie snorted, wishing he'd be in prison for life.

Chapter Twelve

The morning of May twenty-third arrived and Maggie awoke smiling. It was her wedding day. She spent the night at Liv's place and Kyle was at his parents'. Dee came over first thing and brought breakfast while Liv did their hair.

"Phone for you, hon, it's your husband-to-be." Liv handed the phone to her and she went back to artfully pinning up her curls and lacing flowers and ribbon through it all.

"Hi honey! Not having second thoughts are you?" she asked with a laugh.

"Hey, Red, no way. Although I just want to say, yet again, how stupid I think it was to make me sleep alone last night. I haven't slept alone since November. I don't like it."

"Stop whining. It's the last time you'll have to. I didn't want you to see my dress until the ceremony. I want it to be a surprise."

"Okay, I'm sure it'll be worth it. I sure do love you, Red."

"Me too, baby. I have to go. Liv's doing my hair and the phone is in the way. I'll see you in an hour."

"Can't wait."

Maggie hung up and sighed. "He's so wonderful."

"Oh lawd! I thought the weekly Arthur is wonderful updates were bad!" Liv joked.

"Are you talking about my boy?" Polly flounced into the room.

"Hey, Mom. Of course we were talking about Kyle. My, don't you look pretty!"

"Thanks, doll. What can I do?"

"I'm done here. Let's help her get into the dress."

Maggie's dress was antique white silk and satin. Sleeveless, with tiny embroidered French blue flowers along the neckline. The back had a small vee in it with the same embroidered flowers. It gathered into a pleat at the small of her back and the material flowed down and made a modest pool of silk as a train. She opted against a veil and chose to wind flowers and ribbon in her hair. Her bouquet was of silver roses and white magnolias. As a present for Kyle later, she had on a gorgeous cream colored bustier and garter set underneath with pale silk stockings.

Dee and Liv wore French blue dresses of mid-calf length and the groom was wearing a dove gray morning coat with his tuxedo.

"Look at you, girl," Liv whispered as they got her all fastened inside of the dress and she stood before the mirror.

Maggie smiled as she looked at them all. "We sure do clean up nice."

"I almost forgot. Here." Polly handed a velvet jeweler's box to Maggie. "This is from Kyle."

She opened the box and softly gasped when she saw the pair of sapphire and diamond earrings inside. The note said, *something blue and something new.* She put them on and they sparkled in her ears.

"Now for something borrowed," Polly said, "as well as old." She handed her a velvet pouch and Maggie opened it and a diamond bracelet came out. "My mother let me borrow this on my wedding day and then she gave it to me when I had Shane. So today, you'll borrow it from me. And when you and Kyle have your first child, it'll be yours."

Maggie fanned her face. "Oh lord, you're going to make me cry and ruin Liv's make up job! Thank you so much!"

Edward and Tom waited on the front porch as Liv, Dee, Polly and Maggie arrived.

"You look beautiful, hon." her father said.

Edward kissed her cheek and winked at Polly. "You sure do. Kyle is a lucky boy." He called for Matt and Marc who were going to walk with Dee and Liv. She'd asked Polly to be her matron of honor and Shane came to escort her. All three Chase brothers looked at her and cracked grins.

"Wow! You look amazing, Maggie. Absolutely gorgeous," Marc said.

"I'm an idiot," Shane grumbled and Polly nodded and patted his arm.

"You look beautiful, Liv," Matt said and Maggie smiled at the chemistry that always brewed between those two.

"Let's rock, people," she said and they all went to the back doors and the music started as Polly and Shane walked out, followed by Liv and Matt, Dee and Marc.

Suddenly the music changed and she put her hands in the arms of her escorts and stepped outside and everyone stood. She looked out at the gathered crowd of friends and neighbors and then, up to the arbor where Kyle stood, smiling at her.

Kyle's heart stopped when she stepped out onto the back porch. Her dress molded to her body, her hair pinned up in artfully reckless curls and filled with flowers. She looked fey and wholesome and yet earthy and sexy all at once. And she was all his. Her smile flashed at him and he began to breathe again.

Both Tom and Edward placed her hand in his and the rest of the ceremony went by in a haze. Kyle pushed the platinum band onto her finger until it slid home against the ring she already wore and spoke the words that bound their lives together under civil law. She spoke the same words back as she slid a matching band onto his finger.

The minister, who'd married Polly and Edward and presided at the baptisms of each of the Chase children, smiled at Maggie and Kyle and gently turned them to face the crowd of friends and family. "I'd like to introduce Kyle and Margaret Chase."

Kyle's arm encircled his wife's shoulders and he steered her back into the house for a few brief moments of silence and solitude. "I love you, wife," he said, kissing her lips.

"And I love you, husband," she murmured back.

Epilogue

Six months later

It was a Friday night and Maggie, Liv and Dee were all at their usual table at the Pumphouse. Dee was drinking a Perrier because she was six months pregnant with the child she and Arthur conceived the night of Maggie and Kyle's wedding.

Maggie watched Kyle as he bent over to take a shot, hooting as he made it and smacking Shane in the head with the tip of his pool cue. He turned around, feeling her gaze and shot her a look of total unadulterated lust and longing. Her pulse quickened and she smiled wickedly, raising her glass to him in promise.

"Oh god, the two of you!" Liv muttered.

"What?" Maggie asked, laughing. "You expect me to have that in my bed and not have this look on my face?"

"Point taken. I should go, my sister is coming in from Crawford in an hour and I want to pick up my house a bit."

Liv's sister Bea was coming to stay with her for a while, licking her wounds from a bad break up and a lost job. Maggie smiled when she saw Matt cock his head and give Liv a wave and Liv blush and wave back.

"Night then, Livvy. You know, Matt isn't dating Nancy anymore."

"That so? Huh. Perhaps you and Kyle should have a barbecue, you know, a Thanksgiving thing. Give Bea a chance to get back into the swing of things in Petal again."

"And you a chance to hang out with Matt?"

"Something like that."

"All right. I'll call you with the details."

Dee shoved herself out of the booth and Liv helped her stand up. "Arthur is here to pick me up, I'll see you later." She kissed them both and went to her husband who was waiting patiently at the door.

Maggie turned and walked through the crowd to where the pool tables were. She hopped up on a high stool, watching Kyle who tossed his cue to Matt and grabbed her. "Night all. See you Sunday," he called out and pulled Maggie out the front door and practically shoved her into the car.

"Now, I was thinking, Red, that there was a back road with our name on it. I just happen to have the sleeping bags in the back, along with a picnic basket full of food and some sparkling cider. What do you say, wanna neck under the stars?"

She leaned in and caught his lips with her own, pulling his bottom lip between her teeth. "Mmmm hmmm. I'll follow you anywhere. I might even let you get to second base."

He threw his head back and laughed and they drove off, heading for that country road.

Lauren Dane

To learn more about Lauren Dane, please visit www.laurendane.com. Send an email to Lauren at laurendane@laurendane.com or join her Yahoo! group to join in the fun with other readers as well as Lauren! http://groups.yahoo.com/group/laurendaneromantica/

Never read and ebook before?
Try this Romantic Suspense from Samhain Publishing, Ltd.

72 Hours
© 2006 Shannon Stacey
Available in ebook from www.samhainpublishing.com. MSRP S4.50.

Alex Rossi leads a double life, and it may cost Grace Nolan her son.

The Devlin Group: A privately-owned rogue agency unhindered by red tape and jurisdiction.

Grace Nolan walked away from the Devlin Group carrying Alex Rossi's child in her womb and his bullet in her shoulder. But a ghost from the past has kidnapped her son, Danny. The ransom—Alex Rossi. To get her son back, Grace will have to step back into the life she'd left behind and reveal her secret to Alex.

With vengeance for his mother's murder nearly at hand and a deadly substance on the loose, the last thing Alex Rossi needs is to find himself at the business end of Grace's gun. Now the clock is ticking as they race to save a child and stop a madman bent on destruction.

But Alex has a secret of his own, and it may be the ultimate betrayal.

Enjoy the following excerpt…

Alex watched her jump when he opened the door, her mouth opening in a quick exclamation of surprise.

She looked the same, yet so different. Her mass of chestnut curls was pulled back in a loose clip, and she needed no makeup to enhance those big sapphire eyes.

Her body had changed. Her breasts under the lightweight sweater were a little fuller, as were her hips. No doubt the changes lingered from giving birth to her son, but they didn't stop the sudden, hot urge to feel her body under his.

If anything, his want was intensified. The lean girl was gone, and in her place was a woman with a body to make a man want to come home at night.

He stepped back, giving her room to enter and close the door. It was only then he realized she was watching him as well. In his pajamas, probably still coated with the sweat of his nightmare, he guessed he probably made an interesting picture.

Alex watched Grace stare at his body, but he didn't let it get to him. She wasn't here to play. And she looked like hell.

"To what do I owe this pleasure, Grace?" he asked. He made sure the words were slow and lazy, but the back of his neck tingled in warning.

That was fear in her eyes. The list of things that scared Grace Nolan was pretty damn short, and he sure as hell wasn't on it. So what was?

"What are you doing in Key West?" she asked. Stalling—gearing herself up for something.

Instead of moving toward her, trying to intimidate her as he'd done in the past, he stepped back. He might need some room. For what, he didn't know, but he had a feeling he was about to find out.

"Just a job," he said. "It's me, remember? The guy who doesn't know how not to work?"

"Devlin told you I was coming?"

Alex nodded, hating the lie even more when looking her in the eye. "But not why."

She took a deep breath, and he noted the slight hitch. "I need to know...I need—"

Damn. Alex rested his hand on his hip, closer to the Glock tucked at the small of his back. This woman never *needed* anything, especially from him. But today…something was very wrong.

He blinked. Her arm moved. He blinked again, and found himself staring straight down the barrel of her Sig .38.

"I need you to get dressed and come with me, Alex."

He spent a few seconds eyeing the barrel of the gun while he slow-breathed his pulse rate down.

What the hell was Grace into? And who was she into it with? She was supposed to be doing boring-as-hell computer support for the feds, not kidnapping people at gunpoint.

He shifted his gaze to her eyes, and he found no give there. No doubt about it. He either had to pack a bag or incapacitate her.

"I want you to untie that drawstring and let your pants fall to the floor."

"Interesting foreplay technique, sweetheart. New since last time we were together, isn't it? A little rough is one thing, but this…"

"Let the pants drop, Alex. And let the Glock go with them." She knew him well, but he knew her, too. Oh, she sounded cool enough, but he saw the flush on her neck. Saw her nipples harden under the light sweater.

And felt the hot rush of victory. Game over.

With slow, deliberate ease Alex pulled the ends of the drawstrings loose. *Wait for it.*

He ran his thumbs around the front of the waistband, loosening it, and the weight of the Glock drew the silk fabric low on his hips.

Grace's eyes slid down to his groin.

He dove, launching himself at her midsection. He heard the air whoosh from her lungs as he swept his arm up and sent the Sig clattering to the opposite side of the room.

He managed to slip his hand under her head before it bounced off the floor. Grace was pinned under his body, and he squeezed his thighs together just in time to block her jabbing knee.

The Glock had slipped down into the leg of the pajamas now bound uncomfortably around his thighs, but he didn't need it. Didn't want it. He'd shot her once, years ago, and she probably still hadn't forgiven him for it. He hoped never to have to do it again.

He grabbed Grace's wrists and raised them over her head, stretching her body beneath him.

"Tell me what this is about, Grace."

"Get off me," she growled.

Alex saw the muscles in her neck tighten, and barely managed to dodge what would have been a nose-breaking head butt.

"Enough, or I'll put your ass to sleep for a while."

Grace stilled. She'd known him for years—long enough to know he never made idle threats. Staring up at him with those blue eyes, she trembled under him.

"Talk to me," he said in a softer tone. He had never seen this woman desperate. But she was desperate now.

"I need you to come with me. Please don't ask me why. Please."

"I *will* go with you," he promised. This woman who owned a piece of his soul was on the edge, and he sure as hell wasn't going to let her go over alone. "I'll go with you, sweetheart. But you do need to tell me why. And why the gun?"

Her throat worked hard to swallow and her eyes flooded with tears. Against his own skin he felt her stomach muscles spasm.

"What the hell?" He lifted himself from her and she curled into a ball, sobs making her entire body shake. He swore viciously. "What's the matter with you?"

He stood, letting the Glock slip through his pant leg to the floor, and refastening the drawstring at his waist. Then he dragged her to her feet. "Grace, dammit, talk to me now!"

She collapsed against him, and fear pumped adrenaline through his body. He held her for a second, then grabbed her chin in his hands, forcing her to look up him.

Her teeth chattered, and her body shuddered hard. "They took my son, Alex."

Pacific Breeze Hotel
© *2006 Josie A. Okuly*

Available in ebook from www.samhainpublishing.com. MSRP $3.50.

Detective Sean O'Rourke experiences the seedier side of life in 1940's Los Angeles when he falls for Felicia Avery, a beautiful actress in the wrong place at the wrong time.

Felicia Avery arrived in Hollywood with dreams of succeeding in the movie business. But now a powerful movie producer is dead and someone is stalking Felicia through the sunny boulevards and dark alleys of Los Angeles. Her dreams of stardom shattered by scandal, Felicia finds solace in the arms of a handsome detective. Can he protect her from the unknown assailant? Or are her days in Hollywood numbered?

Enjoy the following excerpt…

Nolan stuffed half a cinnamon bun into his mouth. "So are you going to ask Little Miss Redhead to the Policemen's Ball?"

O'Rourke frowned. "That's six months away."

"I have a feeling you'll still be seeing each other."

His partner didn't respond so Nolan got down to business. He pulled a folder out of his desk and handed it to O'Rourke.

O'Rourke glanced at it. "What's this?"

"Come to find out, DeWarner's wife craved a divorce. Got tired of all the rumors about starlets in the pool house. And get this—Mrs. DeWarner's father happens to be the head of the Carmini crime family in Chicago. Supposedly, she ran to Daddy and spilled the beans about Hubby's unfaithfulness. Daddy takes care of problem. Instant divorce."

O'Rourke's eyes narrowed. "Where did you hear that?"

"You think you're the only one with connections in the movie business?"

"Are we talking a professional hit?"

Nolan shrugged. "Maybe."

O'Rourke shook his head. "But if it's one of Carmini's guys, he's back in Chicago safe and sound in the midst of the family."

"I have another theory."

"I thought as much." O'Rourke sighed wearily. He hadn't slept well on Felicia's sofa. Not only was it lumpy and saggy, but he hadn't been able to stop thinking about the lovely girl in the next room.

"Seems another studio was trying to buy him out. DeWarner Junior was keen on the idea but Senior nixed it. Now, Senior is on his way to Hollywood Park Cemetery to join Valentino and the rest of the dearly departed. Junior is the new head honcho—ready, willing, and able to sell off his daddy's studio so he can have more money for gambling and starlets. I heard the old man kept Junior on a tight leash and now the boy has gone hog wild."

"What is it with this DeWarner? Did he go out of his way to make enemies?"

Nolan shook his head. "He didn't have to go far. Most of them seem to be members of his own family."

"So what do we do now?"

"I suggest we pay our respects to Junior."

* * *

C.B. DeWarner, Jr. didn't reside in a mansion like the one owned by his father. Instead, he lived in one of the new downtown apartments which had sprung up since the war. Of course, being the son of a wealthy movie producer had its perks. Junior's bachelor apartment was palatial enough to house a large family. It took up the entire sixth floor of the Sunset Garden Apartments and boasted a three hundred and sixty degree view of Los Angeles. Floor-to-ceiling windows encircled the apartment and opened onto a wrap-around balcony. O'Rourke couldn't help but compare this place to the tiny shoebox Felicia called home.

O'Rourke turned his back on the view and studied the man he had come to question. DeWarner. Jr. had the slicked-back hair of a punk and the wardrobe of a millionaire. His suit probably cost more than most people earned in a month. O'Rourke itched to knock the condescending smirk off his oily face.

Display cases lining one side of the large living area caught O'Rourke's attention. Butcher knives, Bowie knives, switchblades…knives of every description filled the cases. What caught O'Rourke's attention was the collection of knives with ornately carved handles.

"Quite a collection you have." O'Rourke opened one of the cases and picked up a large knife with a beautifully made handle.

"That one looks familiar." Nolan gave O'Rourke a meaningful look.

"I like knives. Nothing wrong with that." Junior's voice was challenging, but O'Rourke detected a hint of nervousness, possibly fear.

"A friend of mine was threatened with a knife similar to this one." O'Rourke held the knife by the blade and then tossed it downward. The blade pierced the wood of Junior's coffee table.

"Hey, what's your problem?" Junior ran to the table and pulled the knife from the wood. "You know how much this table cost me? It's genuine teak from half-way around the world. It probably cost more than you make in a year."

Junior returned the knife to the collection. O'Rourke leaned against the display case. "Your father paid for it, so why are you complaining?"

"Look, will you just tell me why you're here? I got things to do. I'm a busy man."

"Uh-huh." O'Rourke gave him a hard stare.

Junior was the first to drop his gaze. "Like I said, Officers, I'm in mourning. Can we make this quick?"

"Detectives." O'Rourke corrected him.

"Oh, excuse me, *Detectives*." Junior made the word sound obscene.

"Where do you find knives like those? The handle is exquisite workmanship. Must have cost plenty."

Sweat appeared on Junior's upper lip. "You can buy them by the dozen in Chinatown."

"I don't think so." O'Rourke picked up the knife again. "You see, this knife is handmade and signed by the person who sculpted the handle. I have a feeling this signature will match the knife my friend found in her living room."

"I don't know what you're talking about." Junior fidgeted with his tie.

O'Rourke smelled the tension coming from his body in oily waves. "Where were you when your father was killed?"

"What is this?" Anger painted Junior's face an ugly, mottled red. "I was getting my hair cut."

"Witnesses?"

"Of course."

O'Rourke frowned. "Do you have any idea who might want to put your dad out of business?"

"According to the paper, you should ask the little slut who was with him."

A red haze blurred O'Rourke's vision and everything took on the color of blood. Nolan grabbed his arm but O'Rourke shook him off. "Excuse me?"

"I said you should question the slut that was with him. The paper hinted she might have seen the shooter. Who knows? Maybe she did it herself. These gold digging actresses will do anything to—"

Junior never saw the rock hard fist, which slammed into his face and knocked him flat on the carpet.

"Let's get out of this dump." O'Rourke stepped over Junior's unconscious body.

"Please accept our condolences." Nolan took out a business card from his suit pocket and placed it on Junior's chest.